CENTER LINE

CENTER LINE

Joyce Sweeney

DELACORTE PRESS/NEW YORK

Published by Delacorte Press
1 Dag Hammarskjold Plaza
New York, N.Y. 10017

Manufactured in the United States of America

First printing

Library of Congress Cataloging in Publication Data

Sweeney, Joyce.
Center line.

Summary: Five teenage brothers run away from their
alcoholic father in Ohio to search for a new way to live.
[1. Brothers—Fiction. 2. Runaways—Fiction]
I. Title.
PZ7.S97427Ce 1984 [Fic]
ISBN 0-385-29320-8
Library of Congress Catalog Card Number: 83-14322

FOR JAY

CENTER LINE

One

Chris Cunnigan was making a grilled cheese sandwich. You could tell a lot about him just by watching him work. His shirt cuffs were turned back twice, indicating neatness. There was a sureness in the way he flipped the sandwich that demonstrated unusual cooking skill for a sixteen-year-old boy. Just inside the collar of his shirt was the glitter of a chain, the kind used for a cross or religious medal. He was tall for his age, attractive, and clearly took pains with his appearance. And he was restless. As he cooked he shifted from foot to foot, hummed fragments of songs, and paused often to look at the kitchen wall clock.

At twelve thirty exactly he finished the sandwich and put it on a plate. At the same time, his brother Mark came through the front door. Mark was the baby of the family, a slender fourteen-year-old with round expressive eyes and fine, straight brown hair that always hung down in his eyes. Inside the door, he began dropping things: a jacket on the couch, a baseball glove on the dining room table, and a bat, which he leaned against the refrigerator door. He threw himself into a kitchen chair as if the exertion of the morning had been too much for him.

"Did you win?" Chris asked. He pushed the plate with the sandwich in front of Mark.

"What's this?" Mark demanded without really looking at it.

Chris sat down opposite him. "It's your lunch. Eat it."

Mark narrowed his eyes at the sandwich. "I don't like it. I don't want it. Can I have something else?"

Chris frowned. "Eat it. I worked hard to get you that sandwich. I had to kill a man to get you that sandwich."

Mark played with his hair, pulling it back and letting it fall in his eyes again. "If I eat all of this, can I have some cookies or something?"

Chris nodded. "If you eat all this and if you drink a glass of milk."

"Jesus," said Mark. "Where's you-know-who?"

"Shhh," said Chris. "He's asleep in the den."

Mark snorted. "Asleep!"

"Well, he's unconscious. Let's put it that way."

Mark tore into the sandwich and talked with his mouth full. "Where's the rest of Boys Town?"

Chris was up pouring milk. "Shawn and Steve went to the mall to get Steve's art supplies. Rick's in the basement."

"You gave me too much," said Mark, accepting the milk. "What's Rick doing in the basement?"

Chris shrugged. "Who knows? Maybe he's down there taking drugs. I never know what he's doing anymore. He wouldn't even talk to me this morning."

"We lost the game," Mark said. He threw his head back and took the milk in five swallows. "As usual. This is the worst season we've ever had. Ever since the damn Protestants got those black guys on their team."

"It's not like it used to be," Chris agreed. "Nobody could touch us in those days."

"I'm starting to look forward to *school*," Mark said. "Anything's better than getting humiliated over and over."

"You've only got three weeks to wait," Chris said.

"Three weeks till school starts? Are you sure?"

"Look at the calendar."

Mark stopped eating. "That means Shawn's going away in just two weeks, doesn't it?"

"Yes," Chris said, getting up suddenly. "What kind of cookies do you want?"

There was an abrupt groan from some part of the house. Both boys stopped talking and froze. When there were no further sounds, they gradually relaxed.

"Give me some jelly beans," Mark said quietly. "Do you think he's going to wake up?"

"I hope not," Chris said. "I scratched the car last night."

Mark was sticking his hand into a jar of jelly beans, but he stopped in midgrab. "You what?"

Chris looked scared. "I did. I might have been drunk. I misjudged my lane and all of a sudden I heard this grating sound."

"Did the other guy get your name?" Mark stuffed candy into his mouth.

"No," said Chris. "I got out of there."

"Man, that's the worst thing you can do! He probably got your license number. He'll be around here with the police. What do you think Dad'll say about that?"

"You're eating too many of those things." Chris took the jar away from his brother. "I don't think he got the license. I got out of there fast and he was an old guy. He looked kind of stupid. Besides, I didn't hurt his car. It was the Chevy that got scratched."

"So, what are you going to say to Dad about it?" Mark asked.

"I'm not going to say anything and neither are you. Maybe he'll never notice."

"He'll notice," Mark said ominously. "I'm glad I'm not you."

The living room door opened with a crash and Shawn and Steven came in singing. That is, Shawn was singing and Steven was following, since it was a song Shawn was obviously composing as he went along. The refrain went, *If you don't like it, stick it up your ass.* Shawn was the oldest of the five brothers. He was eighteen, big and broad-shouldered with ash-brown hair and brown eyes. His voice was loud and his gestures extravagant. In any group he was the one people noticed first. "Who's home?" he called at the top of his lungs.

Chris tore into the living room. "Shhh! Shhh! Shhh! Dad's asleep and I want him to stay that way!"

Mark was right behind him. "Chris scratched the car!" His voice rang with excitement.

Shawn looked at Chris with wide eyes. "Bad?"

"It's a pretty long scratch. But it's on the passenger side. Maybe he won't see it for a while?" He made it a question.

"He'll see it," Shawn said. "He sees everything. Even bombed, he doesn't miss anything. Listen, don't act like you know anything about it. I'll say I did it."

"No," Chris said. "Anyway, that's stupid. You don't drive."

"I'll say I did it in the garage. I'll say I hit it with my bike. Look, it's better if he thinks I did it. You were just in trouble with him last week. He might . . ." Shawn left the sentence unfinished.

"What did you buy?" Chris asked, deciding to change the subject.

Steve sat down on the couch and opened his shopping bag. He was seventeen, tall like his brothers, but thinner and paler, with thick dark hair and gray eyes. He talked very little, made few sudden moves, and looked afraid most of the time. He was considered a brilliant artist by his high school teachers, so much so that he was getting special permission to take painting classes at the University of Dayton that fall. He said, "We got everything in the store. Charcoals and sketch pads and pastels and acrylics and all these brushes." He took out a handful and fanned them admiringly. "I'm going to take all my old, wrecked brushes and throw them the hell away."

Shawn looked at him fondly. "We even paid for some of this stuff," he said.

"Great," said Chris. "Now that's two reasons for the police to drop by. Did you have anything to eat yet?"

"Yeah, we ate at Woolworth's. Where's Rick?"

"He's in the basement being an angry young man."

Steven had dragged all his art supplies into a corner and was busy experimenting with them. He was clearly no longer aware of the people around him.

Shawn turned to Mark. "Did you win today, son?"

The same groan heard before sounded again, only louder. Everyone froze and Steve stopped drawing.

Chris closed his eyes. "Go back to sleep. Jesus, make him go back to sleep."

"What's going on?" shouted a voice from the den. It was a deep, rough voice. "Chris? Boys?"

"Oh, God, he's awake," said Chris.

"I did it, all right?" said Shawn. "If you tell him about the car, I did it."

"Chris, are you around?" The voice was clearer now, more lucid. "Chris?"

"Yeah!" Chris called. He was shaking.

"Can you come here?"

"He just wants aspirin or something," Mark said. "Don't tell him about the car. Keep your mouth shut."

"Just a minute, Dad!" Chris called. His eyes were wild.

"Don't say anything," Shawn said. "I'll tell him I did it. Tonight, when he's ready to go to work."

Chris looked at him and left the room. They watched him as if he were going off to war.

As soon as he was gone, Shawn and Mark pressed themselves against the wall between the living room and the den to listen. Steve stayed where he was, sucking on the end of one of his brushes.

"Yeah, he wants aspirin," Shawn said, for Steve's benefit.

"Does Chris sound calm?" Steve asked.

"No, he sounds nervous," Mark said. "I bet he tells him."

"No, he won't. He's not that stupid."

A few more moments went by. "They're just talking," Shawn said. "About how bad Dad feels. Chris sounds better now. Wait a minute. Oh, Christ, he's getting ready to confess."

"What?" roared their father's voice. "How in hell did you do that?"

"Oh, God," said Steve.

"Should I go in there?" Shawn asked.

"No, there's no point in your getting killed too," Steve said.

"Why in hell did he tell him?" Shawn said.

"It's our upbringing," Mark said. "We're taught to confess."

"I don't know what the hell's the matter with you!" screamed their father. "You're so stupid! Just when I think I have enough money to get by, one of you ungrateful bastards does something like this!"

"What's Chris saying?" Steve asked.

"He's sorry," Shawn said.

"He's sorry again," Mark said.

"He might be crying, I'm not sure," Shawn said.

"Dad hates that," Steven said.

Then it happened. It was a sound they knew very well. It was a slap.

"Get out of there, Chris," Shawn said.

Chris's voice was raised now. It was angry and frightened at the same time.

"He ought to hit him back," Mark said.

There was more noise. This time the sound of striking was followed by a furniture crash. Chris's voice was audible now. "Dad, please . . ."

Two more crashes. With each sound, the other three boys flinched. Any of them could use his memory and imagination to picture what was going on.

"You're no good!" the father was screaming. "None of you are any good!"

Chris screamed. Something slammed against the wall. Then there was silence.

After a few minutes they heard Chris leaving the den.

He came and stood in the doorway to the living room. His nicely cuffed sleeves were loose around his hands now. He had a small cut on the side of his face and he held his left side protectively. "We ought to get some lightweight furniture for that den," he said. He wanted to laugh, but it came out a sob, and once he started crying, he couldn't stop. He knelt down in the doorway and cried like a child.

Shawn knelt with him. "It's all right, son," he said. "You're okay. He didn't hurt you too bad. You're okay. That's all that counts."

"I wish I were older," Chris said. "I want out of here so bad."

"I wish he was dead," Mark said. "I really do."

"So do I," said Steve. "He's got no right to do that to you."

"Someday you'll all get out," Shawn said. "Just a few more years."

They heard footsteps and all of them froze. But it was only Rick coming up from the basement. Rick was fifteen, falling between Chris and Mark. He was the only member of the family who looked as if he wasn't going to be tall. He wore a Windbreaker and sunglasses, even though he was indoors and it was a warm day. He stood in the hallway with his hands in his jacket pockets, looking at Chris and Shawn on the floor.

"I just wanted to see who it was this time," he said. "I don't want to miss anything." He turned and went back to the basement.

Shawn watched him go. He held Chris very tightly. His eyes looked desperate.

It was after midnight. A half-moon shone in the window. No one was asleep. Rick was sitting up in bed, lighting matches and throwing them into the wastebasket.

Chris was pretending to read, but he was really playing the events of the afternoon over and over in his mind. He pictured himself flattened against the den wall and seeing his father's arm rise over his head and come down across his chest, smashing him hard enough that he fell to the floor. He heard his father shouting at him and then he felt, all over again, the kick his father had given him in the ribs. He played the scene again and again, like a videotape, trying to understand why it happened and what he could have done to prevent it.

Mark was also awake, trying to teach himself to play the guitar. He had mostly given up on his dream of being a professional ballplayer for the Cincinnati Reds. Now he was planning on joining a New Wave band and touring the world. So far, in the three weeks he had owned the guitar, he had learned a C chord, a G chord, and an F chord. He played them over and over in various patterns, hoping to discover a song.

Steve appeared in the doorway of their room. "Shawn wants to see everybody in ten minutes," he said.

So they assembled in Shawn and Steve's room. Rick brought his matches along and continued to play with them during the meeting.

"I made a decision this afternoon," Shawn said. "I've been thinking about it for a long time and now I've made a decision. But you'll have to vote on it. I think we should leave."

Silence. Only the sound of a match being struck.

"Leave what?" Chris asked. "You mean leave here?" Shawn nodded.

More silence. More matches.

"You're out of your mind," Rick said. "Where are we supposed to go? To the orphans' home? To stay with Aunt Ann? Or are we just going to check into a hotel?"

Shawn set his jaw. "We're going. We're not staying

here anymore. We don't have to take this stuff anymore, so we're leaving."

Chris, who sat on the windowsill, was partially illuminated by moonlight. He, of all the boys, most resembled their mother, who had died when they were small children. He had the same large, dark eyes and long lashes and the same expression of calm amazement. Like his mother, Chris always appeared to have just awakened from a beautiful dream. "How would we live?" he asked. "Where would we go? How would we get money?"

Shawn smiled. "Got money," he said. He displayed what seemed to be a very large roll of bills.

"What's that?" Mark squeaked. "Did you rob a gas station?"

"How much is that?" Rick asked.

"Four thousand dollars." Shawn ruffled the money affectionately. "From my own little bank account."

"You're supposed to take that to school with you," Chris said with horror. "It's for school."

"Please pay attention," Shawn said. "I'm not going to school. We're taking a trip together. So, if I don't need the money for Ohio State, we've got something to live on until we get some work."

"This is crazy," Chris said. "You can't just take your college money and run away from home. For one thing, it's illegal."

"It's not illegal for me," Shawn said. "I'm eighteen. I'm an adult. But it is illegal for the rest of you. Which is why we're having this meeting. I want all of you to come with me. But if you don't want to, we won't do it."

"I'll go with you," Mark said immediately. "Let's go to Los Angeles."

"We might. We can go wherever we want. All I know

is, tonight we have to drive like hell out of the state."

"Tonight?" Chris said. "You're talking about tonight?"

"Yes, before he gets home," Shawn said. "Look, we have to get out soon. He's getting worse and worse. He could have broken your ribs today. You were just lucky. I can't stand by anymore and watch all of you get slaughtered. I have to do something. And, short of killing him, this is all I can do."

"You mentioned driving," Rick said. "Are we stealing Dad's car?"

"Yes," Shawn said. "Yes, we are. Any more questions?"

Rick cocked his head to one side. "That's grand theft, Shawn. Runaway is a misdemeanor, but grand theft is a felony. And as you so proudly pointed out, you're an adult. In fact, you could even be charged with kidnapping us. We'll be gone four days, they'll trace the plates, and you'll go to prison for ten years while we end up in some rehabilitation place. Sounds great."

"I don't want you to go to jail, Shawn," Mark said.

"I'm not going anywhere," Shawn said. "Because we'll never get caught. We'll switch license plates. We'll switch them as often as we have to. We'll keep moving. We won't stay in one state more than a month. All we need is four years, until we're all adults. There might even be some states where you're an adult at sixteen. Nobody's going to catch us. Dad's been getting away with assault and battery for eighteen years, so we ought to be able to get away with this."

"I don't know," Chris said.

Shawn leaned forward, directing his whole argument to Chris. "Do you want to stay here and die? Someday, one of us is going to get killed. Do you want to come home someday and find one of us dead on the den floor?"

"No!" Mark shouted. "I'm with you. Even if nobody else is!"

"I'm with you," said Steven quietly. "We haven't got much to lose anymore, the way I look at it."

"Chris?" Shawn asked. "What do you say?"

Chris was still clearly torn. "I don't know. It doesn't seem right. It sounds so dangerous."

"What about what happened to you today?" Shawn asked him.

Chris played the videotape in his head again. Everything out of control. None of it ever made sense. To his horror, he could easily imagine a different ending to the story. It was easy to imagine his father killing him. "I wouldn't let you three go by yourselves," he said, very softly.

"That leaves you, Torch," Shawn said, turning to Rick.

Rick held the stage as long as he could. He struck a final match, slowly and deliberately, and watched it burn. "I'll go with you," he said. "But I bet we get caught."

"That's the spirit," Shawn said. "All right. You've all got one hour to pack. One suitcase per man. No extras unless you ask me. Anything you can leave behind, leave. Tonight, we get out of Ohio and find a hotel and after we sleep, we'll decide where to go. All right?"

"What about my new guitar?" Mark asked. "What about my baseball stuff?"

"Choose one or the other," Shawn said, "and you can have that."

"I'll take the guitar, I guess," Mark said. "But I'll never get another glove broken in like that one was."

"I've got to have something to draw on," Steven said. "Can I take my one sketchbook?"

"Yeah, sure," said Shawn.

"Good. Great start," Rick said. "Let's fill up the car with art supplies and musical instruments. That's pretty slick."

"Look," Shawn said. "I'm in charge here. I don't need you to check on my decisions. They both need those things. Unlike you, they have a soul. If you want to pack a couple books of matches, feel free. Anything extra you want, Chris?"

"No," said Chris. "I don't care about anything in this house."

"All right. We're wasting time. Get to work and I'll be down to check on you in a little while."

An hour later Shawn came down to the other boys' room. "You guys ready to go?"

Mark was grinning. "Chris put a rosary in his suitcase," he said triumphantly.

"I did not!" Chris shouted.

"You did too. I saw you!"

"Okay, okay," said Shawn. "What if he did? He's allowed to have his religious beliefs just like you don't have yours."

"We think he prays, too," Mark said.

"I don't!" Chris shouted.

"You do," Rick said. "I've seen you cross yourself."

"You guys!" Shawn said. "We're running away from home, remember? We haven't got time for an inquisition. We'll have four years on the road or in jail to discuss philosophy. I don't know why you always pick on him for being religious. Just because we're all going to hell doesn't mean he has to go with us. Let's go."

They dragged their things down to the garage and loaded them into the Chevy. It was a little after two in the morning. It was late summer, but cold enough for all of them to wear jackets. Mark put jelly beans in his pockets. He didn't know why.

They did not speak to each other all the time they were loading the car. They were all trying to take in the strangeness of the situation, and memorize their last look at home. They had lived in this house all their lives.

"We have to leave our bikes, don't we?" Chris said. His voice echoed in the garage.

"It's only fair," Mark said. "We're taking his car. He ought to get our bikes."

"It's just a damn good thing he took the bus to work tonight," Shawn said. He could sense they were getting sentimental and he was anxious to get going. "Let's go, Christopher. This is your dream. You get to borrow the car forever." He threw him the keys.

Steven, Mark, and Rick got in the backseat. Shawn sat in front with Chris. As the ignition started, all of them had the same impulse, to suggest calling it off, but each one of them managed to fight it back. Chris backed out of the garage into the moonlight and headed the car south, toward the distant ribbon of light that was the highway.

Two

A light, cold rain fell on Lexington, Kentucky. It was nearly dawn, but the sky was dark, with masses of smoke-colored clouds bunched in the east.

Chris had been awake for hours. He sat up in bed, motionless, watching the rain fall outside the window. As the room began to lighten, he looked around. Shawn and Steve were in the bed next to his, one sprawled, the other curled as tightly as possible. Rick was on the floor, sleeping in a pile of jackets. Mark, who shared Chris's bed, slept so deeply he seemed not to breathe. The pale light made sharply cut shadows on their faces. Perhaps it was the innocent look of all sleeping people, but something filled Chris with fear. They looked like animals waiting for slaughter or one of those photographs of Jewish children sleeping in a concentration camp.

Chris said a quick prayer, not crossing himself in case Mark was secretly watching. Then he got up quietly and stood at the window for a few moments.

There was a large billboard for Jack Daniel's whiskey across the road. Their motel, the Tecumseh, was actually several miles outside of Lexington. They had chosen the most obscure-looking place they could find. The Tecumseh was back from the road and surrounded on three sides by woods. It only cost six dollars a room, no matter how many were in the room. Shawn had expected trouble, trying to put five in a room, but the desk clerk didn't care at all. He'd seen stranger groups than that over the years.

The Tecumseh had a wide gravel driveway leading down to the road. There were a lot of empty liquor bottles down in that driveway. Not just beer cans, but actual glass bottles. Chris deduced that the Tecumseh was a place of mad revels for the people of Lexington.

He put on his clothes, making only a minimal effort to be quiet since all his brothers were heavy sleepers, and left the room, taking the key with him.

He had to walk past the desk clerk to get out the front door. The clerk was an elderly man with a hearing aid and a nose that pointed toward his upper lip. He wore a green cardigan with an interesting assortment of snags in the material. "All your cousins still asleep?" he asked, winking at Chris.

"Brothers," Chris said. "They're my brothers."

"Oh, yeah. I remember now." The old man smiled nastily.

"There's a strong family resemblance," Chris said, blushing. "Anyone can see it."

"Sure there is. Birds of a feather flock together!" The old man giggled and picked up a newspaper. He wasn't going to get into an argument with a queer.

Chris sighed, pushed the door open, and went out into the rain. It was a rain one could stand in comfortably, just a light drizzle. Chris needed to be outside. He craved outside air. The only problem was the cold. He wished he could have brought his jacket, but Rick had been lying on top of it. Hugging himself, Chris walked out to the edge of the gravel and looked at the woods.

It was daybreak now, the sky was as light as it was going to get, a pearl color with gray slashes. The birds in the woods were waking up and singing maniacally.

Chris could see a few of them, deep in the woods, flying from tree to tree. There was a nice smell to the woods, a green and brown smell. Bark and chlorophyll. Everything in the woods dripped water.

Chris wanted to go into the woods, but he felt too much like an intruder. He wished he could feel one with such a beautiful place. He wished at least that he knew the names of the birds he was seeing, but he knew nothing about birds.

Since last night he'd fallen deeper and deeper into depression. He felt that he and his brothers were certainly doomed. They would either be caught and sent home, or they wouldn't survive. Someone would steal all their money. Someone's appendix would flair up and none of them would know what to do. He could not imagine them living safely until everyone was a legal adult. The world was too frightening.

Chris wanted to talk to Shawn about these feelings, but he was afraid of appearing disloyal. Over the years he had established something very dependable with Shawn. There was a certain understanding between them. Shawn was the leader and had all the ideas, and Chris's job was to back him up, to second the motion, to quell doubts in the ranks. Shawn depended on him for that.

But running away was a bigger, more terrifying prospect. This time, Chris thought Shawn was wrong. He was sure they would fail.

The rain fell heavier. *I'm catching cold,* Chris thought. The urge to enter the woods was powerful now, a powerful wet, green urge. It would be warmer there, he thought, where less rain was falling. He shifted his feet on the gravel and reached out with his hand to crush the nearest leaves.

"Have you noticed it's raining?"

Chris turned, startled, and saw Shawn standing behind him, holding his jacket.

"Let's buy you a cup of coffee, son." Shawn handed Chris his jacket. "You look a little cold."

Chris tried to hide his guilty expression. "Just you and me?" he asked. "What about the others?"

"They're asleep." Shawn turned away from Chris and started walking toward the car. "Besides, I want to talk to you alone."

Chris followed him.

They went to a Denny's restaurant several miles down the road.

"How are you today, darling?" the red-haired waitress asked Chris. She took a long time to clean the table in front of him.

"We're fine," Chris told her politely. "We'd both like black coffee."

"Anything you want, sweetheart," the waitress said. She touched his shoulder. "How old are you anyway?" She looked about twenty-eight herself.

"He's only twelve," Shawn said. "So you better watch yourself. I, on the other hand, am thirty-seven and own three oil wells."

The waitress giggled. "You both sound good to me," she said, and minced off to get the coffee.

"We've got to do something about that face of yours,"

Shawn said, "or pretty soon we're going to start getting paternity suits and things. Maybe you should grow a beard."

"I'll try," Chris said. "I don't know whether I can."

"All right," Shawn said. "Let's talk about all these doubts and fears that are tearing you apart."

The waitress brought their coffee before Chris could react. "I get off work at six," she said, smiling at Chris.

"We're leaving town soon," Shawn told her. "We just robbed a gas station down the road, so we don't want to hang around too long, *you* know."

"Oh," she said. She didn't know whether to believe him or not. She didn't bother them anymore.

"What do you mean, doubts?" Chris asked, stirring. "I don't know what you're talking about."

Shawn stirred his coffee too. On both sides it was a meaningless exercise, since neither of them took sugar. "I want you to be honest with me, Chris. You don't have to be afraid to talk to me. It's very clear that you're afraid. You think I've made a terrible decision, taking us all away from home, making fugitives out of us. You think it's more than I can handle."

Chris stirred faster. "Shawn, believe me—"

"And you're right. This is a lot more than I can handle alone. I'm as scared as you are. I don't know what the hell we're going to do, how we're going to survive. We've only got enough money to last a few months and we need enough for years. We've stolen a car, which gives the police a reason to look for us. I don't have any idea, beyond today, how we're going to make it." He looked into Chris's eyes. Shawn had his faults, notably bad temper and imperiousness, but he never lied. He never made any attempt to hide things from people or to delude himself. That was the secret of his self-confidence. He knew, far better than most people, what he was and what he was not.

"If all that's true," Chris asked, "what are we doing here?"

Shawn leaned forward so he could speak quietly. "I'll tell you why. We're here because I'm angry. We're here because I don't think it's right that one human being should beat up on another. We're here because Dad was killing all of us. I've seen all of you changing because of what he's been doing to us. Rick's getting sullen, Steven's a coward, Mark laughs at things that aren't funny, like he's losing touch with reality. You were getting to the point where you blamed yourself for everything that happened. And me . . ." Shawn hesitated, took a drink of coffee. "I think I was starting to be like *him*. I never told any of you this, but there are times when I just feel like *hitting* something." He emphasized his point by striking the table gently with his fist. Chris looked so horrified, Shawn had to avert his eyes for the rest of the speech. "One way or another, we would have all ended up twisted. I think about Mom, you know? How would she have felt if she could see what he's done to us? Maybe, Chris, maybe I'm taking on more than I can handle, but" —Shawn had reduced his voice to a whisper now to conceal the emotion—"you kids don't have any decent goddamned parents to take care of you and you all deserve better. I may kill all of us in the attempt, but I'd like to see some of you get past twenty without getting slugged again."

Chris stared down into his coffee, as if he were able to see the future in it. "One time . . ." Chris said hoarsely, "it was one morning when Dad had a terrible hangover and I was taking care of him. He told me how scared he was about the things he did to us. I guess it was just as frightening to him as it was to us. He told me he had just given Steve a beating the night before, he told me he had pinned Steve on the floor and he had this urge to . . . choke him. He told me how close he came to putting his hands on Steven's throat. And then he asked me, he said, 'Chris, you don't think I'd be capable of actually hurting one of you, do you?' I said, 'I don't know.' "

Shawn and Chris searched each other's eyes. Shawn said, "If someone ever really got hurt, I would have blamed myself for not taking you away. See?"

"Yes." Chris looked down at his coffee.

"You have to understand." Shawn sat back in his seat. "I don't mind if you have doubts. I don't mind if you don't always agree with me. But we need to keep up a certain kind of front for the others. Because if they have doubts, we're in trouble. Rick's ripe for mutiny right now, and Steve and Mark could scare very easily. I need to keep them all feeling brave and confident and believing in me. I need you to set an example for them. If you seem confident, they'll follow."

Chris looked up. "You don't have to worry about me," he said.

"I know," Shawn said. "Next time you get scared, you come to me and we'll go off by ourselves and be scared together, all right?"

"Okay."

Outside, the rain was starting to fall again. People were waiting in line to get a seat in the restaurant now.

"We better get those license plates changed before the FBI catches up with us," Shawn said. "Are you ready to go?"

"Yes."

"Zip up your jacket, son. It's cold out there."

Three

There was little variety in the Indiana landscape. Corn-fields seemed to stretch for miles, broken up only by the occasional farm, with Mail Pouch tobacco slogans painted on the barns. Between the ten-mile cornfields were small towns, always with names that made the boys laugh.

In the town of Laywell, Indiana, there were banners strung across the street that read FROG DAYS: JULY 16TH TO AUGUST 1ST. The boys made a great issue of having missed Frog Days in Laywell, Indiana, and they all had different ideas about how they were celebrated.

Each little town had an immense cemetery adorned with huge, expensive marble and granite markers. The modest cemeteries of Ohio looked pathetic by compari-son. "Death is a serious matter here in Indiana," Shawn said. "People must come from all over the world to die in Indiana."

Most of the roads they used, which looked large and accommodating on the map, were small, twisting, and rutted. Chris found himself driving hand over fist most of the time.

There had been no more rain since Louisville and the sun was shining now, making bright flashes on the hood of the car and blinding everyone except Rick, who had sunglasses.

Shawn fell asleep some time after they passed through Laywell. He slouched in his seat, put his feet on the dashboard, and covered his face with somebody's Fairview High School jacket.

Rick, Mark, and Steve had purchased a road map of Indiana at the last Shell station and had spread it all over the backseat. The three of them had formed a committee to select the town that would be their next home.

"There's Marion," said Steve. "Marion, Indiana. Look at that. That's just twenty miles from here. Do you guys know what Marion, Indiana, is?"

"It looks like a fucking small town," Rick said.

"It's where James Dean went to high school. It really is," Steve said.

"Who's James Dean?" Mark asked.

"Oh, Christ!" said Steve.

"Who is James Dean?" Chris asked over his shoulder.

Steve was overwhelmed by this show of ignorance. "Shawn! Wake up!" he shouted. "I've got no one to talk to but stupid children."

"What?" Shawn mumbled from inside his jacket.

"Tell them who James Dean is," Steve said petulantly.

Shawn pulled the jacket away from his face. "Let's not discuss James Dean until we get Chris off these bad roads." He turned around in his seat. "Have you picked out any place for us to sleep tonight?" he asked the road map committee.

"Indianapolis," Rick said. "The rest of these towns look like annexes from Hell."

"Not Indianapolis," Shawn said. "It's on a main road from Dayton. Where else do you like?"

"Marion," said Steve. "So we can educate these kids about James Dean."

"I don't know who James Dean is, but I'm sick of him already," Chris said.

"I like Muncie," Mark said. "Muncie looks good."

"What makes you say that?" Shawn asked him.

"I don't know. I just looked down and saw it. It's not on any main roads."

"Let's see." Shawn pulled the map into the front seat. "Where is it? Oh, I see it. Hey, that's not a bad choice at all. It's inconspicuous-looking. Not big, not too small, not on any main roads. That's excellent, Mark. I think that's excellent. What do you think?" He showed the map to Chris, holding the place with his finger.

"We're even headed in the right direction," Chris said. "We could be there in a couple of hours."

"All right," Shawn announced. "Now we're Muncie-ites. Mark, we appreciate your good judgment."

Mark was very pleased with himself. "I'm getting a little hungry," he said hopefully.

That brought a collective groan from all other members of the group.

"You've been hungry ever since we left Dayton yesterday," Rick said. "No matter how much you eat, you're still hungry. We just had breakfast two hours ago."

"It was *three* hours ago," Mark said, "and I didn't have that much. It's twelve o'clock. That's lunchtime, isn't it?" He appealed to Shawn.

"If he's hungry, we better stop," Shawn said. "He's growing and everything."

"But *what's* he growing?" Steve asked.

"There's a Lucky Steer restaurant in ten miles," Chris said, indicating a billboard.

"Lucky Steer?" Shawn said. "That's a contradiction in terms."

"Can we go there?" said Mark, who didn't know what a contradiction in terms was; who in fact didn't know what a steer was.

"No," said Shawn. "If you want lunch, we'll have to go to McDonald's. We're spending our money too fast already."

"It's going to run out anyway," Rick said. "Why not spend it fast?"

Shawn turned to say something to him, but his attention was taken by something he saw in the rear window. "Chris? Is that a police car back there?"

Chris squinted at the rearview mirror. "No," he said. "It's the highway patrol."

"Slow down," Shawn said. "All we need is to get stopped."

"It's too late," Chris said, shaking his head. "I can tell by the way he's looking at me."

Sure enough, the cruiser picked up speed and turned the siren on.

"Should I pull over?" Chris asked.

"Yes," Shawn said. "We don't want them to set up a dragnet for us."

The Indiana Highway Patrol pulled up next to the Chevy and a trooper got out. He was young, but looked far from sympathetic. His eyebrows went all the way across his forehead and he had a problem hangnail. He chewed on it during the whole conversation.

Chris had to look up into the sun and squint in order to talk to the patrolman, which took away the advantage his innocent face usually gave him. He tried to compensate for this loss by adding extra sweetness and humility to his voice. "I realize we were speeding, sir," he said contritely.

The patrolman leaned up against the car and folded his arms. "If you knew you were speeding, why'd you do it?" He gave his hangnail a bite.

"We were in a hurry, sir. I know it was wrong. You can go ahead and give me the ticket if you want, but I was in a hurry because my little brother was getting sick. We haven't eaten for twelve hours and we wanted to hurry and get him some food before he passed out or something." Sincerity rang in Chris's voice. He was a gifted liar.

The patrolman hunched over and peered into the car. "Which one of these is your brother?" he asked.

"They're all my brothers, but this is the one who was feeling sick." Chris indicated Mark, who had already leaned his head against the backseat and who was staring at the ceiling with an expression of feeble pain.

The patrolman straightened up and addressed Chris again. "What are you and all your brothers doing out on this highway?" he asked.

Chris's eyes had adjusted to the sunlight by now and he opened them as wide as he could. "We're moving to Muncie. We're going there to live with our aunt and uncle." His voice dropped low. "Our mother and father were killed."

The trooper was instantly transformed. He stopped chewing on his hangnail and looked at the boys anew. All of them performed well. Shawn looked sullen, staring out the front windshield. Rick looked away suddenly, and, again showing his flair for the dramatic, Mark put his face against Steven's shoulder.

"What happened to your parents, boys?" asked the trooper quietly.

"The house burned down," Chris said. "They said they couldn't save anything. We were all at school."

Mark allowed his shoulders to convulse at this last statement.

"So you're going all alone to your aunt and uncle's?" The trooper was fascinated. He would repeat the whole story to his wife tonight.

"Yes," Chris said. "We're kind of taking care of each other right now."

That was a nice touch, Shawn thought. He stored in his mind for future reference that Chris was a good liar and that Mark could act.

"Where was your home, boys?" the trooper asked. His entire face had changed. His eyes were kind and warm.

"Louisville," Shawn said abruptly. "We're from Louisville." Chris might be a good liar, but he never would have remembered they had Kentucky license plates. Chris flashed Shawn a quick look of gratitude.

"Well, I hope you boys will be happy here in Indiana," the trooper said. "It's a beautiful state. I've lived here all my life. I certainly hope things work out for you." Just before he left them, he gave the Chevrolet an affectionate little pat.

"Thank you, sir!" Chris called after him. "Oh, Jesus, I feel guilty," he said out of the side of his mouth.

"It's better for you to feel guilty than for us to end up in the Indiana juvenile courts," Shawn said out of the side of his mouth.

They waved good-bye to the patrolman and gave him time to get well ahead of them before they started up again.

"Boy! That was terrifying!" said Mark with enthusiasm. So far, things were turning out like some of the best television shows he'd seen.

"You did nice, Mark," Shawn said. "You did very well without overdoing it. And your brother here . . ." He indicated Chris. "Your brother gets the gold star of the week for that lovely performance."

"I'm going to have to get to a priest," Chris said. "I've got to confess all this fast, in case we get hit by a car or something."

"Don't be ashamed of your creativity, son," Shawn said. "Very few people are that talented. And I hope you're kidding about confession. I don't mind your having this Catholic hobby, or whatever it is, but until we're legal, I don't want you to confess anything to anybody. It's not safe."

"Are you kidding?" Chris nearly took his hands off the wheel. "You won't let me go to confession?"

"It's not safe. How do you know some old bastard priest won't go straight to the authorities with your story? Are you going to tell how you've stolen a car? Do you think that would be smart?"

"Priests don't call the police!" Chris shouted. "Priests are confidential."

"Well, there might be one sneaky, untrustworthy priest in Indiana and we can't afford to risk it. You can tell your sins to me. I'll be fascinated."

"God damn it, I don't like this!" Chris said. "I don't like it at all. What if I die before we're legal?"

Shawn shrugged. "We'll take good care of you. When you're eighteen, you can go to any priest you want and blow his ears off with your accumulated sins. But not before that." Shawn's tone left no room for argument.

Chris turned his eyes to the road without further comment.

They passed the Lucky Steer and pulled into a McDonald's, where they bought four bags of food. Shawn knew he was being overly apprehensive, but it frightened him every time he had to spend money. Of course, in two days on the road they had barely made a dent in his four thousand dollars. But every time money left his hand, he felt a little shiver of fear in his stomach. Each dollar was one dollar closer to the day he would have to think of something else to keep them going.

At the same time, he felt a compulsion to overspend and overfeed them. He found himself asking them if they wanted cookies, or if a medium Coke was big enough. He went out of his way to keep them from feeling deprived.

The McDonald's was on the outskirts of Montresor, another little cemetery-town. They took their lunch to Montresor Memorial Park, which was an acre of grass surrounded by a chain link fence. Inside the park were three benches, four trees, a water fountain, and a toddler swing. In the center of the park was an iron replica of the Liberty Bell with a copper dedication plate that read: *Presented to the City of Montresor by Dr. and Mrs. D. O. Gatling, who believe the American way of Life will never die.*

The boys congregated at the swings, but Steve wandered off to eat by the fence. No one was offended by this, or even thought much about it. Steve was just one of those people who like to be alone.

He, more than any of the brothers, was at ease about what they had done. His home and his father had been nothing but a continuous nightmare for him. He had no remorse about leaving either one. His father hated him and he knew it. He had always been singled out for the worst beatings, the nastiest insults. Something in Steven's behavior had given Donald Cunnigan the mistaken impression that this son was destined to be a homosexual, or at the very least a coward and a sissy. His interest in painting appalled his father and his tendency to cry easily had been enough to send Donald into a rage. It was no exaggeration when Donald Cunnigan told Chris he was tempted to strangle Steven.

Not only was Steve delighted to be leaving his father, he truly enjoyed the prospect of being rootless, even if it lasted for years. He wasn't learning much at school, and what he did learn, he taught himself. He hated routines of all kinds.

Sitting as he was now, in a park in Indiana, on a nice sunny day, leaning against a fence and eating french fries, not knowing where or how he would spend the night tonight, was his idea of perfect bliss.

Off in the distance he could hear the shouts and cries of his brothers, arguing over the food. It was nice they were over there. They were his anchors.

A ground squirrel that had been sitting in a tree nearby began to descend the trunk.

Steven watched the squirrel approach. "Want a french fry?" he asked. He held his hand out, with a nice long McDonald's french fry balanced between his fingers.

The squirrel hesitated, then came close to Steven. It stood about two feet away from him.

Steven was delighted. He didn't know much about animals. None of the boys had ever been allowed to have a pet. "Come on," he said gently, waving the french fry and making an effort not to breathe too heavily.

Back at the swings, everyone had finished his food except Mark, who was finishing up on other people's leftovers. He had eaten two Quarter Pounders (one with cheese), a large order of fries, part of a small order of fries, half an order of Chicken McNuggets, a quart of Coke, two boxes of cookies, half of Chris's ice cream, and everybody's pickles. Mark's appetite was a source of fascination to everyone. They often speculated as to what his real limit might be, because he never seemed to reach it.

Chris, who paid little attention to food, had only eaten half his lunch and had found a way to adapt the toddler swing to his body. He hung upside down on the underside of it, with his legs inserted backward. He used his hands on the ground for leverage.

When Mark had finally finished eating, he took his guitar out of the car and began to practice. So far he had taught himself two songs: Elvis's "Love Me Tender" and a song by Paul McCartney, "We're Open Tonight," both of which had easy chord patterns. He sang these several times over, until Shawn couldn't take it anymore.

"Let's learn something new," he suggested. "Let's expand your horizons." He began to sing *Back home again in Indiana,* slow enough for Mark to try and pick it out. Pretty soon he, Mark, and Chris were all absorbed in perfecting the song.

Rick was disgusted. Bad enough to be in Indiana, without singing about it. He considered all his brothers to be silly and simpleminded. Especially now, facing an uncertain and dangerous future, there they all were, acting like kids on a picnic. The only reason he'd come along was he couldn't face the thought of staying behind with their father. He didn't want to inherit Chris's job of taking aspirin to the old bastard. Rick had never been beaten as much as the other boys. Donald Cunnigan seemed barely aware of Rick's existence. Sometimes he would call him "Chris" or "Mark" by mistake. Rick wouldn't admit it, but he actually felt resentful when another brother got slugged. At least it was recognition.

Secretly, Rick was waiting for a good chance to get away from the others. He thought he would take his share of the money, or a little more, and leave in the middle of the night. He could go to Chicago or some big city and find some way to make money. He knew he could take care of himself. Staying with his brothers was just a minor inconvenience that he would endure for the time being. But he wouldn't stay with them too long. He was sure sooner or later they'd do something stupid and blow the whole thing.

In the fifteen years he'd been alive, Rick had managed to strangle nearly every loving impulse that came into his brain, until they had almost stopped coming altogether. He didn't really love any of his brothers. Shawn was the only one for whom Rick had any respect, because Shawn had a good mind, but it was a mind clearly held back by too much sentimentality. Shawn rarely acted in his own best interest, a thing Rick could neither understand nor forgive.

Rick strolled over to the west perimeter of the park and took out a cigarette. He had a feeling this was his last pack. Cigarettes would be just the kind of expense his nonsmoking brothers would want to cut out. With this in mind he made the most of what he had, taking lots of little drags. He was amazed by people who lit cigarettes and let them burn away, just wasting them. Rick never wasted anything.

From his vantage point Rick had a perfect view of Steve, the squirrel, and the french fry. By now the squirrel had crept to within inches of Steve and was waiting to see if Steve would compromise and drop the fry on the ground. Steve looked like a child on Christmas morning. He was entranced.

"Well, isn't that cute," Rick said to himself. "In any group of jerks, you can always count on Steve to be the jerkiest." He smiled to himself, sucked hard on the cigarette and threw it away. Then he dropped into a crouch.

Steven had not seen him at all. The squirrel's mouth was just millimeters away from the french fry. He was close enough now to be encircled by Steve's arms. Very tentatively the squirrel opened his mouth and aimed it at the french fry, leaning forward and back again, to see what Steve would do. "Go ahead," Steve said softly, "I won't hurt you." The squirrel opened his mouth and leaned forward again, revealing tiny teeth.

"Aaaaaaaaaaah!" Rick lunged at them, waving his arms and screaming. The squirrel shot up into the tree without hesitation, climbing all the way to the top and glaring down at the two boys.

"Did I scare your little friend, Stevie?" Rick asked. He was too guarded to laugh, but he allowed himself a mocking smile.

"You bastard." Steve was already on his feet. "What the hell did you do that for?" He looked ready to fight, which delighted Rick.

"I'm so sorry, Steve," Rick said. "Was that squirrel a close friend of yours? Did you have a close personal relationship with that squirrel?"

"God damn you," Steve said. He shoved Rick hard enough to knock him down.

Rick scrambled back to his feet and punched Steve in the stomach. It hurt, but Steve was able to grab Rick by the wrist and force him to the ground, coming down on top of him.

So the fight became a classic ground struggle, each one trying to stay on top and, if that was not possible, to land as many blows in the other guy's rib cage as he could.

It only took a few minutes for their battle screams to alert Mark, Shawn, and Chris, who came running.

In a family of five boys, breaking up fights is something everyone learns how to do. It only took them a few seconds to pry Rick and Steve apart.

"What happened?" asked Shawn, who was holding Rick and pinning his arms.

"He was doing something queer with a squirrel and I disturbed him," Rick said, smiling malevolently.

Shawn looked incredulously at Steven. Surely there was a better story than that. Steve opened his mouth in outrage, but realized there was nothing he could say. Nobody would understand. None of them.

"Great," said Shawn. "The FBI is probably after us and you guys fight over a squirrel. That's really good."

Chris, who was helping Mark to restrain Steven, said, "We ought to get going. I'd like to get to Muncie early so we can find a hotel."

"That's right," Shawn said. "Are you guys all finished so we can get on with things?"

"I was never upset to begin with," Rick said. "He's the one who blew up."

"I'm ready to go," Steve said, spitting out the words. He shook loose of his brothers and started for the car.

"I'm not sitting next to him," Rick said with great sincerity. "He's crazy."

"Good," said Shawn. "We'll put you in the trunk."

Unfortunately for Chris, they took several wrong turns and didn't get to Muncie until after sundown. Muncie is not an easy city to approach in daylight, let alone in darkness.

"For God's sake!" Chris yelled. "What do I do now?"

"Wait a minute," said Shawn, who now had command of the road map. "I'm not sure which road we're on now."

"Well, we've changed roads six times in the last five minutes!" Chris shouted. "Are you sure you know what you're doing? You said we were practically there fifteen minutes ago."

"We are practically there," Shawn shouted back. "We're going around it. I just can't find a road that goes into it."

"Maybe there is no way into it," Mark suggested, giggling.

"It's probably never been needed," Rick said. "We're probably the first people who ever wanted to go into Muncie voluntarily."

"Would someone please tell me what to do?" Chris screamed. "Are we on our way back to Ohio or what?"

"I can't tell you what to do until I know what fucking road we're on," Shawn yelled. He and Chris both had marvelously powerful lungs.

"Well, figure it out!" Chris shrieked. "That's your *job!*"

"There was a sign," Mark said. "We're on Route Sixty-seven."

"So what do I do?" Chris demanded.

"Well, I'm not sure," Shawn said. "If it's the Sixty-seven that's southwest of town, you should look for something marked Thirteen East. If it's the Sixty-seven that's northeast, you should look for Three South."

"How do I know which one I'm on?" Chris was near hysteria.

"Which way are we going?" Rick asked. "Are we going north, south, or what?"

"Where's the North Star?" Mark asked, sticking his head out the window.

"It doesn't make any difference which way we're going if we don't know which road we're on," Steven pointed out, "because we don't know if we're going toward Muncie or away from it. See, you have to have at least two factors in order to know what you're doing because the highway runs both ways."

"Shut up! Shut up! Shut up!" Chris screamed.

"There was a sign that said Sixteen," Mark said quietly.

"Turn! Turn! Turn right!" Shawn screamed.

Chris threw his weight against the wheel in order to make the turn. "I'm having a coronary," he whispered. "What do I do now?"

"Look for something that says Three North and then look for something that says One South."

"I thought you said we were near this damn city."

"We are! There's just a lot of roads."

"There's Three coming up," said Mark. Then he added, "It's certainly a good thing *I'm* here."

Chris turned the wheel again. "I'm afraid once we get into Muncie, we'll never get out again."

"Bite your tongue," said Rick.

Route 3 ended at Route 1. Route 1 was not marked North or South. It just said Route 1. Chris slowed the car to a stop. "Which way?" he asked Shawn.

"South."

"It's not marked. It just says One."

"Well, just go south."

"Should we look for the North Star again?" Mark asked.

"Just guess!" Shawn yelled.

Chris guessed. There were a few more tense moments

while they drove through the outskirts of town, but finally they crossed a river and the lights of Muncie came into view. There was a general sigh of relief and Shawn threw the road map into the backseat with contempt.

"There's a hotel, stop there," Steve said. "I'm exhausted."

"Where?" said Chris.

"Down there. That building that says Hotel."

"I don't know. . . ." said Chris. "It doesn't have a name. It just says Hotel."

"It's a generic hotel," said Rick.

"Just go there for tonight. We can look around tomorrow," Shawn said.

They pulled into a parking lot that resembled a Bronx alley.

"Look," said Rick. "The fire escapes don't go all the way down."

It was true. The building was about six stories high, with a crumbling stone facade. The fire escape extended from the sixth floor down to the middle of the third, then ended abruptly. A ladies' pump was wedged in the wrought iron.

"So what?" Shawn said. "You go halfway down and jump. That's obviously what that lady did."

"You don't see the rest of her, do you?" Steven asked.

"I don't want to stay in this hotel," said Chris.

"You older guys are always the first ones to panic," Mark said. "I'm not afraid to stay here."

"Neither am I," said Shawn. "Come on."

The hotel had apparently been built in the 1920s and had not been cleaned since then. The huge lobby had frayed red carpet and a cracked, damp-looking ceiling. There was rust on the pay telephone. The front desk was the kind of huge wooden monster usually found in old public libraries. There were holes in it, just the right size for bullet holes. A man stood behind the desk, looking into space as if it were an activity.

The boys dragged their luggage up to the desk. "Does this hotel have a name?" Shawn asked. He thought he ought to know in case they wanted to call the police during the night.

The man had to pull his attention away from looking into space in order to talk to Shawn. "Charles," he said.

"Come again?"

"Charles. That's the name of the hotel. Charles." The desk attendant had a pale face and gray eyes and long wisps of blond hair surrounding a bald spot. He wore a cardigan sweater similar to the one worn by the desk clerk at the Tecumseh Motel in Lexington.

"Charles?" Shawn said. "The hotel is called Charles?"

"Do you call it Chuck for short?" Mark asked.

With effort the desk clerk focused his attention on Mark. "No," he said seriously.

Chris, who stood at the back of the group, felt someone looking at him. When he turned, he discovered a Latino boy about his own age who was staring at him and sucking a toothpick. He smiled at Chris, a slow, broad smile. Chris edged away.

"Could we maybe have a couple of rooms?" Shawn asked tiredly. "Or are you all booked for the season?"

"You want rooms?" the clerk asked.

"Yes." Shawn had begun to raise his voice and gesture. "We five people want somewhere to sleep."

"I can put all five of you in a double room," the clerk said. "It's cheaper. Two double beds. None of you are very big. You'll fit."

"Good," said Shawn. "Fine. Give me the key, please."

"How long do you want the room for?" the clerk
asked.

"We don't know," Shawn said. "Tonight for sure.
Maybe for four years." He turned to Steven. "We might
want to spend our whole time here. No cop is going to get
information out of this guy."

"Are you good for it?" the clerk asked. "Thirty dollars
a night."

The Latino boy was now gently trying to take Chris's
luggage from him. "Do you work here," Chris asked, "or
are you stealing my suitcase?" The boy smiled, showing a
perfect set of teeth.

"I'll pay you one hundred and fifty dollars in ad-
vance," Shawn said. "That's five nights. Will that be
okay?"

The clerk thought it over. "Yes," he said. "I'll get your
key. You have to take the sixth floor. All the other floors
have water damage." He laid the key on the desk.

Shawn wanted to know what caused the water damage, but he was too tired. "Where's the elevator?" he
asked.

"It's broken," the man said. "Miggle here will take you
up in the manual elevator." He gestured toward the
Latino boy.

"*Miguel*," said the boy savagely. "My name is Miguel,
you old fool."

"That's what I said. Take them up in the elevator."
The clerk turned to Shawn. "We got to hire them," he
explained.

"You lie with horses, old man," said Miguel, dragging
luggage toward the manual elevator, which was a kind of
iron cage with fraying cables.

"What kind of elevator is this?" Chris asked. He was

sorry for every bad thing he'd said about the Tecumseh Motel.

Miguel laughed. "It's an old one, man. It's a dangerous one. You better pray to God before you get on it." He loaded the luggage and herded the boys onto the elevator. Then he said something in Spanish, crossed himself, and closed the cage. He jerked a lever and the elevator shook violently.

None of the boys had ever ridden in a manually operated elevator before. Chris pulled out his St. Christopher medal and held it in both hands. "It looks," he said in a tremulous voice, "as if you're holding this car with just the strength of your arm."

"Maybe I am, I don't know how it works," Miguel said. "I know if I let go of this thing, we all see the basement real fast." Meanwhile the elevator was jerking and shaking its way upward.

"That old guy at the desk, is he crazy or what?" Rick asked.

"He's stupid, man," said Miguel. "He don't have no other excuse that I know of. It's okay with me. I'd rather work for a stupid man than a smart one. Are you all related to each other?"

"We're brothers," Shawn said.

"I thought you all looked alike," Miguel said, jacking the elevator past the fifth floor. "You all got the same kind of eyes. Except this one." He looked at Chris with affection. "This one has eyes like the Holy Virgin, if you excuse the blasphemy."

Chris edged into the corner of the elevator.

"Okay, here we go!" said Miguel as they approached the sixth floor. "Sometimes I hit the floor good and sometimes I don't. We'll see how I do tonight." He jerked the lever. The car lurched to a stop two feet below the sixth floor. Miguel laughed. "You can't get out of that unless you're kangaroos," he said. "Wait a minute, I can do better." He tried again, this time coming about a foot and a half above the sixth floor. "It's not good, but it might be the best you get. You better get out." He helped them all out of the elevator and kicked their luggage into the corridor. "You guys need anything in the night, you call my name. I sleep down the hall. And lock your door. We got some strange ones in this hotel this week." He held out his hand.

"Thank you for everything." Shawn gave him five dollars. He thought Miguel was a good one to have on their side.

"Thank *you*." Miguel gave Chris a parting smile and left.

The room was pretty much what they had come to expect from the Hotel Charles. All the furniture had a Salvation Army look and there was a carpet stain, which Rick would swear was human blood.

"There's dirt on the walls," Mark said, examining closely.

"If any of it moves, hit it with your shoe," Shawn said.

"I'm not ever riding in that elevator again," said Chris, sitting on one of the beds. "Tomorrow, I'm gonna find the stairs."

"I don't think there are stairs," said Rick. "I didn't see any. You'll have to use the fire escape and jump."

"What do we do when we want to go down in the elevator?" Shawn asked. "Call Miguel on the phone?"

"Was he looking at me funny?" Chris asked.

"Yes," three of them answered.

"If he wants to take a walk with you, don't go," Rick said.

"Especially if he wants to take a walk to the rest room," Shawn said. "Speaking of which, have we got one?"

Mark was checking doors. "Sort of. We have a sink and a shower thing like at the Y. We're missing part of the toilet."

That got a reaction. "Which part?" Shawn demanded.

"The seat. Somebody ripped it off the hinges."

"Just make sure it flushes," Shawn said. "That's all that really matters."

They undressed and managed somehow to fit everyone into the two beds. Chris was the only one who did not immediately fall asleep. He sat up in bed, looking out the window at the lights of Muncie. There were some nice-looking prostitutes sitting on a public bench across the street. Chris wondered just what sort of neighborhood they were in. He got up and pushed a dresser against the door, just in case. Even when he finally fell asleep, the smile of Miguel haunted his dreams.

Four

The following morning Chris, as usual, was the first to wake up. He resented his brothers' ability to sleep late, in the same abstract way he resented their inability to drive. It put one more responsibility on him. If, for example, the room were on fire, he, Chris, would have to be the first one to deal with it.

The room was not on fire, though, just dirty. Chris pulled up the shade and looked at the grim little cement plaza across the street. The two whores from last night were gone and in their place was an elderly black man. He was sitting on a stone bench reading a paperback book. To the right, one could see downtown Muncie, which was dominated by a six-block open-air mall. To the left was a railroad yard. Straight ahead was the river and the road that had brought them into Muncie.

The day was sunny and the river sparkled. Chris was anxious to go out and do something. He looked hopefully at his brothers, but they showed no sign of waking anytime soon. He dressed, took ten dollars from Shawn's wallet, dragged the dresser away from the door, and went out to look for adventure.

The first thing he found was Miguel, down in the lobby

eating instant coffee from the jar with a spoon. The dim-witted desk clerk had abandoned his post.

"Good morning, Cunnigan," said Miguel, still grin-ning. "You want some coffee?" He offered Chris the jar and the spoon.

"I don't think so," Chris said. "I usually put water in mine."

"You ought to try it this way," Miguel told him. "Pure hits of caffeine. Pure, legal American drugs. I'll tell you something so you remember it. There is no drug for my money to hit you like caffeine. You can take all the il-legal, expensive stuff and I'll take a jar of Folger's crystals anytime. No one seems to know this but me." He put another spoonful in his mouth. "But don't get the freeze-dried. It don't taste as good."

"I'll remember that," said Chris.

"So anyway"—Miguel leaned toward Chris—"what can I do for you today, Cunnigan? You decide you want to come down here and ask me for a date?"

"No." Chris leaned back the other way. "I don't do that. I'm just learning how to do it the regular way."

Miguel laughed. "I like both ways," he said happily. "I like any way you can do it. Equal opportunity for all!"

"What kind of hotel is this, anyway?" Chris asked. He thought the subject should be changed.

Miguel laughed. "It's a shitty hotel, man. Can't you see that? All the whores in Muncie use this hotel. All the perverts of Indiana travel to this hotel. I've seen things come in here, I don't know if they were man, woman, or animal. One time—"

"I get the idea," Chris said.

Miguel screwed the lid on his jar and put it under the couch where he was sitting. "Tell me, Cunnigan," he said.

"What bad thing did you and your brothers do, that you hide out in nasty hotels?"

Chris hesitated. "We just left home," he said. "You know. I don't really want to talk about it."

"Okay," said Miguel. "As long as you aren't a band of killers, I don't care. I respect your privacy. I'm not curious about people's affairs. How long are you going to stay here?"

"I don't know. We haven't talked it over. I guess we'll stay a few weeks and then go somewhere else."

"Just before the police get here, right? But don't tell me about it if you don't want to. I'm not a curious person."

"Maybe when we know you a little better, all right?" Chris said.

Miguel shrugged. "Whatever you want. It's not important to me."

"Where's the best place to eat breakfast around here?" Chris asked.

"You can eat at the Perkins on Route One. Nobody ever died from eating there. You cross the river and follow that long road. Good place to pick up girls."

Chris smiled at him. "Thanks. I'll see you later." He got up.

"Cunnigan . . ." Miguel said coyly.

"What?"

"You strike out with all the girls, I'm here tonight. I could show you some new things." His smile was mocking.

"I'll keep it in mind," Chris said.

Chris had always been a restless person. His mother had resorted to tying him to things when he was little. If he was let loose, he would walk in any direction indefinitely, and she was always losing him in stores He never seemed to have any destination in mind. He just liked to keep moving.

He stood on the bridge and watched the sun rise over the river. A sign on the bank of the river said WHITE. He assumed that was the name of the river, White. Just like the hotel was simply Charles, the river was simply White. There were lots of trees along the riverbank. It was pretty there. Chris just stood for a while doing nothing. Then the prospect of picking up girls gradually overwhelmed him and he moved on, following the road that had brought him into Muncie.

Shawn woke up a half hour later. He counted heads, saw that Chris was gone, worried about it for a few minutes, then decided it was probably all right. When he checked his wallet and saw ten dollars missing, he felt better. Chris was just out for breakfast.

He woke Steve up. "I'm going out," he said. "I'm going to the library to look up some stuff. When these children wake up, feed them, but don't spend more than twenty dollars. I'd rather you didn't go more than five or six blocks from the hotel. I'll be back in two or three hours. If Chris comes home before I do, tell him he's in trouble for going off like that. I'll see you."

Shawn received directions in the lobby from Miguel and went east, in the direction of Ball State University.

Steve watched him go, then took out a pad and pencil and began copying one of the pictures on the wall, a painting of an elkhound struggling to walk through a blizzard. The caption under the painting said *Courage*.

At Perkins, Chris was on his third glass of orange juice. Miguel had steered him right, the place was obviously close to a high school and was crawling with young

boys and girls at this hour. But Chris was in no hurry. He
wanted a group of three girls who looked unattached,
Protestant, and sexually active. He had all morning to
make a good selection.

A very promising threesome had just walked in the
door. They all had high school rings, which made them
between sixteen and seventeen. Chris had observed that
most girls stop wearing their high school rings when they
hit nineteen. They had the unmistakable round-shoul-
dered posture of Protestants. All the Catholic girls he
knew had straight backs and they always told Chris they
were on the pill when they weren't. He had learned to
invest his time only with Protestants.

The girls shuffled in with an uncertain, high school–
girl rhythm, sort of bumping into each other, and sat at
the counter. All three were prodigious slouchers. Chris
smiled slightly.

The girls were already aware of him. They had glanced
at him when they came in the door and now they were
flipping their hair and shifting their shoulders, the way
girls do when boys are looking at them.

Chris knew enough to take his time. He wanted to look
at them for a while, sort them out in his mind. He especially liked the one on the far left. She was very short,
about five foot one, with blond blunt-cut hair and bangs.
She had a small, turned-up nose and she knew how to
dress. She wore a blue velour top with a deep V-neck.
Her figure was enhanced by the fact that she was five or
six pounds overweight, and she had the slightly flushed
complexion of a definite pill user. *That one's mine*, Chris
decided.

He selected the one in the middle, a trim, auburn-
haired girl who dominated the conversation, for Shawn.
He thought she looked intelligent.

That left the one on the right for Steve. She had a waterfall of dark curls hanging down her back and very long fingernails and she sneered a lot, but Steve wouldn't have anything to say about it. He'd just have to take what he got.

Chris gave his head a quick shake to put all the hair in place, then swaggered over to the counter and sat next to the blonde. The three girls went into an immediate frenzy. The blonde turned away from Chris and made some kind of face at which they all giggled.

"Good morning, ladies," Chris said. Since they were such great gigglers, he thought he'd give them something definite to laugh at.

The blonde turned to him and sparkled her blue eyes at him. *Yes,* he thought, *that one is definitely mine.* "Hi," she said. Her voice was high and chirpy.

He gave her a smile, which he knew made him look devastatingly beautiful. "I wonder if I could buy you ladies a cup of coffee?"

More giggling. He had them all sewn up except for the brunette. She was still sneering. *That one's definitely for Steve,* he thought.

"We're here for breakfast," said the blonde. "You want to buy us breakfast?" She threw a triumphant look at her friends.

Chris smiled again. "Anything you say," he said. He felt wonderful.

Back at the hotel, Mark woke up hungry. He rolled over, ran into Rick, and pulled back. Then he sat up and looked at Steven, who was still drawing the elkhound.

"Where is everybody?" he asked.

"Shawn went to the library and Chris's whereabouts are unknown."

"What time is it?" Rick demanded, his face buried in the mattress.

"It's nine o'clock," Mark said. "Chris must have found the Muncie whorehouse."

Steve looked up from his sketch. "I think this hotel is the Muncie whorehouse."

Mark threw himself out of bed. "I want to eat," he said. "Can I have some money?"

"Six dollars," Steve said. "I'm going to stay here and draw for a while."

Mark dressed, put on his guitar and Rick's sunglasses, and left.

Chris, meanwhile, was making lots of progress. He had found out the blonde's name was Bonnie, the auburn one was Pat, and the sneerer was Cindy. They were all juniors at (God help them) Ball High School and they intended to cut school this morning. Clearly, Chris thought, they needed some excitement in their lives.

"I have a couple of brothers," he said, deciding it was time to talk business. "We're new in town and we'd love some company for dinner tonight." He found that insincere politeness was very effective with girls this age.

Bonnie was all for the idea. Eagerness shone in her blue eyes. Chris was deeply in love with her. "Are your brothers as cute as you?" she asked.

"Well..." said Chris, "almost."

"Where are you going to take us?" Cindy demanded. She was all business, that one.

"Anywhere you want," Chris said. "My brothers and I are independently wealthy."

"If that's true," sneered Cindy, "you ought to buy yourself some new clothes."

Chris gave her a look. It was a shame Rick was too

young for this stuff. He would make a perfect match for Cindy.

Pat, the auburn fox, leaned forward. "Instead of dinner," she said in a low, slightly hoarse voice, "why don't you and your brothers come over to my house tonight? My mother works swing shift. We'd have the house all to ourselves." Her smile had an unmistakable meaning. Chris wondered if he was targeting the wrong girl after all.

"Well, I don't know," he demurred. "I mean, your mother might not approve of you girls entertaining men in your house all alone."

"Listen," said Pat. "She makes me get out of the way when she has men coming over. This is only fair. You guys just come to my house tonight. We'll have a pizza sent over or something. I know how to get into the liquor cabinet."

This girl was a real pro. "Well, if you think it would be okay," Chris said happily.

"Just a minute," Cindy said. "Are you guys crazy? We don't know this guy or his goddamned brothers. How do you know they aren't some kind of criminals?"

"Look at his face," Bonnie said. "Does he look like a criminal?"

Chris tried not to look like a criminal while they evaluated his face.

Pat yawned and stretched. She had a lazy, catlike quality that was very sexy. "It's all right, Cindy," she said. "For once, let's have a little fun."

Cindy shrugged. The battle was over.

"You'll have to give me directions to your house," said Chris, taking out a pen. He was a happy man.

Mark bought his breakfast in the Muncie Mall: a Coke, three Snickers bars, and a bag of Fritos. He ate his meal sitting on one of the mall's concrete benches. Then he chewed up all the ice in his paper cup, turned his guitar around to the front, and began to play "Love Me Tender." He sang very quietly at first and then with increasing volume. People passing by glanced at him and didn't seem annoyed, which gave him confidence. In fact, their glances seemed particularly warm, even affectionate. *Maybe I've got talent*, Mark thought. He threw himself into the song.

One of the shoppers stopped in midstep and came toward Mark. It was a middle-aged man in a business suit. Mark thought maybe it was a plainclothes policeman who would tell him to move. He decided to ignore the man, singing louder and avoiding his eyes.

The man reached inside his suit coat. For a terrible moment Mark was afraid he was reaching for a gun. The man took out his wallet, removed a dollar bill and dropped it into Mark's empty Coke cup. "Very nice, son," he said softly.

Mark opened his mouth to say something, then it dawned on him. It was the sunglasses. People were thinking he was blind. He looked at the money in his cup, thought the situation over a few minutes, then began to sing "We're Open Tonight," being careful to look straight ahead and not watch his fingerwork.

When Shawn came home from the library, he found only Rick and Steven. Steve was now drawing Rick, who was making his face as sullen as possible.

"You can't learn anything about the law from lawbooks," he announced. He threw himself on the bed and

picked up the telephone. "I saw Miguel downstairs," he
added. "He wonders when Chris is coming back."

"Chris has a budding romance on his hands," Steve
said. "You've got funny eyebrows, you know that?" he
asked Rick.

"Why don't you kill yourself, like artists are supposed
to?" Rick asked him.

"I need the number for Information and Referral,"
said Shawn into the phone. "Has anybody heard from
Chris yet?"

"We think he's getting laid," Rick said. "Mark went to
the mall and he stole my sunglasses."

"You guys ought to get out," Shawn said, dialing
again. "This is one damn beautiful city."

"What's the university like?" Steve asked. "Did you see
the art department?"

"I didn't happen to notice," Shawn said. "Hello? Yes, I
need to know, is there a local Runaway Hotline?"

"What are you doing?" Steven cried.

"He's turning us in," Rick screeched.

Shawn covered up the mouthpiece. "Shut up," he said.
"Yes, I've got that. Thank you." He hung up. "If you
want information, you go to the source." He dialed a
third time. "Hello? Hi. I'm a teenage runaway."

That made even Rick laugh.

"Yes. No, I don't want to give you my name. I want to
know about the law here in Indiana. I came from another
state. My question is, if caught, would I be extradited to
my home state or tried here in Indiana?"

"This is adorable," Steve said.

"I see," said Shawn. "And what would happen to me
then? Oh. Oh. Okay, I see. What? No, I'm doing fine.
Yes, I've got everything I need. A message to my par-

ents? No, I don't think so. Thank you." He hung up. "We'd be tried and sentenced in Indiana. The usual procedure is that we'd be returned to our parents and the court would recommend some sort of punitive action, such as detention."

"It's too bad you didn't mention the stolen car," Rick said. "I bet that would change the situation a little."

"I think the best thing to do is not get caught," Shawn said.

Rick stood and stretched. "Well, I've restrained myself as long as I can. I've got to see this beautiful city. I'm going for a walk."

"I'll come with you," Steve said. "Shawn?"

"No, I'm very tired all of a sudden."

Steve and Rick walked west from the hotel, in the direction of the railroad yards.

Mark stopped playing for a minute and glanced quickly at his cup. It looked like about fifteen dollars. *I'm going to have to learn some new songs,* he thought.

"Where do you want to go?" Steve asked Rick.

"I don't know," said Rick. "I'd like to buy some cigarettes."

"You better ask Shawn about that first," Steve said.

"Oh, he can fuck himself," Rick said. "You bastards don't smoke. You can't possibly understand."

"If we walked the other way, we could see Ball State," Steve said hopefully. "I'd like to see what it looks like."

"Forget it," Rick said. "Besides, what do you care about a college campus? You're just another high school dropout now, thanks to your brother."

"I don't know," said Steve. "If we stayed here awhile,

if we were working maybe, I might be able to audit some classes."

Rick stopped walking in order to laugh at his brother properly. "You don't think we have enough money for cigarettes and you're going to audit classes?" he said. Steven could be such a fool, he thought.

"I didn't say now," Steve said. "I meant if we got money somehow."

"Yeah. When the tooth fairy comes."

That was the end of that conversation.

They walked deeper and deeper into the western section of Muncie. It was predominantly black and poor and everyone in the street looked at Steve and Rick as if they didn't belong.

Steve was nervous, but Rick seemed determined to continue on this course and Steve didn't want to appear afraid. He stuffed his hands in his pockets and even walked ahead of Rick. After all, he was two years older and at least a half inch taller. He didn't need to feel dominated by this little creep.

Then, without any warning, three young men stepped out of an alley and formed a triangle around Steven. They were white, blond, tall, and possibly all related to one another. They looked to be about nineteen or twenty. Their eyes were frighteningly pale, like those of a Weimaraner. One of them had a bike chain in his hand.

"Hi, kid," said the bike-chain holder. "You're new around here, aren't you?"

Steve didn't think it would be smart to answer. Instead, he gave the bike-chain holder a quick, gentle shove and broke to the right. One of them grabbed his arms and held them behind his back. Steve managed to kick loose from him, but all three continued to surround him, not leaving any possible escape route. There was no question that the chain was a weapon and that Steven was a selected victim.

"Rick!" Steve shouted. Rick was frozen in his tracks, only about ten feet away. "Come here!"

Rick didn't move. He seemed to be watching the scene unfold as if it were on television.

Steve was amazed. Back on Cornell Drive there was never any question. If a Cunnigan got in a fight, any other Cunnigan in the vicinity would help him without hesitation.

Rick took a step backward.

Someone grabbed one of Steven's arms. "Rick!" he shouted, disbelieving. "Come *here!*"

The assailants were amused by this. "Well, *Rick*," said the chain holder. "You want to fight too?"

Rick hesitated one more second, then turned and bolted in the direction of the hotel.

The chain holder grinned at Steven. "You don't pick your friends very good." He turned to his companions. "Let's get back off the street."

Rick ran as if he were being chased. He was aware he had committed an unforgivable crime, but how could anyone with an instinct to survive throw himself into a fight? His feet hurt from pounding the sidewalk. He felt as if his heart might be giving out.

Miguel was asleep on a couch in the lobby. Rick didn't bother with the elevator, just ran up the stairs and pounded on their door.

Shawn was still there alone. Rick couldn't get his breath. He just stood in the doorway and coughed and looked hysterical.

"What's the matter with you?" Shawn said. "Where's your brother?"

"I couldn't help it," Rick gasped, hanging on to the doorframe for support. "I couldn't help it."

Shawn grabbed his shoulders angrily. "Where is he? What's the matter with him?"

"This street. Six blocks west. Some guys . . ." Rick didn't get any further. Shawn literally threw him out of the way and took off for the stairs.

Rick let his body sag against the wall. His ribs hurt from running.

Shawn found his brother lying in the alley where he had been beaten. His assailants were long gone. He had pulled himself into a sitting position and was staring into space. His shirt was ripped in two places and his jacket was gone. He had been repeatedly punched in the mouth. Shawn was used to scanning beating victims for injuries. Other than a horrible look of resignation on Steve's face, he was basically all right. He looked at Shawn with neither surprise nor emotion. He had been expecting him. "They took twelve dollars off me," he said. "I'm sorry."

Shawn knelt down on the pavement and examined one of the tears in Steven's shirt. "What else did they do? What did they hit you with here?"

"A chain. Just a little bike-chain. They didn't hit me in the head with it." Steve knew as much about medical emergencies as Shawn did. It was their family heritage. Steven's eyes changed suddenly from resignation to anger. "Where's that little bastard?" he demanded. "Back at the hotel?"

"Yes. At least he came and got me."

"I'm going to beat shit out of him," Steve said. "I've got a right. There were only three of them. They had reflexes like vegetables. If you had been here, or Chris or any-body, I would have been okay. I would have gotten away from them."

"I know," said Shawn. He felt tired, weighed down. "But you don't want to hurt him. He's your brother."

"He's *not*," Steve said with a violence that was unusual for him. "The rest of you are my brothers, but he's noth-ing. He's not even a human being."

"Yes, he is," said Shawn, but without much conviction. "He's just got some problems."

"I hate him," Steve said. His eyes had a cold look. "I always have. I never said it, but I do."

Shawn sighed. "Are you good enough to walk?" he asked. "We better get out of here."

"I can walk if I lean on you a little," Steve said. "Somebody did something to my spine. Kicked me or something."

Shawn hesitated. "Steven, they didn't do anything else to you, did they?"

"Like what?"

Shawn was uncomfortable. "They didn't do anything *funny* to you, did they? I mean, they weren't fags or any-thing like that?"

It took Steve a minute to understand the question. "Oh, God. No. I would have lost my mind."

"Well, come on." Shawn put his arm around Steve and helped him to stand. "We ought to get out of this neigh-borhood."

Steve stood up shakily. He hurt all over. "Don't let go of me," he said.

"Come on," said Chris. "Tell me what's going on. Where is everybody and why do you have that guilty look on your face? Did you sell them to the gypsies?"

Rick was standing at the window. "Lay off, will you? I don't know where any of them are. I don't know anything."

"Yes, you do. Spill it, little boy. I want to know where everybody is and what you've done. Now."

"If you don't shut up, I'm going down to the lobby!" Rick shouted.

Chris decided to try a different tactic. "If you tell me your secret, I'll tell you mine," he suggested.

"Your secret is undoubtedly how you got laid this morning and I don't want to hear it." Rick tried to imagine what it would be like if those guys had killed Steve. No one would ever talk to him again. It would be horrible.

Chris, meanwhile, was hurt. He thought people enjoyed hearing how he got laid. "All right," he said petulantly. "Just see if I ever do you a favor. I was getting ready to fix you up with someone, but you can just forget it now."

Rick whirled from the window. "Will you—"

The door opened. It was Shawn and Steve.

Rick didn't look at them. He looked back to the window, his whole body stiff with fear.

"Holy Christ!" said Chris. "You're bleeding!"

"He's all right," Shawn said. "He got in a little fight."

"Jesus Christ, I guess he did." Chris went to them and examined Steven's face, holding it gently with his hand. "Look at him," Chris said over his shoulder to Rick. "Somebody really socked him."

Rick didn't turn from the window or move.

"He knows about this," Shawn said quietly. "Move. I want to get him to bed. He's all bruised."

"You know about this?" Chris turned on Rick. "What do you know about this?"

Rick turned to Chris in a rage. He opened his mouth but couldn't find what he wanted to say. He ran from the room, slamming the door.

"What in hell is going on?" Chris demanded.

"I'll tell you in a minute. Help me get his shirt off him," Shawn said. "He got hit with a chain a couple of times."

"Jesus," said Chris. He sat on the bed beside Steven and brushed the hair out of his eyes. "You gonna be all right?" he asked.

"Sure," Steve said.

"I wish I'd been there with you," Chris said. "We would have shown them."

Steve looked at Shawn. "You see?" he said.

Shawn shrugged. "I know."

The door opened again. It was Mark. His face was alight. "Guess what?" he said. "I made forty dollars today!"

Five

"We've got a situation here, I hope everybody realizes it."
After the excitement of Steven's bruises and Mark's
money had died down, Chris's mind returned to practical
matters.

"What's wrong?" Shawn asked. He sat at the foot of
the bed where Steve was recuperating. Mark had taken
Rick's place at the window. Rick was still out.

"Well, I'm not being disrespectful about your injuries,
Steve, but you see, I got very, very lucky today and we
three had a date with some very nice girls tonight and
now there's only two of us."

"Oh, shit," said Steve. "Were they cute?"

"Cute," said Chris, "and eager and all on the pill by
my best guess. And one of them had an empty house for
us to play in. I can't even talk about it without getting a
lump in my throat."

"Don't say any more," said Steve. "I can't stand it.
What did mine look like?"

"I'd better not tell you," said Chris. There was no point
in telling Steve he'd reserved a sneerer for him.

"Really, Steven," said Shawn. "Did you have to go get

yourself brutalized today? Why couldn't you have
waited until tomorrow, when the fun was over?"

"I don't know what to tell them," said Chris, "unless
we let two of them have *me*."

"Want to invite Rick?" asked Shawn, with a slightly
crooked smile.

"I wouldn't invite Rick for a walk through Hell," Chris
said.

"Well, then, unless we take Miguel, we're up shit
creek," Shawn said.

"That's too dangerous," Steve said. "He might get excited and attack Chris."

Mark had been very quiet through all this. At some
point in the conversation he had turned from the window
and begun inching toward Shawn. "I could go," he said.

That made everyone laugh.

"You don't understand," Chris said. "This is *girls* we're
talking about. It's not like when we need an extra person
to play softball. I mean, it wouldn't be nice if one of those
girls thinks she's got a date and finds out she's going to
baby-sit instead."

"I'm fourteen." Mark had adopted a tone of quiet dig-
nity. "I don't see anything so *ludicrous* about it." He used
the word *ludicrous* on purpose so they would understand
he wasn't a child.

Chris was still laughing. "These girls are seventeen.
They expect certain things. These girls strike me as being
more expectant than most. They expect things a boy of
your age just can't deliver. Do you get my meaning?"

Mark took a step toward him, defiantly. "If my memory is correct," he said, "you started bragging about your
conquests at fifteen, so I'm not too far from the qualifying
age."

"There's a lot of difference between fourteen and fifteen," Chris said.

"Maybe you're just afraid I'll beat your record," Mark said.

"Mark, you're just too young!" Chris shouted.

"Let me go and we'll find out if I'm too young!" Mark shouted back.

"Children!" Shawn called. "Neither one of you is making a good case for your maturity."

"Tell him he's too young!" Chris said.

"I don't know that he is," Shawn said. "I mean, he knows better than we do what he can handle. It seems to me if he were too young to do it, he wouldn't be so interested in doing it."

"Yeah!" said Mark.

"Who knows what he might be capable of?" Shawn went on. "Look at the facts, genetically speaking. We're a family of child prodigies. Steve and I both started at sixteen. You amazed the whole family by starting at fifteen. Who's to say Mark can't do it at fourteen?"

Chris folded his arms. "I'd have to see it to believe it," he said.

"You aren't going to see anything!" Mark shouted.

"Because you aren't going to do anything!" Chris shouted back.

"Christopher *John!*" Shawn shouted. "If I didn't know better, I'd think you were afraid of having your record broken. Why can't you encourage your brother the way Steve and I encouraged you?"

"Yes. Encourage me." Mark giggled.

"Christ," said Chris.

"Besides," said Shawn, "it's either Mark, Rick, or Miguel. Or nothing at all."

Chris considered this. "Do you want to borrow my razor?" he asked Mark bitterly.

"Oh boy!" Mark said. "I'm gonna get laid!"

Steve sighed. "And with my girl, too."

"I appreciate it, Steve," said Mark happily.

"All right," Chris said resignedly. "If you're going to do this, you've got to know some things. The most important rule is, don't do anything until you're absolutely sure she's using some kind of birth control. Go slow, let her make a lot of the moves. Then she can't blame the whole thing on you. Tell her a lot of nice things, even if they aren't true. Especially afterward. They get hysterical if you don't."

Mark frowned with the effort of memorizing all this. "Anything else?"

"If anything tickles," Chris said, "don't laugh."

"I feel like we've witnessed some history here today," Shawn said to Steve.

"The torch has been passed," Steven said.

Pat's house was in the same neighborhood Steve had been beaten in. It was next to an all-night Laundromat. She answered the door in a sheer blouse and cigarette jeans. "Who's this?" she said, indicating Mark. Nothing was going to get past her.

"It's all right," Chris said. "He's fifteen and a half. People always mistake him for younger."

Chris could tell Pat didn't believe this, nor did she care. It was obvious she had picked out Shawn for herself, since Bonnie was interested in Chris. They could stick Cindy with Mark.

Both the other girls were already there. Bonnie had on a fuzzy pink sweater, meant to look like angora. Cindy wore a black tank top. Shawn and Chris knew from experience that clothes of this type meant the girls were ready for action. Mark was beginning to be frightened. Cindy was taller than he, and when she found out she was slotted for Mark, she began smiling at him in a very nasty way, like a trainer about to break a new horse.

Despite their vast sexual experience, none of the Cunnigans had ever dealt with girls who were as cooperative as these three. After about four glasses of Cointreau all around, Pat suggested they split into pairs for the rest of the evening. She handed out room assignments like a camp counselor. As Shawn said later, it was like visiting a whorehouse, except the girls wore tennis shoes.

"What's that thing you wear?" Bonnie asked several hours later. She had turned out to be a perfect match for Chris; cheerful, enthusiastic, rapid to climax, and willing to experiment. They were resting between rounds.

Chris was propped up on an elbow, petting Bonnie abstractedly. He was wondering if Mark was all right with Cindy. "What thing?"

"That necklace thing you took off." She rearranged his hands so he would pet her where she wanted to be petted.

"My St. Christopher? I always wear that. That's my saint. I was named after him, before they kicked him out of the Church." It made Chris nervous to talk about religion in bed. He was still working out whether he considered premarital sex a mortal sin, and until he was sure, he didn't want to think about it.

"You're Catholic?" Bonnie said. Her tone of voice was funny.

"Yes, I am." Chris stopped petting her. "Is there anything the matter with that?"

Bonnie sat up in bed, gathering the sheet around her. They were in Pat's bedroom and the bed was a little small for the two of them. "Well . . ." she said hesitantly. "I'm just surprised. I don't know too many Catholics."

"Well if it bothers you, we can stop right now," Chris said, annoyed. He had just been ready to start in again and she had to pull something like this.

"I just don't know," Bonnie said. There was a tortured look in her blue eyes. "Don't you people worship *idols* and things?"

Chris sat up. "No!" he said, his voice high-pitched with indignation. "I certainly don't!"

"Well, I didn't know," said Bonnie defensively. "That's just what my mom and dad say. And that you pray to people instead of God. And that you try to buy your way out of Hell."

"I'm going to put my clothes on now, Bonnie," said Chris, starting to get out of bed.

"Wait a minute." She detained him gently with her hand.

Chris pushed her hand away. "Bonnie, I can't do anything with you if you're going to attack my religion. I'm sorry."

"Wait a minute, for goodness' sakes," Bonnie said. "Can't we talk about it? I'm just telling you what they taught me in church. Maybe it isn't true. Maybe I've just never heard the truth." Her eyes were as round as a child's.

Chris was moved. "Well, I'm certainly not an idolater," he said, trying to look deeply hurt.

Bonnie rolled onto her back and looked up at him. She reached up and stroked his chest. "I'm sorry if I hurt your feelings, Christopher," she said.

Chris had a feeling she was partially excited because of his new, forbidden status. He sighed and let his body fall against hers, thinking for just a moment of that long confession he was going to have to make in four years.

"I'll warn you right now, I don't come," said Pat. She and Shawn were in the master bedroom, her mother's room. She was sitting up in bed in a black lace bra and panties, twisting her hair into a rope while she watched Shawn undress. "I don't even enjoy sex very much," she added. "I don't even know why I do it."

Shawn stopped in mid-undress. "Well, I don't want to just go through the motions here," he said, sitting on the foot of the bed. "I mean, if you're not even going to try and have a good time, I don't want to bother."

"That's very liberated of you," she said. She grew tired of twisting her hair and tossed it behind her shoulder. It was a lovely shade of auburn, like a fox's coat.

"I'm not trying to be liberated," he said. "I'm just not going to try and get worked up while you lie there and read the newspaper or something. We can go in the other room and watch television if you don't like sex."

Pat clearly wanted to discuss her problem. "I want to like sex," she said. "I try to like it. When we were talking to your brother this morning, I was already planning this. I don't even know your last name, and yet I can't wait to invite you to my house and drag you in here and get my clothes off. I don't know what's wrong with me. I always hope I'll get interested, but somehow I don't."

"Maybe it's because you talk so much," Shawn suggested. He wanted to make her laugh.

"I don't know what it is." She flipped her hair in a gesture of frustration. "Look at you. You're good-looking. You're nice. I want to do it with you. But if you were to touch me right now, I wouldn't feel a thing."

Shawn sighed. Why did he always get the crazy ones? He was having enough trouble worrying about what Cindy might be doing to Mark. "I'm no psychiatrist, Pat," he said wearily. "I mean, if there's anything special you want me to do for you, I'll do it, but I don't know you well enough to try and psychoanalyze you."

"I think it's my mother," Pat went on eagerly. "Because she's such a whore. All she does since the divorce is bring these big studs around. Right in front of me. She doesn't care what I think of her morals. She brings them right in here and doesn't even blush."

"Well, your mother's entitled to a sex life," Shawn said sadly. He knew he wasn't going to get much out of this girl. *I'll bet Chris has had twenty orgasms by now,* he thought bitterly.

"She doesn't give a damn about me," Pat went on. "She calls me names. She's never said one single nice thing about me."

Shawn couldn't take it. He just couldn't take it. "Maybe you should count your blessings, Pat," he said tensely, "because my father used to beat the shit out of me."

"What?"

"He beat me. Kicked me and punched me and I used to bleed all over the floor, Pat, but I still manage to get it up." He realized to his surprise that he was in some kind of rage. It didn't sound like him talking at all.

"They'll hear you in the other room," Pat said, horrified.

"I don't give a fuck if they do!" Shawn yelled. "I'm so goddamned sick and tired of hearing people whine and cry about their bad childhoods and how it's ruined their lives. Has anyone ever hit you with their fist, Pat? Do you even know what that feels like?"

She was cringing against the pillows now. She shook her head no.

"Of course you don't! You haven't suffered as much as you think, have you? Maybe you'd like to hear about my mother while we're at it. Would you like to hear that story?"

Again she shook her head no.

"My mother got thrown through the windshield of a car. I got to see it happen. Did you ever see anything like that, Pat? Do you know what a car accident looks like?" He was near hysteria. His breath was short.

Pat shook her head for the third time. She was crying.

"So just don't tell me how bad your life is. I don't want to hear it." His frenzy had spent itself. He was slowing down now.

Pat watched him, as if he were a dangerous animal. When he didn't give any sign of starting up again, she leaned forward slightly. "Shawn, I had no idea," she said softly.

"Well, now you do," he said. "And you don't see me letting all that stuff mess up my life, do you?"

"No," she said. She edged toward him.

"You have to live your own life while you've got it," he said. "Let your mother be a whore. It's got nothing to do with you."

She was close enough to touch him now. She put her arms around him from behind and gave him a long, caressing hug. "If I had only known what you'd been through," she murmured, "I would have been ashamed to talk about my little problems." She rubbed her hands over his body. "Growing up without your mother, beaten by your father . . ." She rubbed her head against his shoulder, like an affectionate cat. "You poor little boy." And as he turned his head to kiss her, she began to feel what she had never felt before.

Cindy looked at Mark. Mark looked at Cindy.

"How old are you anyway?" she asked.

Mark was terrified. He felt he might have been all right with someone like Bonnie, but this girl was bigger, older, taller, and much more cynical than he could possibly handle his first time out. He could see she had a mean streak. He felt that if he lied about his age or experience, she would do something cruel and horrible to him. He panicked for a few seconds, then said, "I'm twelve."

Cindy's mouth dropped open. "Twelve!" she said.

Mark hung his head and tried to look youthful and sheepish. "Yes. My brothers do this to me all the time, forcing me to do things with girls. They think it's funny." He looked up to see how she was taking this.

Cindy was completely taken aback. "You mean they fix you up with girls as a joke?"

He kept his head down. "Yes. I guess because I look a little older than my age. One time, I was alone with this girl and she . . ." He pretended he couldn't go on for a minute. "She did something awful to me. She *hurt* me."

"You poor little thing," Cindy cried. She threw her arms around Mark, completely smothering his face in black tank top. "You poor sweet little angel." She held him out at arm's length. "Your brothers must be monsters."

"No, no," he said generously. "They don't mean it. They don't realize. . . ."

She cuddled him like a toy. "Well, someday, Mark, you'll be older and they won't be able to tease you that way. I just hope all this won't make you hate women or anything like that."

"I hope so too," Mark said enthusiastically.

She smiled at him warmly. "We can make sure it doesn't. You come over to the bed with me and I'll show you some nice things. Would you like that?"

"I don't know," said Mark, trying to look fearful and not laugh at the same time. "What are you going to do to me?"

She settled herself on the bed. "Would you like to learn how to french-kiss?" she suggested.

He went to her with mock reluctance. "I'll try it," he said bravely.

Cindy put her arms around him and he thought happily that it would only take one more year and then Chris was going to get some real competition.

Rick stood in his favorite position: by the window, with his hands in his pockets, looking at nothing. Indeed, there was nothing to see out the window because it was night and the lights were on in the room. All he could really see was his own reflection and the reflection of Steven, in bed behind him. He appeared all the more ridiculous because he had his sunglasses on.

Steven had been sleeping heavily. He woke up momentarily, saw Rick, and felt a little pity for him, mixed in with the anger. "Why don't you take those stupid things off?" he said.

Rick turned to him, facial expression hidden behind the glasses. "Mind your own business," he said. Actually he was crying, but he didn't want Steve to know that.

He had been crying not out of sympathy for Steven, who was going to be fine in a few days, but for himself. No one would ever forget that he had deserted a brother in need. No one would ever forgive him for looking out for himself as he had. The rift between him and the others had widened again. Soon they would begin to hate him, if they didn't already.

Not that he would have done anything differently. He couldn't imagine anyone stupid enough to throw themselves into someone else's fight. He knew perfectly well that was what they expected of him, but he couldn't imagine how their minds worked to arrive at such a conclusion. He couldn't help it if self-preservation came first with him. He hadn't wished any ill for Steven. But he would never risk getting beaten up for him either.

He could imagine the things they had said about him already. Chris and Mark especially. They were such righteous little bastards. Shawn might have defended him, but weakly. Whatever had been said, he knew he was moving further and further away from them. He knew he would have to leave them someday, before it came to the point where they asked him to leave.

Steven, meanwhile, was feeling sorry for Rick. He didn't understand him at all, but he felt sorry for him. It must feel awful to be so much on the outside, to be so hated. "I don't blame you for what happened today," he said.

Rick turned to him again. Again his expression was unreadable. "You're the only one," he said. "The rest of them think I'm some kind of monster."

"You just panicked," Steve said. "Lots of people do things when they're afraid and not thinking straight."

Rick knew this wasn't true. He could have had five

years to think it over and he wouldn't have helped Steve. "They all want an excuse to hate me," he said, shrugging. "This gives them a good one."

Steven felt an unusual tenderness for Rick. Usually there was a mutually understood hatred between these two, but Steven could imagine how lonely Rick must feel at a time like this. Maybe no one had ever shown Rick enough love. Maybe he was caught in a hopeless cycle. He had been fairly nice as a little kid. Maybe if someone would be his friend, he'd do better. "I'm not angry with you, Rick," Steve said gently. "And I certainly don't hate you. What happened today is just history as far as I'm concerned. In fact, do you know what?"

"What?"

"I'm glad you did what you did. I would have felt badly if you were hurt on my account."

Rick turned back to the window. Steve assumed he was overcome by emotion, but in fact he simply couldn't bear to hear any more of that kind of talk. It was terrifying to him. They were always saying things like that. *I'm glad it was me and not you. I'll tell Dad I did it.* How could he ever feel part of a group whose thinking was so screwed up, so wrong? They were all crazy and only he was sane. He could never be one of them. Rick thought to himself that he would have to get away from them soon, so they would never have to find out just how different he was.

Six

Steven turned his head to one side, still half asleep. Outside the window, showers of leaves were falling. In the bright sunlight they took on the colors of coins: copper, silver, brass, bronze, pewter. A wealth of them, falling in heavy waves whenever the wind blew. Steven had to think for a moment to figure out that it was September.

He moved his right arm experimentally. He had taken most of the beating on his right side and he checked every morning to see how much of the soreness was gone. At first he had enjoyed his confinement. It gave him a chance to be alone, to draw and daydream undisturbed. But now, after a week, his muscles began to crave exercise and he envied his brothers, who left the hotel by ten o'clock every morning and wandered off in any direction they wanted. The arm was not very sore at all today, much better than last night. He tried sitting up in bed and felt new strength in his chest and shoulders. The feeling of recovery was always miraculous to Steven. It seemed strange to him that once you had damaged a human body, it would find some way to make itself well again. His entire childhood had been a testimony to the recuperative powers of the human body. He found it ironic, too, that now, having run away from Donald and their past, he should find himself in bed recovering from another beating.

Determined to make a complete recovery, Steven stood up and stretched his whole body. There was only a light pull of pain in his right rib cage. *I'm going out today,* he thought.

Miguel came into the room without knocking. Miguel was a source of amazement to Steven. At first he had seemed to be some kind of juvenile delinquent, but since Steven's injuries, for some reason Miguel had assigned himself to be a day nurse. He visited the room at least three times a day, bringing coffee and doughnuts and 7-Ups and magazines and, once, a gin and tonic from the hotel bar.

For a while Steven had been terrified of all this kindness, thinking Miguel had rape in mind, but Miguel showed no sexual interest in Steven. He was loyal to Chris in that respect. He seemed more than anything to crave conversation. He would stay for hours, sitting on the end of the bed, asking Steve's opinion about the Catholic Church and life after death and the space program and anything else that came into his head. Occasionally he would offer to sell Steve a joint, or mention, in passing, what sentence he'd gotten for robbing this or that house, but mostly he talked philosophy and gave medical advice. By the end of the week, Steven had come to think of him as a close friend.

"Hey, Cunnigan!" he shouted this morning. "It's Cruller Day at Dunkin' Donuts!" He brandished a sack. "Hundreds and hundreds of crullers for only a dollar sixty-nine!"

"I feel good today," Steven said. "I'm going out somewhere today."

Miguel frowned sternly. "You go out carefully, Cunnigan. You stay off that west side, okay?"

Steve sat down on the bed. "I just didn't know the neighborhood," he said. "Now I do."

"You should have asked me," Miguel said gravely. "You should not wander around a strange town like that. I wouldn't have gone on the street you were on. Not even to pick up a hundred-dollar bill from the sidewalk."

"Well, I know better now," Steven said. He opened his coffee and took a sip.

"Listen," said Miguel. "You should carry a knife or something. I really mean it. All you Cunnigans just wander around like babies waiting for someone to jump you. I happen to have two switchblades I could sell you. I'm not trying to make money, I'm *concerned*." He divided the crullers between them. There was an odd number and he gave the extra one to Steven.

"We don't need anything like that," Steve said. "I wouldn't use a knife on anyone if I had to. We're all good fighters. Really. I just lost out because there were three guys against me. If there had only been *two*, I would have been all right."

Miguel looked at Steven out of the side of his eyes. "Or if your little brother had helped you," he said.

Steve wondered who had been talking. "He panicked. It happens." He made his voice as casual as possible.

"I don't know about that," said Miguel. "I like *all* you Cunnigans, but *that* one is a little sneaky. I wouldn't give him my wallet to hold while I went on the Ferris wheel."

"That's my brother you're talking about, Miguel."

Steven said it in such a way that his emotions could not be gauged.

"I understand," said Miguel. "I have some brothers somewhere myself. If anyone said anything against them, I'd kill him. But still, I know which ones of them I trust and which ones I don't."

"Let's change the subject," Steven said. "I want to go and get some art supplies today. Do you know of a store around here that would have things like that?"

"Art supplies! You mean like pencils and things?"

"Yes."

"You could go to Kelso's in the mall. That would be close. They sell things to teachers. Of course, this is not a place where *I* do a lot of shopping, but I guess they would have artist's things."

"That's great. I could visit Mark."

Miguel laughed. "You *should* see Mark. Mark has to be seen to be believed. He sits on a bench and does Stevie Wonder. It's terrifying. I gave him a dollar yesterday myself. He just looked into space and said, 'Thank you, sir.' What an actor!"

"We've been living off his income," said Steve proudly. "I mean, I guess it's wrong, what he's doing, but ..."

"Nothing is wrong until the police catch you," said Miguel. "Never forget that. Do you want me to go out with you today and protect you from nasty street elements?"

"No," Steven said. "I appreciate it, but I feel like being alone."

Miguel smiled at him and rose to go. "You give my very best to your brother Chris when you see him," he said.

When he had gone, Steve got up again and stretched as hard as he could. All the pain would be gone by tomorrow. He opened the window and let the wind blow in on him. It was beautiful fall air, as clear and pure as water. He couldn't stand the room another minute. He put on his clothes and went out.

Just walking, just feeling his muscles work together, was a joy. The mall was fairly crowded, mostly with young mothers pushing strollers. They were happy because, like Steven, they had an excuse for goofing off. As long as they had those young children to care for, they could spend all their time wandering the streets, taking life as it came, not having to be at schools or jobs. They were all dressed in the most comfortable of jeans, the loosest of shirts, the simplest of hairstyles. They pushed their children along and would stop for hours, if they wanted to, in front of a jeweler's window, counting the diamonds on a watch. They were free.

Steven was in a mood that bordered on euphoria. There was nothing like being in pain and having the pain stop to make you appreciate life.

The mall was open-air. It was blocks and blocks of stores, all of which fronted on a secluded little walkway. Steven thought that was much nicer than an enclosed mall. There were geraniums dying in tubs all along the walkway and old-fashioned lampposts and even a fountain, clogging up because too many people had made wishes and thrown pennies in. Every block or so there was a concrete bench, on which the young mothers and bums and delinquent children and all the other free people were sitting: smoking, eating, and staring into space. It was a whole colony of people just like Steven, who loved to go off by themselves and do nothing.

Then he saw Mark. He was sitting on a bench at the far end of the mall, playing his guitar. At first it was hard to believe it was really Mark, because he had become a different person for this role. His eyes, behind Rick's sunglasses, were convincingly blank, focused on nothing. He was singing "Cry Like a Baby" and using his body to keep rhythm, the way Ray Charles does. When someone came close to him to put money in his cup, he would jump, as if startled to find anyone near him. As Steve walked closer Mark gave no sign of recognition at all, just continued to stare at the same point in space. Steven stepped directly in front of him, only about three feet away. Mark kept right on singing. He didn't even smile. His voice, Steve noted, was not bad.

When the song was over, Steve said, "That was very good, young man."

"Steve? Is that you?" Mark lifted his eyes to a level somewhere in the middle of Steven's chest.

"God, you're talented," Steve said.

"Thank you. I practice a lot."

"I've got to get out of here," Steven said. "You're giving me chills. Do you know where Kelso's is?"

"I've been told it's in that direction," said Mark, pointing sloppily in the direction of the store.

"I'll see you," Steve said, laughing.

"Not if I see you first," Mark giggled.

Once inside the store, Steven lost all track of time. It was a store devoted to school and art supplies. It had shelves and shelves of fascinating things; teacher's plan books and accordion folders and silver stars to paste on students' papers. There were Catholic instruction books that made Steve shiver and there were felt-tipped markers in hundreds of colors, even metallics. Steve took his time, working his way through the first floor of the store and then climbing the stairs to a loft where the real art supplies were. The whole upstairs smelled like unfinished wood and acrylic paint and linseed oil. It was like an opium den for Steven. He went on a binge of the senses, ruffling blank pages in sketchbooks, testing brushes against his hands, uncapping paints to look at the colors. It was quiet and desolate in this part of the store and there was no artificial lighting, just an attic-type window that let a huge shaft of sunlight slant across the room. To Steve, the atmosphere seemed almost holy.

He had to decide carefully. He had told Shawn that he was tired of making pencil sketches and wanted to do something else for a while. Shawn said anything that cost under five dollars and wasn't too messy. Of course, that eliminated painting. But there were charcoals and pastels and crayons and markers, all clamoring for Steve's attention. He felt dizzy from the importance of the decision he had to make.

Then he saw a display of steel pens and bottles of ink. It was perfect. Neat, portable, totally different from the soft lead of a pencil, and something he hadn't done for years. He would draw Chris first. Chris was made for pen and ink. He could already picture the drawing he would make.

"Excuse me." A voice near him made him jump. He had thought he was all alone in the loft. It was a girl, whom he estimated to be his own age, standing only a foot away from him. It might have been just a product of his mood, but it seemed to Steven that this was the most fascinating-looking girl he had ever seen. She was bone-thin and very small, with graceful lines in her body; a long waist, tapered fingers, a pretty neck. Her hair was just shoulder-length and apricot-blond, with rows and rows of tight waves, as if she had braided it wet. She wore a black leotard, jeans, and sandals, although it was really past the sandal season. Where most girls would have decorated such an outfit with chains or rings or earrings, this girl wore no jewelry, not even a belt. Her jeans were embroidered across the front pocket in small peach-colored letters that announced her name, *Amy*.

Steven noticed all these details and recorded them in his mind, partly because he found her so attractive and partly because artists record and memorize all the beautiful things they see.

She smiled at him, a little embarrassed. "I want to get at the X-Acto knives," she said. "I've been waiting for ten minutes for you to move, but it kind of looked like you were going to stand there all day." She was making fun of him, but in a friendly way. Her voice was musical. She punched certain words, the way professional announcers are taught to do.

"I'm sorry, Amy," said Steven. Then he realized he had made a mistake in using her name, even though she advertised it.

She cocked her head at him. "Are you one of my students?" she asked. "I don't recognize you."

"No," he said, wishing he were back home in bed again. "I read your jeans." The way he said it, it sounded like a confession to the most hideous sex crime of the century.

"Oh!" She looked down and laughed. "You're very observant."

Steven stepped out of the way so she could get her knife. A shower of apricot hair fell across her shoulder when she reached.

"You're awfully young to be a teacher, aren't you?" Steven asked. He was having trouble breathing.

"I'm twenty-six," she said. "Is that too young to be a teacher?" She had become defensive.

"No," said Steven. "I thought you were younger." He

was convinced he had never said so many stupid things to one person in his whole life.

"I wish I were," she said. Steve couldn't tell how she meant that.

She showed signs of getting ready to go to the cash register, so Steven said, to detain her, "Where do you teach?"

"Ball State," she said. "This is my first year. That's why I jumped down your throat. I'm still a little insecure about it. I teach painting and ceramics. Do you go to Ball State?"

"No," he said. "I'm not a college student." He decided to leave it ambiguous just what he *was*.

"Oh. I was going to try and recruit you for one of my classes." She smiled. Her smile was nice. Just a little curve of the lips.

"I wish I could afford to go," he said. "I haven't ever had any proper training. You can only go so far by yourself."

"That's true." She had become thoughtful. She was thinking of something else. "What's your name?" she asked.

"Steven. Cunnigan."

"Do people call you Steve?" she asked. All the while she was clearly thinking of something else, something totally unrelated to their conversation.

"Yes."

She focused her eyes on him again. They were green. "I'll make a deal with you, Steve," she said.

Steven was ready to go out and murder all her enemies, if that was what she wanted. "All right," he said.

"I could give you some lessons, if you'd like. I could give you painting lessons, just work with you a little. We could do it on Saturdays or something, maybe at my apartment."

"I couldn't afford to pay you," he said. He was almost shaking. He couldn't believe this nice little girl was going to come right out and make a sex deal with him, yet he was almost sure that was what she was leading up to.

"Well," she said, suddenly becoming shy and girlish in her manner, "I was thinking about a deal. I'd like to paint you."

"You want me to sit for you in exchange for lessons?" Steven couldn't read her eyes at all. He couldn't tell if that was really what she wanted or not.

"Yes," she said. "I'd love to paint someone like you. You have a nice quality. A sort of fiftyish quality."

"I look fifty?" he said.

"No. I mean the 1950s. The way you stand on one foot. There's a guardedness about you. A sort of Brando-like quality. Like . . ."

"James Dean?" he pleaded.

"Yes, that's it. Like James Dean."

Steven *was* shaking now. "It's just my brother's jacket," he said. Shawn had given him his black motorcycle jacket after his own had been stolen in the fight.

"Well, whatever it is, I'd like to paint it," said Amy. "I'll give you good lessons. I'm a good teacher. Is it a deal?"

Her eyes were still unreadable. He couldn't tell if she was lying about her intentions or not. He didn't much care. "Sure," he said.

She smiled that curved smile again. "Good," she said. "Would you like to come home with me now? We could start this afternoon. Unless you have someplace else to go."

"No," he said. "I don't have anywhere to go."

She turned to go to the cash register and Steven followed her, watching the light reflections on her hair.

Amy's apartment was the space over someone else's garage. It had huge windows. Steve sat on the carpet and Amy sat cross-legged on her couch, drinking iced tea and fiddling with her sandal. As they talked Steven watched the window behind her head. The wind was making leaves fall in spirals.

"Let me make a quick sketch of you," Amy said. "Just to see how it comes out."

"If you let me draw you at the same time," Steve said.

She was a good painter. Her paintings were hanging all over the apartment. He could learn from her. She did two things he especially admired.

One thing was knowing when to quit. Steven had a tendency to torture his paintings until there was nothing left of them, but Amy's paintings looked as if they had been painted fast, with a minimal number of strokes. She knew how to get it right the first time.

The other thing he admired about her work was the way she signed her paintings. Big black letters across the bottom of each canvas, saying AMY LEWIS. Whether it marred the painting or not, she made sure that name could be read from a distance. Steven rarely signed his paintings, not from forgetfulness as much as from shyness. He wondered if she could teach him to have confidence in his work. He wondered if that skill could be taught at all.

"Don't draw the bruise on my face," he said.

"I'm not." She sucked on her lower lip while she worked. "How did you get that?" she asked.

"I was in a fight," he said, hoping she wouldn't probe.

"You look so young," she said. "How old are you?"

"Seventeen," he said. He saw no point in lying.

"Oh!" She looked up. "I thought you were out of high school."

He kept his eyes on his work. "I dropped out," he said.

She wanted to catch his eye, but he wouldn't let her. "Why would an intelligent boy like you drop out of school?" she asked.

He looked up, making his face expressionless. "I had to," he said.

She didn't have the nerve to push it any further. She went back to her work. "You seem very mature for seventeen" was her final comment.

Steven decided to fight fire with fire. "You've never been married?" he asked.

She smiled. She knew what he was doing. "No," she said. "Someone used to live here with me, but not anymore." She got that faraway look on her face and Steven realized that this was what she'd been thinking about back in the store.

"Why did you break up with him?" he asked, using the same friendly tone with which she had interrogated him.

She looked up. "I had to," she said.

They both smiled.

"I'm finished with you," Steven said. "Are you finished with me?"

They showed each other their sketches. They had each drawn the other one to look much more beautiful than they actually were.

Seven

"Hello, Cunnigan." Miguel didn't have to look up to know it was Rick. Rick's shoes never made any sound on the stairs.

Miguel was stretched out on his favorite couch in the lobby, reading *The Star*. The old desk clerk was on duty, cleaning his counter with Glass Plus.

Rick waited for Miguel to move his legs, then sat down beside him. "It's very lonely up there," he said.

"All your brothers are home," said Miguel.

"There's no one up there who wants to talk to me."

Miguel pretended to still be half interested in *The Star*. He had learned that people give you much more information if you appear uninterested. "Cunnigan, you look depressed," he said. "I think you worry too much about those other guys. If they don't like you, they don't like you. Live with it. This old horse who runs the hotel hates me, but I don't lose any sleep."

"That old horse isn't your brother," Rick said.

Miguel looked sideways at Rick. "You don't fool me, Cunnigan. You hate those brothers worse than those brothers hate you. You hate everybody except you. So don't waste your depressed act on me."

Rick gave Miguel a look, but didn't say anything.

Miguel put his newspaper aside and pretended to look at his fingernails. "Maybe you need a little something so these small things won't upset you."

Rick smiled a little. "What kind of something?"

"I don't know," said Miguel, stretching. "Different people unwind in different ways. If, for example, you like to smoke ..."

"No, I don't like that stuff," Rick said. "It just makes you giggle."

Miguel put his magazine aside. "But I'll bet, Cunnigan, there's *something* you like."

Rick pretended to think. "Yes, there are a few things I like. Raindrops on roses, whiskers on kittens, diet pills, warm woolen mittens ..."

"Uppers!" Miguel said happily. "I wouldn't have figured you for uppers."

"Keep your voice down," Rick said, looking nervously at the desk clerk, who had a clog in the spout of his Glass Plus and was trying to clean it with a toothpick.

"Relax, Cunnigan," grinned Miguel. "Uppers to him is just teeth." Miguel was happy. He had discovered a new source of income without really trying. "I'll bet back in Ohio all you could get was those little pink pills for fat ladies. But this is Muncie, Indiana, Cunnigan. This is the big time." He fished in the pocket of his jeans and displayed a large all-black capsule.

Rick's eyes widened. "What's that?"

Miguel smiled. "It's candy, man. It's licorice. You eat some and you can go over to the west side and outrun the trains. Would you like to try some, Cunnigan?"

Rick sat back. "I don't know," he said nonchalantly.

Miguel was having a wonderful time. He knew a desperate man when he saw one. "Of course, really good candy like this costs money. I have to keep a supply on hand for all the whores and perverts and other guests of the hotel. So, if I were to give you this thing in my hand, you would have to reimburse me." He shook the capsule around in his hand.

Rick was tired of playing. "How much, Miguel?" he asked.

"It's strong stuff, Cunnigan. Five dollars."

"For just that one? Forget it."

"You heard me. Five dollars. Either that or a date with your brother." Miguel laughed.

Rick looked at him with contempt. "I see," he said. He reached into his pocket and took out a crumpled five.

Miguel gave him the pill. "Thank you, Cunnigan. I thought you'd have to go upstairs and ask your big brother for the money, but I see you have funds of your own."

Rick swallowed the capsule without water. "You're a very inquisitive person, Miguel," he said.

"Don't tell me anything you don't want to tell me, Cunnigan," said Miguel. "I'm not a priest. I don't get paid for hearing confessions."

"No, but you enjoy it," Rick said. "How fast does this thing kick in?"

"Pretty soon."

"I'll be happy to confess to you. I'm robbing my brothers blind. I'm taking ten percent of everything Mark makes. They're all too incompetent to count it right. When I get enough together, I'm going to Chicago."

"What's in Chicago?" Miguel asked.

Rick could feel his heart rate picking up already. *Well worth the money*, he thought. "It's a big city. I'll be able to take care of myself there and I won't need to depend on a band of hypocrites for my survival. I'll be able to do whatever I want."

"You going to be a doctor in Chicago or an attorney?" Miguel laughed.

"I'll do all right. There's lots of ways to make money. You just made five dollars, didn't you?" He could feel it in his blood now. Energy. Force. It was wonderful.

"I see," said Miguel. "You won't miss your family?"

"Family. My mother's dead, my father's an animal, and all my brothers are morons. I don't think so."

"I like a man who knows himself," Miguel said.

"I like a man who keeps his mouth shut about what I tell him," said Rick. He couldn't stand to sit and talk anymore. It made him edgy. He wanted to get out and walk and move. With that pill in him, running would feel like flying. He stood and zipped his jacket. "I'll see you later, Miguel."

"Don't pick up any parked cars, Cunnigan," Miguel called after him. He smiled. Two sources of income: pills and keeping quiet. And the price of both could go up at any moment. It was too bad, he thought, that Chris didn't need drugs.

Miguel stood and stretched and walked over to the front desk. "You want some help with your easy-trigger sprayer, old fool?" he asked.

The desk clerk glowered at him. "Why don't you people go back where you came from?"

"What people are you talking to, blind idiot? There's only one of me standing here. And besides, I came from New Jersey." He went back to his couch. There was no use talking to that old man. He would miss the Cunnigans when they were gone.

Chris walked far ahead of Shawn, at a faster, more excited pace. He loved being out on the streets at night. The lights, coming out of nowhere, made his heart beat fast. He liked to walk under the streetlights, floodlit one moment and dark the next. There was no way he could walk slowly in such an environment.

Even when they were children, he had always walked ahead. When all five of them walked somewhere, they always created the same basic formation. Shawn walked down the center of the sidewalk, decisive, the leader. Steve and Mark flanked him to the right and left, always about a half step behind. Rick hung back, so far back, a casual observer couldn't tell whether he was with them or not. But Chris was like an erratic satellite to the group, running ahead and waiting for them to catch up, walking backward so he could converse with one of them, crossing the street and coming back again, stopping to look at anything that interested him. A walk was never relaxing to Chris, it was a mass of sensations. He was always tired after walking somewhere.

He was careful now not to get more than two blocks ahead of his brother, checking all the time to make sure Shawn was still back there. They were on their way to Pat's house to get laid and do laundry. It had worked out very well, Pat's house being next door to the Laundromat. They could put the clothes in, go next door, and get laid during the wash cycle, and afterward the girls came over and helped them fold. Shawn said it was what marriage must be like. Only Shawn and Chris went on these expeditions. Cindy and Mark didn't seem to feel their relationship had a future.

But the best part of these Saturday nights, for Chris,

was the chance to get out and walk at night. It was better than sex, even. Despite the fact they were on the same street where those guys had attacked Steven, Chris never entertained a thought of fear or apprehension. The darkness was beautiful to him, and could not possibly be a harmful thing. It was even better on a rainy night, when the light reflections cut deep into the street: streaks of turquoise and flame and gold, and the neon flashes from restaurants and bars, but most of all, the streetlights. When he walked in and out of streetlights, it was like taking leaps from fantasy to reality, over and over again. One world was fierce with brightness and the other was dark and loaded with possibility. It was a risk, somehow, defying those two worlds. There was a chance, even if it was only in the mind, that somewhere between the darkness and the light, you would be swept into another world and lost forever.

Chris stopped outside the Laundromat to wait for Shawn. Across the street a bar flashed BLATZ in lilac and BUD in green. Chris took deep breaths of the cold night air and watched the light-show until Shawn caught up with him.

"Let's stay out here just a minute," Shawn said, setting the clothes down by a public phone and pulling Chris a little closer to him. "I want to tell you something and I can't do it in there."

Chris glanced at the people in the Laundromat. "Why didn't you tell me at the hotel?" he asked. He thought it was a little ridiculous that Shawn would want to have a private conversation out on the street.

"This just has to do with you and me," Shawn said. He looked bright and unreal under the Laundromat lights. His breath was visible in the air.

"Make it fast, all right?" said Chris, shifting his weight back and forth. "It's fucking cold out here."

Shawn frowned momentarily at Chris, as if making some final decision, then abruptly reached in his jacket pocket and took out an object, which he displayed for Chris. "Do you know what this is?"

Chris looked at it with horror. "It's a switchblade," he said softly. "Where'd you get that?"

Shawn moved so they were more in shadow. "I bought it. I bought two of them. This one is yours." He extended his hand slightly.

"No it isn't," Chris said, leaning backward. "I don't want anything to do with it."

"I know you don't," said Shawn. "But listen. Look what happened to Steve. That could happen to one of us again, only worse. Someone could get killed. We're going to be in strange towns all the time, walking around streets we don't know, messing around at night. I don't want anyone to be caught alone again, with no defenses."

"So, we're all going to carry knives?" Chris was very upset.

"Just you and I. I don't even want the others to know. There's no point in scaring everyone to death. We'll just make sure nobody goes out anywhere at night, or in an unsafe neighborhood without one of us. It'll be a lot safer that way."

Chris's eyes were fixed hypnotically on the retracted knife. "Look, I understand what you mean, but I couldn't use one of those if I had to."

"Yes, you would. If you were with Mark and someone tried to hurt him, you'd use it, wouldn't you?"

Chris looked up now, eyes wild with fear. "Maybe I would. But I wouldn't want to."

Shawn looked at him a little fiercely. "We're not talking about what anybody *wants*. I *want* to be at Ohio State right now, taking prelaw. I *want* to be living in a nice house, with a normal family. We're talking about what we have to do to take care of each other and make sure no one gets hurt anymore."

Chris's eyes were pleading. "Look, why are you picking on me? Steve's the second oldest. Why don't you give him the knife?"

"He's not as big as you and I don't think he would use it if he had to. He's a pacifist. He'd freak out."

"I would too!"

"No. You're stronger than you think. I know you. There isn't anyone else I can depend on. Mark's too young—"

"Well, Rick then! Rick's a born killer!"

"No."

"Why not?"

Shawn averted his eyes. "I don't trust him enough."

Chris was out of arguments. He ran his hand through his hair. "Okay," he said softly. He let Shawn put the knife in his hand. It was much heavier than he had expected. It would be hard to hide in certain pockets. He transferred it from hand to hand, getting the feel of it. He tried to picture how he would use it on someone. It was painful, but not impossible, to imagine such a thing. He realized that Shawn was right about him. If someone menaced Mark, it would be possible for Chris to pull it out, to use it. This knowledge made Chris's whole body feel tired and sad. "Show me how to get the blade out," he said quietly.

They walked home together that night. Chris didn't feel like going ahead anymore. And the darkness frightened him a little.

Amy fed Steven lemonade and Doritos. She had a monstrous appetite for Doritos, kept bags and bags of them in her cupboard. She built whole meals around them. Her lunch was often Doritos and cottage cheese, and her favorite dinner, when she was alone, was tomato soup with Doritos crumbled over it. She served them plain today, in a bowl, testing Steven to see if he liked them. She had made the lemonade from lemons.

Today she was dressed in white shorts, with bare legs and bare feet and a white blouse knotted over her midriff. She seemed determined to pretend it was summer.

Steve had been coming to her apartment every Tuesday for the past month. Tuesday was her day off from teaching. She would sit him on the couch, where the light was good, and work on his portrait for a few hours. At lunchtime she would feed him and in the afternoon, give him a painting lesson. These days were so perfect, Steven hesitated to believe in them. He never told any of his brothers of the existence of Amy or how he spent his Tuesdays. It seemed that if he tried to connect Amy with the real world, she would disappear.

He watched her now, working methodically on her Doritos, standing at her easel with her legs apart. She always stood to work, and her stance at the easel was brazen, soldierly, feet planted squarely apart, as if someone might try to drag her from her painting. Her legs were beautiful, beautifully proportioned. Steven had never known a short girl before. It was strange and fascinating to see such small legs with all the proportions right. He looked at her legs all the time she painted him. She assumed he was looking down, lost in thought.

She worked in fast, broad strokes, tossing her hair back impatiently when it strayed over her shoulder. When she was tired, she would throw herself into a chair and rest for ten or twelve seconds, then jump up and paint again.

Steve was allowed to watch the progress of his portrait. He thought it was an excellent painting, but it didn't look like him. He could not possibly imagine he looked that good. It looked more like a frail version of Chris.

It was near noon now and Amy was tiring. She cleaned her brush, rather carelessly, and sat down in her resting chair. Steven stretched his arms and legs.

"You must be tired of looking at me for so long," he said.

She piled her hair on top of her head and held it there. "Not really," she said with a little smile.

"Are you about finished with me?" he asked.

Her smile grew. "I don't know," she said.

Steven reached for his lemonade. He could never tell if she was teasing him or not. She was always smiling at him that way and saying little double-entendre things, but he wasn't sure how she meant it. Maybe she had figured out he was attracted to her and she was mocking him. He wanted to ask her right out how she felt about him, but he wasn't ready. He didn't think he could handle it if she said, "I think you're a very sweet little boy" or something like that.

"Your work is improving," she said.

"I still overpaint," he said. "I just can't get anything right the first time, like you do. I guess I should plan better."

"You don't know what you want to do," she said. "You decide too late which way you want to go. I had the same problem when I was your age." Her use of that phrase embarrassed them both. She ate Doritos compulsively for a few seconds. "Steven . . ." she said, "do I seem

old to you? I mean, I know I don't seem *old* but do you
think of me as being your age, or in some different cate-
gory. I mean, I know I'm not your age but . . ."

"I think of you as being lovely," he said. He couldn't
stand to hear her stumble around that way. "I don't think
of you as being any age." He decided to look at the carpet
for a while. He wasn't up to making eye contact with
someone he'd just called lovely.

He heard her voice, through the screen of his own
thoughts. "Steven? Could you think of me as a . . . girl
friend? As a lover?"

A *lover*. He played the word back in his head. It was
a word only women used. Men never had the nerve to say
"lover."

He said, "I wish I were old enough to be a lover of
yours." He congratulated himself for using the word.
True, he was still afraid to take his eyes off the carpet, but
he had said the word. Amy didn't answer right away. It
was terrifying.

"You're old enough," she said. "Ever since I met you, I
thought . . . but I thought you wouldn't be interested in
someone my age."

He looked up. Somehow it had become safe to look up.
Some of the glow of fantasy was gone from her and she
looked like a person now, an approachable, real person.
"I didn't think *you'd* be interested in someone *my* age."

Her eyes were so pretty. She had green eyes. Her lashes
were long, but the tips were blond. You had to be very
close to her to appreciate the length of her lashes. "Steve,"
she said, "would you like to go to bed with me?" She still
talked to him in a teacher's voice, the way a teacher ad-
dresses a student. He didn't mind.

"Yes," he said.

Amy's bedroom was pastel and white. The sheets and blanket were white. On the wall there were pictures she had painted of seashells.

She knew things he didn't know. He made no attempt to hide his innocence. If he didn't understand, he just asked her and she would tell him. At first he felt very virginal with her, but somewhere along the line their roles reversed. Sex seemed to overwhelm her and when they were finished, she would hold him tightly, the way a child clings to a parent in a crowd. After the first time he knew that he would never stop loving her.

They stayed in bed together a long time, just because it was pleasant to do so. She put her underwear back on and sat up in bed and braided her hair. Her underwear surprised him. It was white cotton, almost like a little girl's underwear. The few high school girls he had stripped were all decked out in satin and lace. He wondered if that was something only young girls did. He watched her, thinking how beautiful she was. Her stomach was flat, concave even. He kissed it.

At one point in the afternoon she said, "I've been lonely most of my life."

He had said, "So have I."

She gave him chili and Doritos for dinner and then he began to talk. He had not really talked to anyone for a long time, so there was a lot to say. He talked about how his mother had died and about what his father had done to them, and why they had run away. He told her how he knew he was never going to be a painter now, because he had dropped out of school. He told her how much he loved his brothers.

There had been an unspoken rule among the Cunnigans, that they did not discuss their situation with any outsider. Even as Steven was breaking this rule, he felt guilty, but he knew he had to do it. He knew that from now on he would move gradually further and further from his brothers, until he was completely separate from them. His future was with Amy now.

The policeman was about a hundred yards away, eating an apple. Mark was singing "Sometimes I Feel Like a Motherless Child." He was doing a fine job with the song. A black lady with a shopping bag had stopped to listen and she was crying. Mark had learned that sad songs brought in more money than happy songs. "Send in the Clowns" was very effective with white people and "Motherless Child" worked best with blacks. If any old people came around, he sang "I'll Be Seeing You" and really raked it in. He was proud of the expansion of his repertoire. He worked with the guitar every night, teaching himself new songs. Steven had taught him some very neat stuff from the 1950s, too; a song called "Sheila" and another called "I'm All Shook Up." Mark was ready to consider making the performing arts his life's work.

But today he couldn't sing "Motherless Child" with his whole heart. The policeman made him nervous for some reason. Police were like houseflies to Mark. Some days you could ignore them completely, and other days they drove you to distraction. Today he could almost hear the buzz of that policeman in his ears.

The crying black lady gave him a five-dollar bill. That unnerved him still more. He believed that luck had a balance sheet. If you got too much good luck, something catastrophic was about to happen.

The policeman finished his apple and threw the core into a planter, something only policemen can do, and started to walk in Mark's direction.

Mark began singing "I'm All Shook Up." He thought it was time for something cheerful.

The policeman looked at Mark with extreme interest. Mark had no way of knowing whether he was just being paranoid, or whether he was really in trouble.

"My hands are shaking and my knees are weak," Mark sang with feeling.

The policeman was about three yards away now. He was coming straight for Mark. He intended to say something to him. *"There's just one cure for this body of mine."* Mark wished he'd picked a longer song. There was no way to spin it out either. When that song ended, it just ended.

The policeman stopped in front of Mark and just stood there.

Mark finished the song. He wanted to look up and see the policeman's face, but, of course, he couldn't. He just stared at the policeman's crotch, as if it weren't there.

The cop folded his arms. "Elvis," he said.

Mark pretended to jump. "I didn't realize you were there," he said.

"Really?" said the cop. "I thought you people could sense those things."

"Just about half the time," said Mark uncertainly. "I sure didn't know you were there."

"I heard that Elvis," said the cop, "and I had to come down here and listen. There's nothing like The King, is there?"

Mark assumed Elvis and The King were one and the same. His own musical memory went back about as far as

"Heart of Glass." "Nothing," he agreed. "Except maybe Buddy Holly." He was proud of himself for adding this. Steven often talked about the genius of Buddy Holly. Mark had heard one of his songs, "Peggy Sue," and thought it incredibly dumb. He had a feeling Steven picked his heroes based on how young they died.

"Buddy Holly can't touch Elvis for my money," said the cop, "but I used to love Chuck Berry."

"Yeah," said Mark. He was weary of this conversation.

"Make a lot of money today?" the cop asked, peering into Mark's paper cup.

"I don't know yet," Mark said. He still felt this policeman was trying to catch him out.

"We talk about you down at the police station," said the cop.

Mark suppressed a shiver. "Are you a policeman?" he asked.

The policeman laughed. "That's right, how would you know?"

"What do you say about me at the police station?" Mark asked.

"Oh, well, you know. Everyone's seen you here at the mall. You're here every day. Well, you know, technically what you're doing is illegal—it's like a form of begging. But we've talked it over with our superiors, you know, and everyone agreed we ought to leave you alone, do you know why?"

Mark was sweating. "Why?"

" 'Cause you're such a nice kid. I admire somebody like you who tries to do something constructive. The merchants say you've brought business into the mall. So in a way, you've helped the local economy."

"I wouldn't say that," Mark said.

"Well, most of all you're just a damn nice kid. You hardly ever see any nice kids these days."

Mark was tortured with guilt. And the guilt was just strong enough to break his concentration for a few seconds. And during those few seconds a 727 flew over the mall.

"Jesus," said Mark, not only looking but lifting his sunglasses for a better view, "isn't that beautiful?"

"What the hell—" began the policeman.

Mark didn't wait to hear any more. He bolted, leaving his guitar and money behind as payment for his crime.

After that incident it was generally agreed this was the time to leave Muncie. The part about Mark's being a celebrity down at the police station made it definite. Everyone except Steven seemed rather excited about the prospect of going to a new place. No one quite understood Steven's reaction. He got upset, out of all proportion to the situation, but he wouldn't offer one good reason why they should stay. Finally he went to the bathroom and stayed there for nearly an hour. No one questioned him any further about the matter. They had learned over the years to respect his privacy. It was settled among the other four that they would leave the same night.

Miguel was upset about their leaving. He was losing all his best friends at once. "Now I have to go back to talking to whores and perverts," he said, hoping to make them feel guilty. Still, he knew what it was to be afraid of the police. Before they left, he had two private conversations, one with Shawn, the other with Chris.

Shawn dragged him off to the lobby, giving the others a fake excuse. "I want to know if my brother Rick is on anything," he said.

"Beg pardon?" said Miguel.

"I know you sell stuff," said Shawn impatiently. "If he's hooked on something, you'd know it. Is he?"

"You sure come to the point fast," Miguel said. "No, he's not addicted to anything I know of. He takes speed for fun, but he's not hooked. He only bought two caps from me the whole time you've been here."

"Good," Shawn said. "I was afraid he was really gone on something."

"Shawn." Miguel detained him with his hand. It was strange to hear him use Shawn's first name. Usually he called all of them Cunnigan, as if he couldn't tell one from the other. "I think I ought to tell you—it isn't my business—but Rick is stealing money from you. He told me he's saving up to go to Chicago. He's taking it from you a little at a time." Miguel braced himself. It was always dangerous, he knew, to get in the middle of a family thing.

Shawn fixed him with a long look. "That," he said, "I already knew." And he went back upstairs.

Miguel was sorrier than ever that they were leaving. He felt there were lots of things about them still to be figured out.

Chris was the slowest packer. He was still up in the room packing while the others were loading the car. Miguel kept him company.

"I had a lot of fun at your expense, didn't I, Cunnigan?" he asked.

Chris smiled at him. "I guess so," he said.

"Well, I'm sorry. You're a nice guy."

Chris looked up, surprised. "So are you. We really appreciated the way you took care of Steven when he was hurt. You've been a real good friend."

Miguel got off the bed and started for the door. "Well, come back and visit me sometime," he said. "I'll be here. I'll probably be here forever, unless they put me in prison." He was halfway down the hall by the time he finished this speech.

Chris bit his lip. "Good-bye!" he called. But there was no answer.

They took Route 69 North and at eight o'clock that morning, crossed the border into Michigan.

Eight

Not much thought was given to the location of the Cunnigans' new home. It was generally agreed that any road that led out of Muncie was a good road. Route 69 was chosen in a moment of jocularity, and North because it was easier for Chris to make a north turn than a south one. Route 69 North led them through Fort Wayne and across the Michigan border.

Conveniently enough, they hit Battle Creek at breakfast time, so they took the complete cereal-factory tour, putting up with the humiliation of having to talk to a frog in a baseball cap, all for the opportunity of getting five free bowls of Froot Loops and a wooden ruler that said *It's going to be a great day.* Mark used the ruler to smack various brothers all the way to Lansing, where it was taken away from him.

They considered Lansing as a semipermanent home, but rejected it on the grounds that it had all the wrong fast-food places. They switched routes, reversing the 69 to 96, and drove west to Grand Rapids.

With Grand Rapids it was love at first sight. They approached the city from the southeast, coming in on 28th

Street. The first thing they saw was a new Holiday Inn with a Holidome directly across the street from a Bill Knapp's restaurant. After the horrors of the Hotel Charles and the Lucky Steer, it seemed like paradise. Further exploration of the neighborhood uncovered the Eastbrook Mall. Its cinema featured a teen-horror film called *Death Prom*. There was a pizza place two blocks down the street, and promising signs that said AIRPORT and SPRING LAKE. It was clear to everyone that God had given them Grand Rapids to make up for the indignities of Muncie. After Shawn had recovered from the price of rooms at the Holiday Inn, it was all settled.

In fact, the luxury of the new surroundings brought on a mood of unprecedented extravagance. They booked two rooms instead of one, which meant no one had to sleep on the floor. They spent their first night in mad revels at Bill Knapp's, going all the way from vegetable soup to fudge cake, followed by a viewing of *Death Prom*, which Chris and Steven hated and everyone else loved. The following night they had pizza and took Mark to the airport, where he could watch 727's as much as he wanted, without fear of the law. They finished up the week by having dinner at the Holiday Inn restaurant, Grazin' in the Brass. Dinner for that evening came to $157.28, including appetizers and dessert and three rounds of drinks for everyone who passed the waiter's inspection. The bill would have been more, but Steve didn't have an appetite.

Every euphoria has its letdown, however, and it didn't take long before things began to go wrong. Mark developed a chest cold, which trapped him in the hotel room. He had to endure Chris taking his temperature every fifteen minutes and making him eat hundreds of oranges against his will. The weather turned cold and rainy, so there was little to do except sit around and watch Mark be sick. Needless to say, this put a strain on everyone.

"I want to go to Bill Knapp's tonight. I feel better," Mark said. He sat on Shawn's bed surrounded by Kleenexes, magazines, and Snickers bars. For entertainment he had resorted to restringing his tennis shoes, as this was one of the few things that didn't make Chris scream at him for overheating himself.

"You're not going anyplace," said Shawn, who sat on the floor reading *No Exit*. He and Steve had recently decided to become Existentialists. "Besides, I don't want to spend that kind of money tonight. We've really been throwing it away this month, getting drunk and going to the movies every night. Not to mention the eighty dollars a night I'm laying out so you can all have semiprivate rooms."

"I feel like I haven't been anywhere in a hundred years," Mark whined. He thought an argument would be a great way to liven up the afternoon.

Chris was also on the floor, doing pushups. "I'm bored," he said. "I haven't had sex for a month. I haven't been to church for three months. I haven't—"

"Another county heard from," Shawn said. "What is this, the Complaint Department?"

Mark got a coughing spell and had to go to the bathroom for water.

"You see?" Shawn yelled after him. "And you want to go out in the rain tonight and get sicker." He picked up his book again, satisfied he had put the subject to rest.

Mark wasn't finished, though. "You don't care about me," he said, charging out of the bathroom. "You're just cheap, you bastard!"

"You better be about finished with this little harangue,"

Shawn said, slamming down his book, "because I've still got that ruler. . . ."

Chris was not following their argument. He was still thinking how long it had been since he'd gone to church. "If I happened to die now," he said, "I'd probably go to Hell."

"You wouldn't go anywhere," Shawn said, on behalf of Jean-Paul Sartre. "There isn't any Hell." Mark had gotten him into an argumentative mood.

"You better *hope* there isn't," Chris said.

"I don't know how anyone can say there's no Hell when he's been to Muncie," Rick said. No one paid any attention to him.

"I've got a great idea," Shawn said. "Why don't all of you shut up for the next three or four hours so I can read?"

"Or let's at least change the subject," said Rick. "I think this would be a good time to talk about what we're going to do in three months when all the money runs out."

"How did you figure that?" Shawn asked.

Rick shrugged, as if Shawn were too stupid to have it explained to him. "Pencil and paper," he answered.

"We'll get more money," Shawn told him.

"How?" Rick asked happily. "Two of us are too young to work. Two more of us are high school dropouts. You're the best shot we have and I'll bet you can't get a job digging shit in a depressed town like this one. Christ, you aren't even black. There's no way you're going to get a job. Our best bet is Mark. We should get him out on the streets begging again. With that cough, he might pass for a TB victim."

"I don't understand," Shawn said. "This is some kind

of planned mutiny. You've all met secretly and decided to drive me crazy this afternoon."

"Or we could cut off his legs and say he's a paraplegic," Rick went on, laughing.

Mark objected to that idea. "Why don't we cut your balls off and you can sing in a choir?" he said to Rick.

"How do you know Jean-Paul Sartre isn't in Hell right now?" Chris demanded of Shawn.

"That does it," Shawn said. "Where is that ruler? I'm going to beat all of you!"

Steven had been sitting at the window all this time, watching the rain fall. He had not spoken to anyone all day. Now he turned and looked at each of them. "Why don't you guys ever shut up?" he asked. He asked it sadly, the way Christ spoke to the sleeping disciples in Gethsemane.

"All right!" Shawn yelled. "That's it! It's time we got *your* grievances out in the open like everyone else's. You've been pissed off about something since we left Indiana. Everyone else is dumping shit on me, so this would be a great time for you to go ahead and express yourself. I want to hear everything that's on your mind!"

Steve stood up. "I was thinking," he said calmly, "about all the different ways you can kill yourself." He walked across the room and went into the other bedroom, closing the door quietly behing him.

There was a moment of silence.

"Was that supposed to be a joke?" Chris asked.

Shawn was just staring at the door. "I don't know," he said. "There sure is something wrong with him."

"He hasn't been eating," Mark said.

"You know what else?" Chris said. "He hasn't shown any interest in girls for months."

Rick was bored with psychoanalysis. "Leave him alone," he said. "Maybe he's gay or something."

Shawn gave Rick a withering look. Then he turned back to Chris. "Do you think I should go in there and talk to him? Do you think he has some kind of problem?"

"I don't know," Chris said. "He's always sort of moody like that. Maybe it's just some artists' thing."

"I guess if it was something he wanted to talk about, he would," Shawn said doubtfully.

Mark had taken Steve's place by the window. "It looks like it's starting to snow," he said.

"Keep looking," Rick said. "The wolves ought to be along anytime."

Nov. 12

Dear Amy—

I got your letter yesterday. I still feel very badly about going away and not saying good-bye to you. Even though you say you understand, I know it was wrong to do. But I just couldn't. I knew if I saw you again, I wouldn't be able to leave you and for right now, I have to. I want to tell them about you, but somehow I can't do that yet either. I'm an emotional coward. I feel sort of torn between them and you, I don't know why. I'm just glad you seem to understand everything, or at least say you do.

I turned eighteen yesterday! That's our second birthday since we left home. Shawn was nineteen last month. All our birthdays are about one month apart, all down the line. I think our mother must have been some kind of math genius.

Congratulations on your show. I wish something like that would happen to me some day. It won't, though. I'll probably end up at a Ford motor-assembly plant, the way things are going.

Amy, I miss you an awful lot. If everything weren't so confusing, I mean, if I didn't have this unusual family situation, I'd have found some way to be with you. Right now, I'm taking a risk just writing to you. We aren't supposed to write letters to anyone.

This is getting too long. I love you very much and I think about you all the time.

STEVE

PS: Are you dating anyone? I'm just curious.

Nov. 19

Dear Steven—

No, I'm not seeing anyone, for heaven's sake. You've only been gone two weeks. And I'm in love with you, even though I know you don't believe that.

Don't worry so much about the future. We'll figure something out. Maybe I can get up to Michigan during Christmas vacation. We could meet somewhere and your brothers wouldn't have to know about it. It would be good for both of us, I think, if we had some date in mind when we'll see each other again.

My show went great. I sold three paintings and I've got more money than I've ever had in my life. You can't imagine what it feels like to have your work appreciated a little. And don't you dare say those things about Ford assembly plants. If you want to be a painter, you'll be a painter. You've certainly got the talent. I'd say that even if I didn't love you.

Steven, I think the reason you don't talk to your brothers about me is that you're afraid they won't like the idea. Then you'll find yourself pulled in two directions. I can't imagine them liking the idea that you're interested in a twenty-six-year-old woman, so, you see, there's bound to be some kind of argument. I can understand your wanting to avoid that. I know how close you feel to them. So just wait until you feel ready. If you want to keep us a secret for years, that's all right with me.

But I want to ask you something, Steve. If everything else were equal, would you want to come back to Indiana and live with me? Or would it upset you to leave your brothers? It won't bother me if you tell me the truth. I realize you're very young and you haven't had much stability in your life. I was hoping, though, that maybe when you're a little older, you could come and live here. That is, if I'm not too old and decrepit by that time.

Love, AMY

Nov. 22

Amy—

I read your last letter over and over. I realized I hadn't thought any of this stuff through the way I should have. I've just been going around confused and depressed because I didn't know how I felt. So I forced myself to figure out how I did feel.

I don't want to live with you. I want to marry you. Maybe that sounds stupid, coming from a little kid like me, but that's what I would want. If we tried to live together, both of us would always wonder how much the age difference was bothering the other one. I'd be insecure all the time and so would you. But if we could get married, Amy, and I hope you understand how serious I am, if we could get married, we'd be saying to each other and to everyone else, that we want to be in it for good. That we don't have any doubts or reservations. That we really believe in each other. Do you understand what I mean?

I'm going to talk this over with Shawn as soon as I can. He's having a rough time now. One of my brothers is sick and everybody's bitching at Shawn and I don't want to throw something like this at him. Anyway, I'm in no position to marry anybody at the moment, right? Unless the idea of welfare appeals to you. But if we just give it time, I think we can work it out.

Please take this letter seriously. I mean all of it.

Love, STEVEN

Nov. 30

Steve—

I cried when I read your letter. I did. I'm starting to cry now, just thinking what to say in response. Are you sure you meant what you said? We've only known each other a short time and I'm eight years older than you. No matter how seriously I take you, you're still only eighteen and that's awfully young to be talking about marriage.

Here's my answer. You wait awhile. Talk it over with Shawn and if you still feel the same way after he's told you all the reasons I'm not good for you, we'll talk about getting married.

If we did (and that's a big if, Steven), I would want to put you through school. I can afford it and you need to give your talent the chance it deserves. That would be my only condition.

But listen to me, Steven. I would love to marry you. I

really mean that. But I feel you may change your mind
after you talk to your brothers about it. Let's not say
anything definite for now. For now, just keep writing and
be honest with me and with yourself, all right? I love
you.

AMY

Shawn had the same dream every night, only every
night it seemed a little worse.

They were in the car together, but it was Shawn, not
Chris, who was the driver. The people in the car were
composites of his brothers and their numbers varied.
Sometimes there was only one brother in the car with
him, other times there seemed to be eight or ten of them.
Sometimes the number changed in the course of the
dream.

Shawn was driving very fast on hilly roads. The roads
twisted around hillsides, and sometimes climbed straight
up the side of the hill. Shawn's task was to manipulate the
car successfully and keep it on the road. The car never
had a gas or brake pedal, so Shawn controlled the car
exclusively by turning the steering wheel.

At first he was always in control of the situation. He
was nervous at the beginning of the dream, but coping
with every hill and curve as it came. It took his full concentration, staying on that road.

Then the hills would get steeper and the car would pick
up speed, gathering momentum from the steep down-
grades. The wheel would turn harder and harder, and
darkness would begin to fall, complicating things even
more. Shawn would feel the pressure building inside him,
trying to stay on that road.

The hills steepened into mountains, like the hills of roller coasters. Others in the car would begin saying things to him, issuing warnings. Someone always said, in Chris's voice, "Are you looking where you're going?"

Then the car would crest at the highest possible hill. It was a monstrous hill, so high, it was impossible even to see the valley at the bottom. The car would hesitate at the top of this hill, as if it had a will of its own, then would plunge. It was always at this point in the dream that the steering failed.

Shawn turned the wheel frantically. The car swerved wildly, but stayed on the road. The wind made a screaming sound as it hit the hood and Shawn could feel the lurch of the car all around him.

"Are you all right? Do you know what you're doing?" The other people in the car were afraid. They knew he was no longer in control. Their fear seemed to contribute to the wildness of the car.

"I'm all right!" he shouted, trying to give the wheel a hard right turn. "Just leave me alone! I have to think!"

But the car was swerving crazily now, still picking up speed. He could see the road rushing toward him through the windshield and away from him in the rearview mirror. He was confused, disoriented. The wheel had no effect at all. "There's something wrong with my steering!" he shouted. "What should I do?"

The landscape seemed to hurl itself at the car. Shawn could see the bottom of the hill now, where the road made a tight hairpin turn, a turn he could not possibly make without the use of the steering wheel. "We're going off the road!" he screamed. "We're going to crash!"

Shawn drowned out the sound of the wind and the glass and the metal with his own scream.

"Hey. Hey. Come on, wake up. It's not real. It's all right." Chris was holding him by the shoulders.

Shawn found himself, awake now and safe from car crashes, back in the hotel room. He realized the reason Chris was holding him was that he was shaking uncontrollably and crying.

"God," he said, trying to recover as fast as he could. "That was horrible."

"What the hell was it?" Chris asked. Frustrated that he couldn't steady his brother's shaking, he pulled Shawn against him in a tight hug. "Were you dreaming about Mom?" he asked gently.

"No. Well, maybe. I was dreaming about wrecking the car."

"Well, it wasn't real, so calm down."

"I'm *trying*," Shawn said. He was horribly embarrassed. "Sometimes those damn things are so *real*."

Chris continued to hold him. The trembling was slowing down anyway. "You've had that dream before, haven't you?" he asked.

Shawn pulled away from him. "What makes you say that?"

"You say things in your sleep when you have it. You say, 'What am I supposed to do?' But you sure never screamed like that before. I hope they didn't hear you in the other room."

"No," Shawn said. "They'd be over here by now if they had. They all sleep like bricks anyway."

"You're okay now, aren't you?" Chris put his hand reassuringly on the back of Shawn's neck.

Shawn felt a shock of recognition. Their mother had done that. When they were crying or upset, she always put her hand on the back of the neck, just that way. It was her version of a kiss. Shawn scrutinized Chris in the dark. "Do you remember Mom at all?" he asked.

Chris was surprised by the question, but he figured having nightmares made you a little crazy. "Sort of. Not very well. I was in the first grade, I guess. But I do remember her. Better than Rick or Mark would anyway."

Shawn could feel all kinds of old emotions come up out of places where he'd buried them years ago. The dream had let them loose. "When the accident happened," he said, "I saw that it was going to happen. I never told anyone this. I don't know how Steve remembers it, but what happened"—he swallowed—"I saw that other car before Mom did and I started to tell her, you know? But"—his voice began to break up—"I didn't tell her *fast* enough." Then all his control was gone. He cried like a little child.

Chris was at a loss. This was not the brother he knew and could recognize. This was some private Shawn that was supposed to be kept hidden. He put his arms around his brother again and just let him cry. There was nothing he could say that would make any difference.

Shawn spent himself in a few minutes and began to relax. "It's going to be all right," Chris said. That was always a good thing to say to people, he knew. It didn't mean anything, but it was good to say. After a while Shawn was able to go back to sleep and he slept through the rest of the night.

But Chris couldn't fall asleep again. He could hear Mark coughing in the next room, for one thing. He lay on his back for hours, looking at the ceiling and trying to remember things about his mother.

Nine

Snow fell steadily for two weeks. All the Grand Rapids meteorologists were surprised by it and seemed to have little idea where it came from. Twenty-eighth Street was torn up by construction crews, and when the snow came, it filled up the jagged holes in the street with black muck. It was impossible to either drive or work on the street, so people in the east end were stuck.

Mark's cold settled in his chest and didn't get any better. Then, during the second week in December, on Chris's seventeenth birthday, Mark began to run a high fever. His temperature was erratic, running between ninety-nine and a hundred and three at various times during the day. He slept most of the time, and when he was awake, he had chills. He refused all food except root beer, apples, and candy. Worse than all his other symptoms was the cough. It was a sudden, frantic cough, coming unexpectedly and shaking his whole body with its violence. After a coughing spell Mark was left panting and with a look of secret terror on his face, as if he came face-to-face with death during every seizure.

Everyone else's life revolved totally around Mark and

his illness. He had to be monitored because of his erratic temperature, and his needs were constant and endless. Someone was always running across the street to buy something for him: Robitussin and Kleenexes and aspirin and copies of *Penthouse* and *OMNI* and *Road & Track*. The wastebaskets were filling up with empty root beer cans.

All of this, of course, was a drain on the budget. In only four months they had gone through more than half of Shawn's original four thousand dollars. Without Mark's begging income, that gave them only a few more weeks unless someone got a job. Rick's assessment of the Michigan employment market was accurate: Young transients from Ohio who were vague about their past couldn't get past the first interview. Even for the most menial jobs there was no chance. Just as discouragement had set in, Mark's illness came on in full force and dominated everyone's attention. Shawn's brief mood of fiscal conservatism switched back to extravagance. He went out of his way to spend money on Mark. The room was slowly filling up with medicine and magazines and candy and toys of various kinds. One day Mark was talking wistfully about the penny candy they used to buy at Woolworth's, and that afternoon he was showered with fifteen dollars' worth of jawbreakers and red licorice and burnt peanuts.

A strong sense of decline had gripped them all. The onset of winter, the inevitable drain on the money supply, the hopelessness of getting more money through any legal channel, all these things were underscored and mocked by Mark's deteriorating condition. Everyone knew they had hit the skids and were losing ground. The terror of it was that no one knew how far they had to fall.

Chris took Mark's temperature for the fourth time that day. It was on a climb again. It had been a hundred, then a hundred and one, then a hundred and two, and now it was a hundred and three. "Damn it," said Chris. "It's still going up."

"How high is it?" Shawn sat at the foot of Mark's bed. His face looked worn. He wasn't sleeping.

"It's up to a hundred and three," Chris said. "Like it was yesterday. If it goes any higher, we'll have to start worrying."

"I'm worried now," Mark said faintly. When his fever went up, his voice got softer proportionately.

"Why does it keep fluctuating like that?" Shawn demanded.

Chris was the only member of the family who had any medical knowledge. After their mother died, he had taken over many of her roles. "It's an infection," he said. "His body is trying to fight an infection. I'd say it's either a sinus infection or it might be bronchitis, the way he coughs."

"Well, why doesn't his body fight it off and be done with it?" Shawn asked.

"It doesn't work that way," Chris said. "How do you feel?" he asked Mark.

"Hot from the neck up and cold from the neck down. And tired, but not sleepy. Fed-up tired. And my head hurts from coughing."

"Do you want anything?" Chris asked.

"A simple funeral," Mark said bitterly. For the last few days his sense of humor had taken on a nasty edge.

Rick and Steve were playing cards at the far end of the room. Both of them were terrified of contagious diseases. They didn't quite have the nerve to go in the other room, but they kept their distance. They played their game very mechanically, without any conversation or show of enthusiasm. In fact, neither one had said a word or looked up from the cards in the last hour.

"If he has an infection in his body, what do we give him?" Shawn was determined to get a definite answer.

"Antibiotics," Chris said. "But you need a prescription."

Their talk was interrupted by a sudden and slightly hysterical fit of coughing. Mark's eyes took on a look of helpless fear, as he was trapped for a moment by his illness and thrown out of control. The spell lasted about three minutes, which is a long time to do nothing but cough, then subsided.

"You want cough medicine?" Chris asked.

Mark shook his head, almost afraid to speak. "It doesn't stop the coughing," he said wearily. "It just makes me feel like crying."

"I wish we had Miguel here now," Shawn said. "I bet he could get a prescription."

"We should never have left Indiana," Chris said. "That's when everything went wrong."

Steven looked up for a moment when this was said, then returned his attention to the card game.

"Do you think we could trust a doctor?" Shawn said. "I mean, if you think he's got to have anti-whatevers, we'd better try to get some."

Chris frowned. "I don't know. Doctors like to interfere. Look at all those doctors on television. They examine some guy for gallstones and the next minute they've got him set up with a marriage counselor."

"You mean, you think he'd ask a lot of questions? You think he'd turn us in?"

"For our own good, but I bet he would," Chris affirmed.

"We could take him to a clinic and tell lies," Shawn said. "We could say our mother sent us. Or we could say we were orphans again."

". . . can't go anyplace," Mark said, very faintly.

"What?"

"I can't go anyplace." Mark looked exhausted and impatient with them. "I can't get up. I can't even hold my head up. I can't go out in the snow. Somebody has to come here."

"Then we have to trust a doctor," Chris said.

"But can we?" Shawn asked.

With the last ounces of strength in his body, Mark raised his voice to a broken wail. "Are you people planning to let me *die* while you make this decision?" He looked briefly at Chris, but his eyes rested on Shawn, accusing.

His outburst brought a shocked silence to the room. Since he was six, Mark had blindly trusted, almost worshiped, Shawn's judgment. If Shawn said something, Mark would not question it. No one had ever heard him attack or say anything against Shawn. Everyone was speechless.

Shawn looked at Mark, pained and apologetic. "I don't know what to do," he pleaded.

Mark seemed to deflate with exasperation. He turned his head away and closed his eyes. "Well, figure something out," he said, just above a whisper. "You're *responsible*."

Shawn closed his eyes, as if taking a blow, then got up and went into the other room, closing the door behind him.

Chris, Steve, and Rick exchanged looks. Their expressions were those of men who have been led into a hopeless battle by their commanding officer. The sun had gone down, but no one bothered to turn on a light, so they sat in the dusk together and said nothing. Snow piled against the window, slowly covering the glass. Chris felt desperate, as if his oxygen were being cut off. He took a deep breath and stood up. "I'll go see what he's doing in there," he said, and went into the room he shared with Shawn.

Shawn sat on his bed in the dark. There was a limpness in his posture, as if his muscles had resigned their responsibilities. He stared into space, not reacting when Chris came into the room.

Chris turned on a lamp, filling the room with intense gold light. He approached his brother cautiously, seating himself a few feet behind Shawn on the bed. Then, very hesitantly, he rested his hand between Shawn's shoulder-blades.

There was no reaction. Shawn neither tensed nor relaxed. He was like a paralysis victim.

"You can't do this," Chris said. His voice was soft but urgent. "You can't act like this. They don't know what to do when you act like this."

"Let's tell them the truth and end the suspense," Shawn said in a monotone. "I've failed them. I've failed all of you."

Chris sat up straighter. "Stop it," he said. "You can't afford this. You've got to be strong. You told me, remember? We've got to put up a front for them. We have to make them think everything is all right."

Shawn shook his head no. "I can't." There was a break in his voice. "Don't you see? Everything is crashing around us. I've lost all control of the situation. I can't get us any money and I can't keep us warm and I can't make him well. I can't do *anything*." Chris couldn't tell if Shawn was crying or not.

Chris edged close to Shawn on the bed and rested his body, very tentatively against Shawn's back. There was no protest. He put his arms around Shawn's waist, like a passenger on a motorcycle. He could feel a certain convulsiveness in Shawn's breathing that suggested crying, but he still couldn't be sure. "Why do you always talk about control?" Chris asked. "Why do you always think you have to be in control? You aren't in control of anything. You never were. That's one thing you filthy Existentialists and us Christians have in common. We know we can't control anything." Chris knew it was dangerous to mention religion, but he was desperate.

"So what do you want me to do?" Shawn asked. "Pray? Shall I ask God to send money or give us a prescription for antibiotics?"

Chris felt he was making progress. Arguing was a positive sign with Shawn. "There's no need to be sarcastic," he said. "If you weren't too cool to do it, you could say a prayer that maybe *you* would feel stronger, so you could help Mark feel stronger. How do you think he feels when you walk out of the room like that? It's like you've left him there to die."

Shawn flinched. "It isn't. Don't say that."

"That's how it looks to him, I bet. All he's got to believe in is you. He depends on you. When you crack up like this, that leaves him with nothing."

"So you think I should pray and get full of the Holy Spirit and go out there and heal Mark miraculously, right?"

"Something like that," Chris said.

"Forget it. I wouldn't ask God for change to get on the bus. Religion doesn't work. I used to pray all the time and it didn't do any good. Mom didn't come back and Dad didn't go away."

Chris pulled away from Shawn. "So? Why did you ask for dumb things like that? You knew He couldn't do that kind of stuff. Did you think someone was going to come back from the grave, just for you? What kind of fool were you?"

Shawn looked at him. "What should I have asked for? I lost my mother. What good is God if He won't do anything for you? Why bother with Him at all?"

Chris was surprised at this turn in the conversation. "He could have made you feel better when she died. That's all He can do. That's all He's ever done for me. It just helps to think someone cares how you feel." He paused for a minute, thinking. "It's the same with you and Mark. You can't get us money and you can't make him well. But you could make him feel better. You always have in the past. That's all he really wants from you. That's what we all depend on you for. We don't expect miracles. We just want someone to be there."

Shawn looked into his brother's beautiful eyes, reading them. "Do you think if I would go out there and be positive and confident, that Mark would be able to cure himself?"

Chris nodded. "Yes, I do."

Shawn's muscles had begun to assert themselves again. His slump straightened up. "You think he just needs something to believe in?"

"Yes."

Shawn's face was thoughtful. "You go out and distract

the little brat for a while and I'll be out in a minute, all right?"

"Yeah." Chris was immensely relieved.

When Chris was gone, Shawn lay back on the bed, looking at a corner of the room, where the wall joined the ceiling. "All right," he said out loud. "I hope to Christ You really are out there somewhere, because I need something to believe in too. I'm fucking sick of being the only one in charge."

Mark could feel his temperature go up another degree. He had learned what each degree felt like, and he could always tell when there was a change. Chris had said the last time it was a hundred and three, so now it must be a hundred and four. At this new level the lamplight in the room swam a little and he felt an overpowering desire to let consciousness slip away from him, to end the struggle. At some point soon his body would give up and he wouldn't be able to think anymore. Ever.

Even when their father was punching him out, he'd never had a feeling like this. Because at those times his body at least fought for life. He could depend on it to try and keep him going. But now his body was betraying him. It wouldn't put up a fight. It wanted to give up.

He had really believed Shawn would be able to save him.

Now *he* seemed to have given up, too. He just got scared and went into the other room. He was quitting, just as surely as Mark's body had quit him.

Chris sat on the end of the bed, watching the snow fall. He had that thermometer in his hand again. Mark knew he should ask to have his temperature taken again, since he thought it was rising, but what was the point?

Mark closed his eyes and relaxed, trying to judge how close to death he was. Then he was pulled back by a sudden thought—if he died now, he would probably go to Hell. He had become an atheist when he was eight, because Shawn had become an atheist. But if they were wrong and Chris was right, Mark would have to go to Hell. He hoped he didn't die before he had time to think that situation over a little.

He turned his head to one side and looked at the door to Shawn's room. *That's fine,* he thought, *you just stay in the other room while I die and go to Hell. Don't take any responsibility at all.* He wondered if Shawn was having a nervous breakdown in there. That would be the only acceptable excuse. Maybe after he, Mark, died, Shawn would kill himself out of remorse. That would be pretty good.

Mark felt a tickle at the back of his throat. He willed it away. He wasn't going to cough again and make his head feel any worse. The pulse was banging away in his head now.

He wished he'd gotten himself laid when he'd had the chance. It seemed poignantly tragic to him that he was going to die a virgin.

He decided to vent some hostility on Chris. "What's our brother doing in there?" he asked.

Chris looked at him rather blankly. He simply shrugged.

"Is he freaking out?" Mark demanded.

"No, he isn't," Chris said sternly. "How do you feel?"

Mark gave a perfect imitation of Chris's blank look and shrug.

Chris got the message. He gave Mark a parental frown and shook down the thermometer.

"How long does it take before pneumonia kills you?" Mark asked. "Is it sudden or lingering?"

Chris put the thermometer in his mouth a little roughly. "Quit it," he said. "You're not funny." He went back to looking at the snow.

Mark was furious. Not only was he being left alone to die, no one even wanted to talk about it with him. Shawn was hiding, Chris wanted to look out the window, and those other two were cowering in the corner, as if he had leprosy. It enraged Mark to think about it. If he had to go, they could at least come and cry over him a little. He took the thermometer out of his mouth. "I hate all of you, do you know that?" he said passionately.

Chris looked at him, surprised and hurt. His eyes filled up automatically with tears. "Don't say that," he said. "Why would you say something like that?"

"Because none of you cares about me," Mark said, working himself up. "Not *one* of you."

It was a contest to see which one of them would cry first.

"Yes, we do," Chris said brokenly. "Of course we do."

Shawn came in at that point. He looked calm, cheerful even. "How's our little patient?" he asked.

Mark regarded him warily. He took the thermometer out of his mouth again. "I'm still dying," he said viciously.

"That's what I like to hear," Shawn said. "A patient's attitude has a lot to do with his recovery." He took the thermometer and looked at it. "You're down two degrees," he said.

"I'm *not*," Mark shouted indignantly. "You're reading it wrong! And besides, I had it in and out of my mouth. It's not an accurate reading."

"Maybe not," said Shawn agreeably. "But you look better. Doesn't he, Chris?"

Chris was ready to go along with anything. "Sure. He looks a lot better."

"Not so flushed," said Shawn, eyeing him critically. "Fevers drop pretty fast when they drop. I wouldn't be surprised if you were normal by morning."

"There's no way I'll be normal by morning!" Mark was outraged. "I'm very sick."

"You were," Shawn said. "But you're very strong. I'd guess by about next week you'll be out playing in the snow."

"You're crazy!" Mark said. He was especially infuriated because the arguing seemed to be clearing his head a little.

"Well, I hope you don't drag your feet, Mark," Shawn said. "I was hoping you'd feel better by next week, because soon we'll have to start thinking about Christmas."

"That's true," Chris said. "It's the middle of December already."

"Christmas?" Mark asked grudgingly.

"Sure, Christmas. You know Christmas. 'Hark the Herald Angels Sing.' *That* Christmas. We have to decide what we want in the way of presents."

Even Steve and Rick were interested in this conversation. "You mean we're going to spend money on presents?" Rick asked.

"Of course we will," Shawn said. "We may be outlaws, but we're still civilized. I think each of us should decide on something he really wants, and if it's within reason, okay. I know what I want. I want a new jacket so Steve can keep the other one."

Chris picked up the ball quickly. "I need new jeans," he said. "You can't pick up girls without the right packaging. I'd like some nice tight Calvin Kleins."

"I know what I want," said Rick with rare enthusiasm.

"I want a couple bottles of whiskey. Something decent, you know, not crap. And we can wreck ourselves right up till New Year's Eve."

"I want something to read," Steve said. "Something besides the Gideon Bible and *No Exit*."

Everyone had spoken but Mark. He was torn between his desire to punish them with his illness and his fear of being left off the gift list. "Well," he said. "I did lose my guitar. And just when I was getting pretty good on it."

"Yes, you were," Shawn said. "It's a shame to let talent like that go to waste. Is that what you want?"

Mark lifted his chin. "Yes," he said. "If I live till Christmas." He only said it out of pride. He knew he wasn't going to die now. "Do I get to drink any of the whiskey?" he asked.

"If you live till Christmas, yes," Shawn said. "We didn't eat yet, did we?"

"No," Chris said. "We better go get something."

"Get pizza," Mark said. "And if you get new jeans, I get your old ones, okay?"

"We'll see," Chris said, smiling at Shawn over Mark's head.

Ten

The bar was crowded, even for New Year's Eve. Shawn and Chris had good places at the bar only because they'd started very early in the evening. Since ten o'clock people had been pouring into the Blackhawk, choosing it to be their final resting place until midnight. It was reaching the stage now where everyone had to talk loudly in order to be heard, and no one was terribly offended if someone pressed against or fell on them.

The Blackhawk was Chris and Shawn's favorite bar in Grand Rapids. They liked it because it was very dark, and because the atmosphere allowed for easy, honest pickups. The bartender, who looked about nineteen himself, had no interest in asking silly questions about identification. If you had money, and didn't misbehave or throw up on the floor, you were twenty-one as far as he was concerned.

The decor had been chosen for its ability to look good in the dark. The bar and barstools were upholstered in black leather. The walls were paneled and walnut-stained. There was an antique jukebox with stained glass in the front and there was a statue of a brass hawk standing next to the cash register. Right now the place was still decorated for Christmas, which meant a string of erratically flashing lights over the bar and a garland of gold tinsel around the hawk's neck.

It was just the kind of place Steven should have liked, but he had refused to come. He didn't want to get drunk, he said, and he didn't want to pick up girls. Again, Shawn and Chris were sure something was wrong with him, but they didn't press the matter.

So this New Year's Eve, Steven stayed back at the hotel with the "little" kids, helping them drink off what was left of Rick's Christmas present.

Chris, who looked good on any occasion, was especially sharp tonight. He had his new jeans on, and with them he wore a black pullover and no shirt, showing off a sensual collarbone. The lights over the bar made shadows of his eyelashes against his cheeks. He sat sideways on his stool, in order to talk intimately with Shawn, and one of his feet was propped on Shawn's stool. This pose allowed any interested woman in the room to observe him with one leg stretched and one flexed. He held his Bloody Mary gracefully, with the fingers of both hands curving around the glass. Instead of taking drinks, he held the glass close to his mouth all the time, and occasionally sucked at the rim. This slightly childish drinking style was another woman-pleaser, he had learned. He had already gotten seven separate offers for sex during the course of the evening, but so far had resisted.

Shawn, in his new motorcycle jacket, was nothing to sneeze at either. He had racked up five offers for himself, although three of them didn't really count, as they were rebounds from Chris. He was also trying to resist temptation that night. He and Chris intended to stay together at least until midnight. There was something terrifying about going into a new year with a stranger. Shawn had recently taken to drinking Jack Daniel's and soda. He didn't especially like it, but he thought it was the most adult-sounding thing one could possibly order. Shawn had no time for posing or looking cute when he drank. When a new drink came, he stopped talking, threw it back in one or two gulps, and went right back to the conversation.

The two of them enjoyed getting drunk together. Drinking allowed them to have any kind of intense conversation they wanted, at least until they were too far gone to articulate.

"What's been the best year of your life so far?" Shawn asked Chris. They were already beyond religion and politics and were psychoanalyzing each other.

Chris sucked thoughtfully on his drink. "What summer was it when we were going to Baskin-Robbins all the time?"

"One summer," Shawn said, "no, two summers ago. You were fourteen. That's a funny one to pick. We didn't do anything special that year."

"I know." Chris fingered his drink and set it aside. "It was just a nice time, a nice summer. Mark was finally old enough to act like a human being. I had a bike of my own for the first time, not one of your old ones. It . . . just seemed like we had a nice summer."

"You just like ice cream," Shawn said.

They had begun a game, that summer, to see which one of them would be the first to taste all 131 Baskin-Robbins flavors. Since the flavors rotated every month, it had involved meticulous planning and bookkeeping. They visited the store almost every evening after dinner, each one searching for the flavors he needed to finish his list. For the first month it was a good game, but by July rampant cheating had broken out. Secret deals were made (*I'll eat your pink bubblegum if you eat my licorice*) and in general the game was riddled with corruption. By August no one except Mark could stand the sight of ice cream and the game was dropped.

"I'd never pick that year," Shawn said. "We didn't go on vacation or anything. What about the year we went to Florida?"

"We were pretty little then," Chris said.

"You can remember it," Shawn insisted. "I taught you how to swim. We practiced shaving with Dad's credit cards."

"I don't remember that. I remember Rick trying to drown Steven." Chris giggled.

As usual, Shawn threw his drink back fast and Chris cuddled his in his hands.

"Was Mom on that trip?" Chris asked carefully.

Shawn was too drunk to be upset by Chris's lack of memory. "No. That was after. Look there," he said, wanting to change the subject. He made a line with his eyes to a table across the room, where a lady was staring at Chris. She was a nice-looking woman in her forties with a mane of black, curly hair and heavy makeup. Her fingers sparkled with a series of cocktail rings and she wore a very sharp leather jacket. She looked shamelessly at Chris and smiled.

"Is that wanton look directed at me?" Chris asked innocently.

"I'm afraid you're the lucky one," Shawn said. "Go over and sit with her. Ask her if she'd like to adopt some nice boys."

Chris grinned boyishly. "Well, I can go see what she wants anyway." He jumped down.

"As if you didn't know," Shawn called after him.

Tim, the bartender, decided to keep Shawn company while this was going on. He and Shawn watched together while Chris sat down with the lady and began a very animated conversation. Everything the lady said was hysterically funny, judging from Chris's reaction.

"He's a little young to mess with her, isn't he?" Tim asked. He was a dropout from Michigan State. He had long red hair and a moustache. He was deeply disappointed he had been born too late for the hippie movement.

Shawn watched Chris with a fond expression. "He's just playing around. He gets very flattered by this kind of stuff. He'll be back here in a minute, after he says no to whatever she wants."

Tim sighed. "It must be nice to look like that and have women jump all over you."

"I wouldn't know," Shawn shrugged. "I was given a brilliant mind instead."

"Well, there's something to be said for that, too," Tim said agreeably.

The lady was clearly working on Chris. She leaned close to his face to talk to him and kept touching him in maternal ways, brushing imaginary things off his sweater and so on. He seemed to be suppressing laughter.

"Who would you say is the victim in a situation like that?" Tim asked Shawn.

"Me. I have to sit here and watch it."

The lady put some sort of question to Chris. He lost his amused look immediately. Then he asked her a question. She nodded her head emphatically. He frowned and asked another question. She continued to nod. Chris looked a little stunned.

"She must be telling him she's a virgin," Shawn suggested.

Chris held up one finger, asking her to wait a minute, and started back toward Shawn.

"Whatever she said, he wants to check it out with me," Shawn said.

"If you need a ride home," Tim said, "just whistle." He went to see about his other customers.

Chris looked as if he had received a blow to the head. He climbed up onto his stool and looked at Shawn with disbelief.

"Well?" Shawn asked impatiently.

"She said she'd give me two hundred dollars to drive her home from here," Chris said. He waited for a reaction.

Shawn's voice dropped a few decibels. "She certainly doesn't know the going rate for cabs, does she?"

"Well, she's drunk," Chris said. "But look at all that jewelry. I mean, she's probably good for it." He kept watching Shawn's eyes.

"Are you trying to be naive or what?" Shawn said. The situation had come up too fast and he wasn't sure if he should feel as angry as he did.

"What do you mean?" Chris asked, not quite meeting his brother's eyes.

Shawn decided his anger was justified. "Don't you suppose she means she wants to have sex with you for two hundred dollars?" he asked.

Chris kept his eyes down. "Well . . . I suppose so."

"Is that all *right* with you?" Shawn had to whisper in order to avoid shouting.

"Calm down," Chris begged, terrified someone was going to hear them. "I didn't say yes or anything. I'm just telling you what she said."

Shawn regained control of himself. "There's a name for people who do that stuff for money," he said.

Chris flushed. "That word is for women," he said.

"That's because, up until tonight, men have had too much self-respect to consider it!" Shawn was really angry.

Chris was getting angry now. "What makes you so righteous all of a sudden?" he demanded. "You're the one who doesn't think anything is a sin. I don't know why you're getting so excited about the whole thing. It isn't you who'd have to do it." He glanced back over at the lady, who was discreetly putting on makeup while they discussed her. She seemed to have done this sort of thing before.

Shawn took Chris by the shoulders, forcing him to look up. "You tell me this. Would you have anything to do with that lady if she hadn't offered you money?"

Chris pulled away. "No, I wouldn't. She's too old for me."

Shawn's heart pounded with anger. He didn't understand what had come over Chris. "Chris, please, think about this for a minute. You're going to let this lady take you to her god-awful house or apartment or whatever and you're going to let her undress you . . ."

"Come on. Don't."

"You're going to let her undress you and do whatever she wants to with you, just because . . ."

Chris was near tears. "Well, don't we need the damn *money*?" he said. A few people around them turned and looked to see what was going on.

A look of concern came over the face of the lady in

question. She picked up her handbag and left as quietly and quickly as possible.

Shawn looked as if Chris had slapped him. "For Christ's sake!" he whispered. Then he turned away and hunched over his drink, Christmas lights flashing in his hair.

Chris couldn't remember a time when he had felt so upset. "Well, we *do*," he said softly.

Shawn stared down at his drink, watching bolts of color shoot through the ice cubes. "We don't ever need money that badly," he said.

Chris was afraid he was going to cry. He also faced front, sucking on his drink to calm himself. Neither of them spoke for several minutes.

Then Shawn looked over at him. "I'm sorry," he said. "I'm sorry, Chris. I just feel awful. If things are so bad you feel you have to do things like that . . ."

"I didn't feel I had to," Chris said. "I just, I don't know, wanted to help. We do need money. There isn't much I can do. It was such, it seemed like such a lot of money. It wouldn't have killed me."

"It would have killed *me*," Shawn said. "I don't want you ever to consider anything like that again, all right? Even if we have to steal, it would be better than that. Okay?"

"Okay." Chris sucked on his ice cubes.

"I mean it. Don't ever think of it again."

"I said I wouldn't. Can we go home?"

"You want to go home this early?"

"Yes. I don't feel good." Chris felt totally humiliated. He wanted to go to his room and close the door.

"All right." Shawn put his money on the bar and jumped down. Chris followed him.

It was a cold night, with a sky so clear, it made the stars seem unnaturally bright and swollen. There was no one on the street because it was nearly midnight. They walked to the car without talking.

Chris pulled out of the parking lot and turned south on Division Avenue. There was no traffic at all. The world was completely deserted except for the two of them.

Shawn knew how Chris felt, but he thought anything else he said would make it worse. It was touching, he thought, that Chris was willing to make such a drastic sacrifice for the cause, but it was frightening that he was feeling that desperate. Something had to be done, Shawn knew. They couldn't go on this way. Soon all of them would be thinking that way, doing things they wouldn't ordinarily do, just for survival. Shawn felt he had to find a solution and find it right away.

It didn't help that he was drunk. He couldn't think straight. Everything in his mind ran together: the coldness of the air and the brilliance of the stars and Baskin-Robbins ice cream and the way his ice looked under the flashing lights and the siren in the distance and the summer they spent in Florida . . .

Shawn looked up suddenly. "Christopher," he said. It was a vision, opening before his eyes. He couldn't imagine why it hadn't come before, but it was there now, glowing in his mind.

"What's the matter?" Chris asked. "Are you going to throw up?"

"Christopher! What's wrong with us?" Shawn asked.

Chris's embarrassment was getting pushed aside by curiosity. "I don't know," he said. "What's wrong with us?"

"We're crazy!" Shawn said. "We've got to be crazy!"

"No, we're not," Chris said. "We're just drunk."

"No, listen to me," Shawn said.

"I will, as soon as you say something."

"What are we doing here?" Shawn asked excitedly.

"At the corner of Twenty-eighth and Division?"

"No! No! No! How did we get to Michigan? What the hell are we doing in Michigan?"

"You are far gone. We just followed the road and we ended up here. Do you remember now?"

"Ended up. You see? We just drifted here like idiots. Chris, think for a minute. If you were sick and cold and you needed a job and winter was coming on, where would you *not* go?"

Chris was catching on. "Michigan."

"Right. What the hell are we doing here in the snow? It's January. Even birds have better sense than us. We've got the run of the country. Why are we in the coldest, most depressed state in the Union? Why?"

"Because we're crazy!" Chris said happily. He liked it when everything fit together this way.

"Right! You know where we could go? Where it's warm and there are lots of jobs for kids our age and where the police would never find us?"

Chris was perfectly set up now. "Where?"

"Florida."

This time Chris was able to call more of that distant vacation back to mind. He could remember the ocean now, rolling away to infinity, and the warmth of the sun. He could remember the freedom of only having to wear enough clothes to be decent, going barefoot all the time. He could remember standing in surf up to his knees and drinking a Coke out of the bottle. He could remember a feeling of steady, unwavering happiness and well-being.

Even their father had been reasonably cheerful on that trip. "Florida," he echoed softly.

"We *have* to go," Shawn said, sewing up his argument. "All we have are these little jackets. We can't go through January and February up here. So we have to go somewhere. And you know what else I think? I think the legal age might be lower down there. It's in the South."

Chris was entranced. "Let's go tell them," he said.

Shawn leaned back against his seat. "I hope this doesn't seem like a good idea just because we're drunk," he said happily. "Hey, is it next year yet?"

Chris looked at his watch. "Fifteen minutes ago. We missed it."

"One year down and three to go."

Chris looked over at him. "I think we're going to be all right."

"I do too," Shawn said. And for the first time, he really believed it.

"I understand perfectly," Rick said, sipping his coffee. "It's inspiring. Moses and Aaron went to a bar and got ripped and had a vision of a new Promised Land."

It was the first day of the new year, two thirty in the afternoon. Shawn and Chris had been the first ones up and had brought coffee, doughnuts, and a glowing description of the state of Florida to the other three.

There had been three different reactions. Mark was as excited as his hangover would allow. Rick, naturally, took a cynical view, and Steven had stopped eating, drinking, and paying attention to his surroundings. Shawn and Chris were doing their best to cope with all three reactions at once.

"Do you like it here in Michigan?" Shawn asked Rick.

"You'd prefer to stay here? Be my guest. Chris and I are going to Florida, but anyone who really loves Michigan is welcome to stay behind."

"Well, I'm not staying in any fucking Michigan with *Rick*," Mark said emphatically. He believed the whiskey last night had killed the last germs that were in his body. He was ready for a new life.

Shawn couldn't figure out what was the matter with Steve, but he decided to let that slide while he shored Rick up. "Well, I hope you have fun up here. You'll probably get a good job in a truck assembly plant, just before the next blizzard hits. Write to us now and then."

Rick smiled. None of them suspected that someday he would run away from them. His plan had been considerably slowed down, but it was still there. When no money was coming in, it was harder to embezzle, but someday he'd have his freedom. "Oh, I'll go with you," he said. "It's interesting to see all of you moving from town to town, encountering failure at every turn."

"That's what I like," Shawn said. "A unified group. Except Steven's being very quiet."

Steve looked up as if lights had been turned on him. He looked at Shawn with his clear gray eyes and spoke directly to him, as if no one else were in the room. "We better have a talk," he said.

Shawn let everyone else drop too. "You want to go in the other room?"

They got up with no other discussion and left, closing the door behind them.

"Which of us is going to listen at the door?" Rick asked after a decent interval.

"We better not," Chris said. "We weren't invited."

"We could just be quiet and see if we hear anything by accident," Mark suggested.

"And I could go and sit there by the door," Chris added. "Nobody told us we had to stay away from the door."

"If you're tired, you could even lean against the door," Rick advised. "Steve's got a low voice."

"Shut up and let me listen," Chris whispered. "Steve's talking and talking," he said. "Shawn isn't saying anything."

"Make sure they can't hear *you*," Mark said.

"He's still talking," Chris said, even more softly. "I never heard him talk so long without stopping."

"Well, what's he saying, fool?" Rick demanded.

"Shhh . . . I can't . . . he's talking low even for him. It sounds like he's telling a story. Shawn isn't interrupting him at all. That's unusual. It's a guilty tone of voice, like a confession."

"Shut up and listen for *words*," Rick said.

Chris listened attentively. "He said either 'make sure' or 'mature' . . . 'class' . . . 'letter' . . . 'special.'"

"They're talking about the post office," Mark said.

"You're not getting the important words," Rick said. "Listen for things like 'I got her pregnant' or 'hooked on heroin.'"

"Do *you* want to listen at the goddamned door if you're so smart?" Chris said, forgetting to be quiet.

"Just wait till Shawn says something," Mark advised. "You'll be able to hear him."

Chris leaned hard against the door. "He just now asked a question. But I didn't get it. Steve said, 'Twenty-six.'"

"That could be the price of something," Mark suggested.

"Or the minimum sentence," Rick said.

"Shut up. Shawn asked a long question. He's talking real low, too, so this is something serious. They both sound sad. Wait a minute. . . . Whatever he asked, it made Steven mad."

". . . how I *feel?*" Steve's voice carried through the wall.

"No, I don't." Shawn's voice carried easily too. "You're crazy. You can't know someone two months and be sure of anything."

"It's a girl," Chris said.

"Or twenty-six girls," Mark said.

"Or a girl who's twenty-six," Rick said.

"My God, that's it," Chris said. "He's got an older woman somewhere."

"I wish you'd give me a little credit!" Steven shouted, so loudly it made Chris pull away from the wall.

"I just can't let you go down there and live with her!" Shawn shouted back.

"My God!" Mark said. "Down where, Muncie?"

"That's right, I don't." Shawn's voice was vicious. "I don't want to know anything about it. You just go ahead and leave, if that's what you want. I'm not your father. I don't care what you do."

Chris bit his lip. He was frightened. Then he realized the other two were looking at him and he tried to make his face impassive.

"I hoped you'd at least try to understand," Steven begged.

Shawn's voice began to lower in volume. But it was no friendlier than before. "I *don't* understand. You just do what you want."

Then there were no more audible sounds behind the door.

"Are they saying anything else?" Rick asked.

Chris listened hard. "No."

"What are they doing?" Mark asked. He looked completely terrified.

"Maybe one of them killed the other," Rick suggested.

"I don't *think* so," Chris said angrily. "Wait a minute. Steve said something, real quietly. I didn't get it. Shawn didn't answer him."

"This is boring. Let's have some more screaming," Rick said.

"There. Shawn said something. It didn't sound too nice. Now it's real quiet again. There. Steve said something else. Shawn said, 'Of course I do.' Now it's quiet again. I think they're making up. Steve's talking. He's saying all kinds of stuff. I can't make any of it out. They've shifted around in the room, somehow. Shawn's talking. He said *my* name. I wish I could have heard that part. He said 'you and me' . . . 'frightening' . . . 'family.' I think the worst of it's over. I think he's going to let Steven go."

Mark sat up straighter. "You mean, for real? You think Steven's going to leave us?" Now that the excitement was dying down, they had time to let the reality sink in.

"Well, I guess so. Wait a minute . . . Shawn just said something about how Steve could always come back if he wanted to. God, he *is* leaving us." Chris looked a little pale.

Rick didn't care one way or another. He'd always thought Steven was a lost cause anyway. "Well, that sure broke up the afternoon. I'll see you guys later. I have to get something at the drugstore." He got up and left.

"There'll only be the four of us," Chris said softly.

"I thought we were all going to stay together until we

were legal," Mark said. "This is like *Ten Little Indians*. You don't think we'll all end up separated, do you?"

"Of course not," Chris said. "I don't want to go live with any woman and Shawn wouldn't do anything like that either. Steve was always a little strange, you know."

"Yeah. But Shawn's nineteen. What if he would meet somebody and fall in love? *Then* what would we do?"

Chris looked scared. "He wouldn't do that. You know he wouldn't."

"What's going on in there now?"

Chris listened. One of them was crying. "I don't know," he said. "Maybe we ought to get out of here for a while. I'll take you for a drive."

"All right. Chris?"

"What?"

"Let's make a promise. I mean, just to make sure. Let's promise that no matter what else happens, you and I won't get married until I'm eighteen. Okay?"

Chris looked at him. Sometimes he thought of them as all being the same age. He forgot, sometimes, that Mark was still a child. "Yes," he said. "Absolutely. No matter what else happens."

Just before he left the room with Mark, he glanced back fearfully at the door that blocked his older brothers from his view.

Eleven

Even on the map, which was now heavily circled, battered, and marked up, Florida had a promising look. It
wasn't like the rest of the country, all bound in and land-
locked. Without discussing it, they all shared a mythical
belief that once the Florida state line was crossed, no one
would ever be cold or hungry again and they would be
magically invisible to the law.

So, renewed by having a goal once again, they hit the
road on a Monday night and drove straight through from
Grand Rapids to Muncie, where the first and most difficult leg of the trip had to be completed—the dropping-off
of Steven.

They were mostly silent during this part of the ride,
like men on a grimly dangerous mission. No one knew
what to say to Steve, because what he was doing seemed
strange and wrong. None of them believed his relationship with Amy was a good thing.

Steven couldn't talk either. All he could think was that
in a few hours they'd be leaving without him and he
didn't know when he'd see them again. At the same time,
another part of him was elated at the thought of see-

ing Amy again. Even though the situation was supposed to be resolved, he still felt torn. Also, he didn't really want his brothers to meet Amy. He felt sure they'd hate her and then he'd hate them. He felt sick, thinking about it.

Muncie had an eerie familiarity in the dawn. This time they had no trouble navigating at all. They followed the White River into town and took a sentimental drive around the Hotel Charles. They considered visiting Miguel, but Chris didn't think that was a good idea.

Steven directed them to Amy's apartment. They saw her through a haze of sleepiness and fatigue. She wore pink corduroy overalls and a white angora sweater. Steve was relieved to see that she did have winter clothes. She gave them Twinkies and hot chocolate and insisted they sleep a few hours, so they collapsed on her living room floor like corpses and slept through the morning while Steve and Amy renewed their acquaintance in the bedroom.

When they got up again, around three in the afternoon, Amy fed them again, hot dogs and Doritos and Dr Pepper, and they had a chance to talk to her and decide if they hated her or not.

Mark was easily won over. As far as he was concerned, anyone who kept that much junk food around the house was all right with him. Chris was impressed with her looks. In the past he'd seen Steven fall for some pretty frightening-looking girls, but this one, he thought, was outstanding. Rick liked her simply because she was taking Steve off their hands. It was Shawn who seemed to have a problem. He tried to be polite, but there was an antagonistic edge to everything he said. At one point he asked, "How long have you lived over a garage?" Steve spent most of the afternoon looking out the window and pretending he was somewhere else.

Amy didn't seem to resent Shawn's attitude. She answered any questions he asked with no sign of anger, and later, when they were talking about how they had left home, she said something about it being a heroic act, and after that Shawn seemed a little less hostile.

Shawn was aware that a long good-bye would be hard on Steve, so when he thought they had stayed the proper amount of time, he said something about getting to Chattanooga by nightfall and started herding everyone to their feet. He hugged both Steven and Amy, which set the precedent for the others. "He's allergic to penicillin," he said sternly to Amy.

"I can tell her what I'm allergic to," Steven said. "For Christ's sake!"

"I wasn't going to give him any tonight anyway," Amy said, smiling. She gave them a bag of Mars bars for the road, which cemented her friendship with Mark forever.

The first few miles out of Muncie were difficult ones. Even though Steve had never talked much, there was a gap in the rhythm of their conversation because of his absence. Mark complained of too much space in the backseat. He didn't know what to do with his legs.

Shawn was very quiet. He didn't talk for miles, just looked out the window. Then he turned to Chris rather abruptly. "Just don't *you* get any ideas about this kind of stuff!" he shouted.

Chris jumped. "Don't worry!" he cried. "I'd die first."

"Everyone says that," Shawn said bitterly. "I've heard Steve say that very thing."

"I'm not ever getting married!" Chris insisted. "And certainly not tonight!"

"Well, just make sure you don't," Shawn said. "I don't want all you bastards doing crazy things like this."

Chris couldn't understand why he was being singled out for such strange accusations. "I don't even know anyone," he pointed out.

"Who am I supposed to talk to now?" Shawn continued. "He was the only one of you who had half a brain. Now I'm stuck with an altar boy, a cynic, and a little kid."

"Who's little?" Mark demanded. "I'm as tall as anyone in this car, almost."

"It'll be all right," Chris said. "We'll see him pretty soon."

"Yeah," said Shawn. But they both knew that wasn't true.

They took Interstate 65 through Louisville, Bowling Green, and Nashville, into the mountains where the landscape was unbroken but for tourist traps and truck stops. The road was full of surprises during this stretch. The car would round a turn and find itself on a cliff, with clouds below. The highway would rise on an incline and whole cities would appear in the distance. The beauty of the landscape was reassuring to them. It convinced them of the rightness of their plans. They felt things would just get more and more beautiful until they reached Florida, which would be some kind of paradise.

They stopped in Chattanooga to feed Mark, at a place called Truck City. The truck drivers seemed amused with the boys and even tolerated the Top 40 music they played on the jukebox. Everyone noticed how much warmer it was here than in Michigan. They made a point of walking around with their jackets unzipped.

When they crossed the Georgia border, all of them assumed most of the trip was behind them. The first city in Georgia was called Ringgold. In Ringgold they talked about it being just a few more hours to Florida. But a few hours later they were only in Atlanta. Valdosta, the last city in Georgia, was still 225 miles away, according to the road signs. After a while they began to wonder if they really could get all the way to Ft. Lauderdale without stopping. It had seemed like a much shorter distance on the map.

"It's fifteen miles to King Frog," Mark said. Out of boredom he had developed an obsessive interest in road signs. "That's twelve signs for them, so far."

"Who's got the record?" Shawn asked him. "Rock City?"

"No." Mark consulted his notes. "There were only thirty-eight signs for Rock City. Historic Ruby Falls is in first place with fifty-two signs. King Frog still has a long way to go."

"Aren't we out of gas yet?" Rick said. "I really need a cigarette." The others had voted in a rule that Rick couldn't smoke in the car, so he had to wait until they stopped somewhere. It was just another example, he thought, of how they ganged up on him.

"Half a tank," Chris said cheerfully. "Hey, if anyone sees a patrol car, sing out the color. I want to know what to watch for."

Rick was in bad shape. He'd miscalculated the number of diet pills needed for the trip and had run out, with no idea when he could get more. He'd been messing up lately, taking more than he used to. He'd always tried to limit himself to one or two capsules a day, but lately, just for the fun of it, he'd been having five and six a day. Now he needed that many just to keep from getting sick. He'd taken the last pill back in Chattanooga and his body was clamoring for another one. His head hurt and he felt hot and dizzy. The lights outside the car blurred together and his brothers inane conversation jarred his nerves.

He had known he was making a mistake, letting his habit get out of hand like that, but somehow in Michigan, up there in the snow, he'd felt desperate. Besides, when Mark was sick, they'd been sending him to the drugstore all the time and the temptation to stockpile was just too great. Rick switched back and forth among all the popular diet aids on the market, but his favorites were extra-strength Dexatrim. They kicked in fast and they lasted longer, too. He'd kill for one now. He was beginning to sweat. Even if they stopped somewhere, he knew he couldn't buy anything. There was always someone hanging around watching everything he did. It was infuriating.

Anything would help at this point. If he could just get out of the car and get fresh air. If he could smoke or have a cup of coffee, anything like that would help. Rick knew if he had to go on much longer, he was going to vomit.

"Look at that one," Mark said, scribbling. *"Crazy Jack's. Fireworks, ammunition and hams."*

"Could you keep quiet for a while?" Rick asked.

"Fuck you," Mark answered. "Here we go. Fourteen miles to King Frog."

"What is King Frog?" Chris asked.

Mark reread his notes. "It's part motel, part restaurant, part gas station, and I think they sell sportswear and towels."

"Why would anyone name a truck stop King Frog?" Chris asked.

"I'm not kidding, guys," Rick said. "I could really use a cigarette. Aren't you hungry, Mark? Don't you have to go to the bathroom, Chris?" His voice was getting shrill.

Shawn turned in his seat and studied Rick. "What's the matter with you?" he asked. "You're pale."

"I'm fine!" Rick shouted. "I just want a fucking cigarette!"

"Pull over at the next place," Shawn said to Chris.

"No!" Mark cried. "If we're going to stop, I want to go to King Frog. It's only eleven miles."

"Next stop," Shawn said firmly. "He looks funny to me."

"He looks funny all the time," Mark whined.

They stopped at a Chevron station. Chris filled the tank and used the bathroom. Mark collected change from everyone and went to look at all the vending machines. Rick took out a cigarette and walked away from the car, around toward the back of the service station. Shawn decided to follow him.

Rick stood at the very edge of the asphalt, looking out over a field of weeds. He was looking up at the night sky, his face brightly lit by the tall revolving Chevron sign. There was a warm wind blowing, mussing his hair.

Rick had to concentrate very hard to get the cigarette back and forth to his mouth without shaking. *I'm not going to make it,* he thought.

Shawn stopped a few feet away from him. "What's really the matter?" he asked.

Rick put his hand up to his heart, Shawn had frightened him so badly. "Nerves," he said. He didn't have his sunglasses on, so he looked away.

Shawn took a step toward him. "You need a pill, don't you, son?" he asked.

Rick couldn't keep his hand from shaking then. "What are you talking about?"

"Let's don't mess around, Rick. I know what you take. Are you out of them?"

Rick nodded, still looking away. The breeze blew the hair away from his face.

He looks like me, Shawn thought. "You've been taking too many of them, if you're in this shape," he said.

Rick looked up. He was grateful for the lack of recrimination. "I know," he said. "It got out of hand."

"If you keep up this way, you know what'll happen to you, don't you?"

Rick nodded. "I'm going to straighten it out," he said. "I just wish I could get one now so I won't . . . I don't even know what happens when you crash real bad, do you?" He looked at Shawn pleadingly.

"I don't have any idea," Shawn said. "Maybe convulsions or something. I just don't know."

"Shit," Rick said. "What are you going to tell them if I . . . if it gets real bad?"

Shawn ran his hands over his face. "It won't," he said. "I've got a pill for you."

"You what?"

"I've got one. I've got a package. I knew you were on them, and I didn't want something like this to come up, so I bought a package for you. I'm just going to give you one, though."

"That's all I want, really. I just want to make it through tonight. Christ, how did you know about this?"

"I just knew." Reluctantly, Shawn handed the capsule to Rick. "Listen, you better mean what you say. I want you to get yourself off these things as fast as you can, because they can really hurt you."

Rick swallowed the pill without water. "I will, I swear it. Honestly I will. It was just tonight . . ."

"I know." Shawn turned and started back toward the car.

"Shawn?"

Shawn stopped and turned. Rick had not called him by his name in years.

"Thank you," Rick said. For just a minute Shawn could see into Rick's eyes, but it happened too fast and there was no time to interpret what was there.

"Just forget it," Shawn said. "And get off those things. I've got enough trouble." He walked rather quickly back to the car.

Chris was tired. It was time for dawn, but no dawn was coming. There was nothing yet but the dark sky and the falling rain and the monotony of the center line, stretching out in front of the car. If the sun would come up, Chris thought, he could keep going. Or if he could turn the radio on. But he didn't want to wake anyone up, so he left it off. The silence and the sameness were hypnotizing him. He was sure he was right on the edge of consciousness, and that any time he might fall the other way and wreck the car.

He didn't know if Rick was still awake or not. They hadn't said anything to each other for hours. Chris felt lonely and frustrated and put-upon. He always had to be the driver and stay awake and do all the work. Shawn, who was always talking about his responsibilities, was collapsed against the passenger door, sleeping like a baby. It wasn't fair. Childhood trauma or not, Shawn ought to learn how to drive and do his share.

Chris had to figure out how old Rick was. He would be

sixteen soon. Maybe then he could get a license, if Shawn would permit that. Shawn had a paranoid fear that all the established institutions of the world were working with the police to track them down. They couldn't use banks, schools, churches, or doctors, so it seemed unlikely Shawn would want to send Rick to the Bureau of Motor Vehicles.

Chris forced himself to pay attention to the center line. If he could just concentrate on driving and not think about other things, then his mind wouldn't wander and he wouldn't fall asleep. The center line was all that mattered. Stay to the right, and everything was fine, cross it, and you kill everyone in the car. If Chris started to fall asleep, the car would invariably drift to the left and he would have to jerk it back. He had spent hours now, struggling with himself and with that line, trying not to cross it.

The rain made a gold mosaic on the windshield. One of the wipers always squeaked, the same pitch and the same tempo, over and over. The center line went on and on, broken for a moment to allow for passing. There were no other cars right now. Chris was all alone.

A strange, self-indulgent sadness overtook him. Lack of sleep always brought Chris's emotions to the surface. He was filled with self-pity. He wanted to cry.

He remembered a rainy night when he was five years old. He couldn't sleep, so Steve and Shawn were staying up talking to him.

Then their mother had come into the room. Chris could remember her vividly, as she looked on that night. She was soft and flowing. Her movements were fluid. Her face was pretty, vulnerable, innocent-looking. Like his own. Her hair and eyes were the same brown as his own. She was an adult, female, saintly version of the way he looked now. She had leaned over him and he told her how he couldn't sleep.

She had smiled and said, "You get that from me. I have trouble sleeping too." And she had hugged him and made sure he was covered properly, and just before she left the room, she said something to Steve and Shawn that made them laugh.

Chris could feel, all over again, the way he had fallen asleep that night, easily letting go of consciousness, hearing the sound of the rain grow dimmer and dimmer, everything around him warm and secure. Knowing his mother would take care of him.

He jerked the wheel hard to the right. The center line had been under one of his wheels. He could have killed all of them. His adrenaline surged up and subsided into anger. No one was taking care of him now. He had to take care of himself and all of them as well. It wasn't fair. Other kids his age were worrying about history tests and who to take to the prom. But here he was, responsible for all his brothers' safety, driving all day and all night and now into the next day, wanting to sleep, living like a fugitive, afraid of the police all the time. It wasn't fair. Angry, resentful tears came into his eyes. He wanted to be five again. He wanted his mother back. He wanted to scream and wake everyone up.

He knew he had to get control of himself. It was hard enough to drive in the rain, without crying on top of it. He had to see. He had to keep track of that damn center line.

"Rick, are you awake?" he asked quietly.

"Yes." Rick sounded wide-awake, in fact.

Chris was glad he hadn't started crying. "Talk to me, I'm falling asleep."

"All right." Rick leaned forward so he could talk quietly and not wake up the others. "I've been confused for the past few miles. Did we cross the Georgia border yet?"

"Yeah. The Florida sign was only on the other side of the road. We're near Lake City now."

"Oh. Okay." Rick rustled the map quietly, squinting down at it so he wouldn't have to turn on the light.

"How much longer does it look like?" Chris asked.

Rick calculated. "Four hours? Maybe five. Lauderdale is way down there. It's near Miami."

"You mean until noon? I'd have to keep driving till noon? I can't do it. I just can't do it."

"So pull over and sleep awhile. What difference does it make?"

"Well, we *said* we were going to try to drive straight through. . . ." Chris looked resentfully at Shawn.

"Well, so what? The people who said that are sleeping. Why should you make a martyr out of yourself? If you're tired, pull over and sleep. *He* doesn't know if the car's moving or not."

"You're right," Chris said. "Besides, it isn't safe for me to drive the way I feel."

"Just do it," Rick said. "Quit arguing with yourself. There's an exit for you right there."

Chris shifted the car into the exit lane. "I don't know how you're keeping awake," he said. "You seem to be in better shape than me."

"I have a lot of self-discipline," Rick said with a sort of laugh.

Chris pulled into a roadside rest. There were several trucks parked there while the drivers slept. Chris always felt safe in places with lots of truck drivers. He parked and listened to the rain for a few minutes. "Rick?"

"What?"

"Can you remember Mom at all?"

Silence. The rain started coming down harder.

"I'm just asking because Shawn's always asking me. I can only remember her a little. I was wondering if you could remember her at all."

"I remember her," Rick said tonelessly.

"Really? You were only five when she died. What do you remember?" Chris turned to look at Rick.

There had been a look of pain in Rick's eyes, which he erased the minute Chris turned around. "Just general things," he said. "Nothing specific. You better go to sleep. You look horrible."

Chris cuddled against his seat. "You should, too. You haven't slept the whole trip, have you?"

"I don't feel like sleeping," Rick answered.

Chris didn't say any more. Rick listened to the rain. It was turning into a downpour. It was a good thing they had stopped. Nobody could drive in this. Rick put his head back and looked at the acoustic holes in the ceiling.

He could remember picking up the stopper from a perfume bottle and looking at his mother through it. It reduced her to colors: pink and white and brown, swirled like taffy. She was only barely recognizable as his mother, a sensation Ricky didn't like, so he put the stopper down and looked at her the normal way. "Where are you going now?" he had asked crossly.

She smiled at him, then went back to putting on her mascara. "Shopping," she said. "Your brother needs new shoes."

"Which brother?" he asked suspiciously.

"Steven."

"I need new shoes too," Ricky said. He held up his foot for her to see. There was a small hole in the toe of his tennis shoe.

"Yes, but Steven's shoes are more important because he has to go to school. When you're in the third grade like he is, we'll make sure you get some nice shoes too."

Ricky snorted. He was used to empty promises of that sort. He knew perfectly well all the good stuff went to the older ones. When he got to the third grade, he would probably have to wear the very shoes they were going to buy for Steve today.

His mother finished her makeup and gave herself a lingering look of approval in the mirror. Then she leaned down and put her hands on her knees so she could speak directly to Ricky. "I want you to be a good boy while I'm gone and not hit your baby brother anymore. I want you to promise."

Lately, Ricky had been punching Mark for no apparent reason. "I won't," he said.

"And also"—she spoke a little hesitantly—"don't do anything to, you know, antagonize your father. He doesn't feel well today, so try and stay out of his way."

Ricky knew the truth about his father because Shawn had explained it to him. What his mother was really saying, Ricky knew, was that his father was drinking that morning, which meant he might go crazy and hurt him. "I won't," he said again.

"That's my baby." She smiled and her face was radiantly beautiful. "Play nice with your brothers until I get home."

Ricky was hoping for a kiss. "I swear I will," he said enthusiastically.

Since she didn't kiss him, he followed her downstairs,

still hoping. In the front hall, he discovered not only Steven putting on his jacket, but Shawn doing the same thing. Ricky flew into a righteous rage. "Why is he going?" he demanded.

His mother leaned down to him again. "Ricky, please try to be a nice boy," she said. "Shawn has to go because he knows what kind of shoes kids are wearing and I need his advice."

Shawn, who was nine, went over to Ricky and lifted him a few inches off the ground. "Quit acting like a brat," he said. "I have to go. You don't want Mom to buy Steve some kind of queer-looking shoes, do you?"

Ricky looked bitterly at Steven, who was zipping his jacket and looking at the floor, trying to stay out of the controversy. "Yes!" Ricky said defiantly.

Shawn set him down. "Look, kid, you're not going and that's that. If you be good and play nice with the other guys, I'll play catch with you when we come back."

This was a pretty special offer. "With just me?" Ricky asked.

"Just you," Shawn said solemnly. "Not with Steve or Chris or Mark. Just with you. All right?"

Ricky relaxed a little. "All right," he said.

Their mother smiled at Shawn. "You're so good with them," she said. She gave Shawn a kiss.

That started Ricky up all over again. "Where's my kiss?" he asked indignantly.

She knelt down. "I'll tell you what," she said, trying to emulate Shawn's technique. "If you don't hit your little brother while we're gone, I'll give you a special kiss when I get home."

Ricky wasn't sure of the propriety of this. It felt wrong to him that a kiss should be included in this kind of bar-

gaining. "What will I get if I do hit him?" he asked, just trying to get the terms straight.

She laughed. "Then I might not come home," she said. And all three of them left, laughing at what she had said.

Ricky watched the car pull out with a disgusted look on his face, then took stock of his options for the afternoon. His other brothers were up in the bedroom. His father was getting drunk in the den. There was nothing on television at this time of day. Ricky decided to go upstairs.

Ricky was disgusted at having been born into such a huge family. His parents, especially his father, were always forgetting which one he was, calling him by someone else's name. He sensed somehow that he was not as important as some of the other ones. He felt like a minor character and that made him resent all his brothers, especially Mark, who commanded attention just by being smaller and stupider than the rest of them. Ricky thought that was a pretty cheap way of being noticed. Besides, if Mark hadn't been born, he, Ricky, would have been the baby and all sorts of special attention would have been his. Lately he had taken out his feelings by punching Mark, which not only drained off his resentment but also focused a lot of attention on him. When he hit Mark, his brothers would yell at him, his father would spank him, and his mother would console him for getting spanked. Sometimes they would discuss him for days, have whole arguments built around why he did what he did, ignoring the other boys as if they weren't there. Even though the technique had its drawbacks, it was the only thing Ricky had found so far that worked.

Ricky pushed open the bedroom door and went in.

Christopher was lying on their bed, on his stomach, reading a Spider-Man book. He was absorbed in the book and didn't bother to look up when Ricky came in. Ricky was mad at Chris lately. He and Chris used to be pals, but when Chris started school, he suddenly wanted to hang around with the older guys. Reading also had widened the gulf between them. Chris loved to read and Ricky didn't know how.

"Hello," Ricky said, very sarcastically.

"Hello," Chris said, not looking up. "Are they gone?"

"Yeah." Ricky walked over to Mark, who was sitting in the middle of the rug, playing with a truck. Instead of running it along on its wheels, Mark was just banging the floor with it. "God, you're stupid," Ricky said to Mark.

Mark only understood things in a half-assed way, but he knew an insult when he heard one. He also knew which brother had been hitting him lately. He made a rude noise at Ricky.

"You do that again and I'll sock you!" Ricky said eagerly.

"Leave him alone," Chris said, still not looking up. "I'm supposed to watch you guys and not let you fight."

"What'll you do if I hit him?" Ricky asked.

Chris still would not bother to look around. "I'll cream you," he said, "then I'll tell Dad and he'll cream you again."

Ricky considered this. It sounded like a pretty good deal. First he would get Chris's undivided attention, then Dad's, then Mom would have to have the whole thing explained to her, and with any luck, Shawn would want to have it out with Ricky too. "I'm gonna hit him," Ricky said.

Chris didn't move a muscle. "You better not," he said in a bored voice.

That sealed it. Ricky made a fist, then a thought occurred to him. He remembered what his mother had said before she left. If he hit Mark, she wouldn't come home. Ricky was pretty sure it was a joke, but what if it wasn't? She had been laughing about it, but maybe she was serious. Ricky didn't know what he would do if she didn't come home. She was the only person in the family he really loved.

Meanwhile, Mark was getting confused, waiting to find out if he was going to be hit. To get things moving again, he threw his truck across the room, knocking a wheel off.

"Hey! Be careful with that!" Ricky said. "That's my truck!"

"It isn't your truck," Chris said in that same impersonal tone of voice. "It's everybody's truck. It was Shawn's truck first."

Ricky felt Chris was disagreeing with him just to be mean. "Is there anything that's just mine?" he cried angrily.

"Just your lousy personality," Chris said, still reading away, "and we don't want that."

It was too much. Everyone was against him. Ricky punched Mark as hard as he could on the arm.

Mark was used to this and knew how to react. He threw back his head and began to cry as loudly as he could.

Chris jumped up, throwing the book aside. "Did you hit him?" he demanded. "Did you?"

"Yes," Ricky said, trembling a little. If he could just get through the painful part now, he would get what he wanted.

Chris grabbed him by the shoulders and shook him. "Why do you keep doing *that?*" he asked.

Meanwhile, Mark was testing the full capacity of his lungs. His crying was more like a series of screams.

"Dad's going to hear that for sure," Chris said. He gave Mark a hug to calm him down. "Shut up, you idiot," he said.

"Are you going to tell him?" Ricky asked. He was anxious to get the painful part of the ordeal over and get on to pleasanter things. The last time his father had spanked him, his mother had rocked him on her lap for a whole evening.

Chris looked uncertain of his duty. "No," he said. "I guess I'm not going to tell him." He hated to see people hurt.

"You're not?" Ricky demanded.

Mark was bored with screaming. He got up and went to look for the wheel of the truck, which had rolled under the bed.

"No." Chris let go of him. "You're probably sorry you hit him anyway, aren't you?"

"No!" Ricky said.

Chris was tortured by this moral question. "Well, I'm not going to tell him. Just, please don't hit Mark again, okay?"

Ricky felt defeated. "Okay," he said sadly.

Chris climbed back onto the bed and picked up his reading as if nothing had happened.

Ricky thought things over. The only thing to do was to go down and tell Dad himself. It would be scary, but it would work. Dad had certainly heard that screaming, so he'd have to punish Ricky if he confessed. "I'm going downstairs for a while," he said.

"All right." Chris wasn't even listening.

Ricky had to hesitate at the den door to get his courage up. What he was doing was extremely dangerous. Shawn had explained the whole thing to him. When Dad drank that stuff, he didn't know how much he was hurting people. His spankings were terrible. He used shoes and books and he never knew when to stop. You always felt you were going to die before it was over. Remembering the last time and how much it hurt, Ricky felt something lurch in his stomach. But then afterward, in his mother's lap, that made up for all of it. She had forgotten all about her little Mark, as if Ricky were the only child she had. Ricky pushed the door open.

His father was on the phone, talking in a very low voice. There was an empty bottle of stuff on the desk beside him. Ricky could tell it was a serious phone call because his father's face was white and frightened and his voice was very low, not like normal. He kept saying over and over, "How could that be?"

"I hit Mark," Ricky said doubtfully.

Ricky's father did a strange thing. He reached down and put his hand on Ricky's shoulder in a sort of caress. He had never done anything like that before. Ricky knew something earthshaking was happening.

"I just don't see . . . What about the boys? Yes, I know. No, of course I'm not. What do you think I do, just sit around and drink all day? Of course I can. I'll be there in half an hour. I just have to get a sitter. Are you sure those bastards are doing all they can? You know, you have to watch . . . Yes, yes, I will." He hung up.

Ricky had never seen his father look so scared. Sometimes when he drank, he got strange looks on his face, but never one like this. Ricky forgot all about the spanking *he was trying to get.* "What's the matter?" *he asked.*

Dad looked at Ricky as if he didn't recognize him. "They had an accident," *he said.* "Somebody sideswiped the car. They're at St. Elizabeth. I have to get a sitter." *He got up, then sat down again, clearly confused.*

Ricky didn't understand. He thought his father was saying Mom had wrecked the car, but the word side-swiped confused him. And he couldn't imagine what St. Elizabeth had to do with it. "Is Mommy hurt?" *he asked, trying to get to the heart of the matter.* "What's she doing with St. Elizabeth?"

His father was trying to think and the question distracted him. "Listen," *he said.* "I have to get a sitter. I have to get over there. You go play with Ricky and Mark and don't worry." *He picked up the phone again.*

"I'm Ricky," *Ricky said.*

It was the middle of the night. Shawn was standing over him, trying to wake him up. Ricky sat up, trying to figure out what was going on. He had never been awake in the middle of the night before. The night-light made the room into a cavern of long, tall shadows. Ricky could see something was terribly wrong. Steven was sitting in the window seat, hugging himself and rocking back and forth, staring at nothing. He had a bandage on his head. Chris, in bed next to him, was crying. Not quiet, dignified crying, but shameless, brokenhearted crying. Only Mark looked normal, asleep with his fist in his mouth.

And Shawn was the most frightening of all. There was something wrong with his eyes. They looked huge and scary, all black, with no colored part. Ricky found out later it was because they had given him medicine at the hospital, because he'd gone crazy and started tearing up things. Now he just looked big and empty and confused. "I have to tell you something," he said.

Ricky tried to put things together in his mind. They had had a sitter all afternoon. It was mean old Mrs. Adams from next door. She had told them that Dad and Mom and Shawn and Steve were at the hospital, but she wouldn't say anything else. Chris had yelled at her, trying to find out what was going on, and she had slapped him. Then evening came and still no one came home. The phone kept ringing. Mrs. Adams had to stay and give them dinner. Every time the phone rang, Chris would demand to know what was going on, but Mrs. Adams wouldn't tell him.

Now it was the middle of the night and Shawn was going to explain things to him. And then it all came together in Ricky's mind. He realized what had happened. It wasn't a joke. She hadn't been joking. He had hit Mark. It was just like the sister had explained to him in Sunday school. If you did something wrong, you had to pay the price. "Mommy isn't coming home, is she?" he whispered hoarsely.

Shawn looked a little stunned. "How did you know?" he asked softly. "Did you hear me talking to Chris?"

Ricky shook his head. "She won't ever come home, will she?" he asked.

Shawn touched him. "No, she can't," he said. "She can't come home anymore."

"I know," Ricky said. A sob came into his throat but didn't quite come out. "Shawn, I hit Mark today, but I'm sorry I did it." He let himself fall back against the pillows. The room with its weird light and shadows looked just the way he imagined Hell. Chris's crying had an unearthly sound to it.

Shawn petted him a little. "Don't worry about that now, Ricky," he said. "It isn't important."

Rick looked at Chris, who was limp and breathing very deeply. "Are you still awake?" Rick asked him hopefully. But there was no answer.

Twelve

They ditched the car in Jacksonville. It was a risk, a relief, and an act of faith. Without a car, they surrendered their mobility and committed themselves, at least for a while, to the state of Florida, but giving up the car also meant the burden of grand theft was finally lifted.

Chris was given the responsibility for disposing of the car. He left it parked, with the keys in the ignition and one window rolled down, in the parking lot of a twenty-four-hour supermarket. As a theatrical touch, he went shopping at a nearby drugstore and left a sack of cheap items in the backseat. The clear impression was that some poor sucker had left the keys in the car while he went shopping. They were sure this guaranteed the car would be stolen, rather than picked up by the authorities.

Once that was done, the plan was to hitchhike down the east coast of Florida until they found a place they liked. Ft. Lauderdale was no longer written in stone. They decided any beach with lots of women and not too many police would be fine.

Hitchhiking scared them. Back in Dayton, Ohio, at

Cornell Heights Elementary School, they had seen dozens of little training films about teenage hitchhikers who were beaten, dismembered, and tossed into woodland areas. There had also been a memorable scene in the movie *Death Prom* where a female hitchhiker had her throat cut. It didn't take too much imagination to think what might happen to four boys hitchhiking with a couple of switchblades and nine hundred dollars in cash. Shawn was even more terrified of sexual perverts. He refused all rides from people of either sex who smiled at Chris.

They rode from Jacksonville to St. Augustine with a somber, middle-aged man in a herringbone jacket. He drove a Mercedes, which assured Shawn he couldn't be a thief or a pervert, but he had a horrible disposition.

"How come we can't see the ocean from here?" Mark had asked him.

"Because it's somewhere else," the man had said bitterly, and that was the only conversation they had with him.

In St. Augustine they were picked up by a man in his early twenties. This man was much more talkative than the Mercedes driver. His name was Max Buckner and he drove an old red Maverick. He was a sales rep for a trade magazine. He had recently graduated from Penn State, where he had been a football star. He had blond hair, cut very short, a square body, and broad shoulders. He was always hunching and shrugging and twisting his shoulders as he talked, as if afraid someone might tackle him at any moment.

None of the boys were interested in Penn State or football or what it was like to rep a trade magazine, but they learned a lot about all three, because Max Buckner enjoyed talking about himself.

"Sales," he said. "The oldest profession in the world and the most basic. It's the only thing I'll ever do, because I respect it. It takes character to be a sales rep. It takes guts. Do you know what sales really is?" He turned all the way around in his seat to see if anyone knew what sales was. No one seemed to. "It's one man pitted against the other, in the purest, most primitive sense. I'll tell you guys something. Nobody really wants to buy anything. People want to hang on to their money, but they're weak. That's the great rule all salesmen must know. It's the job of the salesman to work on that natural weakness, and exploit it for all it's worth. You've got to make people think they want something, whether they do or not. You've got to create an illusion, at least until the money changes hands. You can imagine what an art that is."

If anyone in the backseat had an opinion, it was not expressed.

"I go into people's offices every day," Max went on, "and they say to me, 'Why should I advertise in *Tire and Rubber Digest*?' It's my job to come up with a bunch of reasons why they should. You guys remember that for when you grow up. That's how it's done."

"None of us are going to be salesmen," Shawn said coldly.

"Well, I'll tell you something else," Max said. "No matter what job you have, you're still basically a salesman. That's the truth, when you think about it."

"It's hard to apply that concept to brain surgery," Shawn said.

Chris decided it was time to change the subject. "How far down the coast are you going, Max?" he asked.

Max looked at Chris as if he were insane. "Are you kidding? I'm going to Daytona. Isn't that where you guys are going?"

"Why should we go there?" Shawn asked.

Max turned his incredulous look to Shawn. "It's race week, little boy, *race week*."

Rick caught on. "The Daytona 500?"

Max shook his head in horror. "Jesus!" he said. "You guys must be from Kansas or something."

"We're from Brooklyn," Shawn said. "Actually, we just escaped from a juvenile correction facility up there."

Max believed him. "Really?"

"Yeah," Shawn said, very seriously. "We had to beat up a guard to get out, but we got out. We've escaped from other places before. They can't build one that'll hold us, can they?" He appealed to his brothers, who made affirmative noises.

Max began to give them searching looks in the rear-view mirror. "That's pretty interesting," he said nervously. "Did you guys commit any special crime, that they would want to put you in one of those places?"

Shawn laughed the macho laugh of a hardened criminal. "I guess we did," he said. "We got put in this last place for aggravated assault. It was a reduced charge. We beat up a guy in an alley." Shawn had to be careful not to look at Chris, who was about ready to giggle.

"Wow," said Max. The color was leaving his face. "Did you hurt him bad?"

"I think we've said enough about it already," Chris said in a threatening tone.

Max was terrorized by now. He could hardly keep the car in the right lane. "I'm not trying to *pry*," he said. "If anybody knows how to mind their own business, it's me. I don't care what you guys did in the past. That's just history. Sometimes it might seem like I'm asking a lot of questions, but that's just because my sales training . . . I'm very interested in people . . . What . . . now, don't answer me if you don't want to . . . What would make you guys beat up that guy the way you did?"

Rick shrugged. "We just didn't like the guy," he said.

"He talked too much," Mark added, pleased with himself.

Max was very quiet for the next few miles.

They drove on A1A now, the coast road. The scenery was very uniform. The highway was closed in on the left side by thick hedges of sea oats. The boys knew they were sea oats because every two miles there was a sign saying UNLAWFUL TO PICK SEA OATS. The right side of the road was pine trees and billboards, mostly for Marineland, Palm Coast, and Cocoa Beach. No one looked to the right, however, because the left side held their attention like a magnet. Behind those sea oats, everyone knew, was the Atlantic Ocean.

They could catch glimpses of it now, when there was a break in the hedges or when the highway rose on a hill, just quick, teasing flashes of it, but what they saw was thrilling to them. It was frothy and gray and it went on forever. The immensity of it was compelling. One could not look at something that large and not be drawn toward it. The windows in Max's car were down and no one wore his jacket anymore. It was seventy degrees in the middle of winter. Everyone, even Rick, was beginning to feel elated.

Suddenly the sea oats and pine forests vanished and there was a city, or rather a series of hotels and malls and causeways. The ocean was clearly visible now, frothing crazily in the wind. At the first traffic light a banner saying WELCOME RACE FANS was strung across the street.

"This is Daytona?" Shawn asked Max.

"Not quite," Max said. "This is Ormond Beach. It's a separate city, but it's really like a suburb of Daytona.

There's a million little communities around here: Holly Hill, Port Orange, Ponce Inlet."

It was like hearing poetry. Traffic poured into Daytona and Ormond. Max had to slow to fifteen miles per hour, so the boys got a good look at everything. "This is the strip," Max said. "The main drag. This is where all the hotels and restaurants and bars and you-know-what-else is. The farther south you go on the strip, the better the action is. This is all part of the peninsula. If you want to go over to the mainland, you cross one of those causeways. But you don't want to go over there. That's where the townies go. The beach and the bars are here."

The strip had them all fascinated. There were hundreds of hotels, huge palatial complexes next to three-room dives. Most of the hotels and motels had aquatic names: The Schooner, The Pirate's Cove, Coral Inn, and Mark's favorite, The Riptide. Many of the hotels had large statues of friendly turtles or pearl divers or pirates to beckon motorists in. All of them had billboards spelling out the advantages of each particular place: olympic pools, giant waterslides, disco on the roof, and so on. The smaller places, which could not brag of those things, simply said CLEAN ROOMS or TELEVISION. Every one of them had a sign saying WELCOME RACE FANS.

Between hotels were restaurants, bars, and a series of identical-looking souvenir stores, all with different names. Seashells, Indian River oranges, and Confederate flags were clearly the best-selling souvenirs.

"I hope you can find a place to stay," Max said. "The hotels get pretty booked during race week." He pulled into a McDonald's parking lot to let them out. "One other thing," he warned. "The whole town is crawling with cops this week, so be careful." Max drove away from them, looking relieved at being alone again.

They tried five hotels before finding one with a vacancy. It was called Corsair. Not The Corsair, just Corsair. They liked the sign out front, which showed a rather degenerate-looking, grinning pirate. They had to share a room but were promised the adjacent one right after race week. Like all the hotels on the strip, Corsair fronted the ocean and each room had a balcony overlooking the water. After about ten minutes of their pretending to move in, they were unable to resist the call of the ocean.

The beach was crowded with people and dogs and parked cars, but the boys hardly saw those things. They looked at nothing but the ocean. Still gray and foaming, it was hypnotic, frightening in its power to charm. Most of them had been very small on the previous trip to Florida, and none of them had remembered how amazing an ocean can look. Compared to the rivers of Ohio and Indiana and the lakes of Michigan, it was powerful stuff.

Shawn walked straight into the water without hesitation, until it was just below his knees. He stood almost reverently, watching the waves and learning the rhythm of them. The sea was immense and pale and the sky was the same color, broken only by the graceful flight of seagulls. At the horizon the line between sky and sea was blurred, indefinite. Everything moved with an unfailing, well-rehearsed rhythm. There was a pattern Shawn could understand, and as each wave hit his legs he felt more and more a part of it.

Shawn waded farther, letting the water get above his knees. It was clear, beautiful water and polished, fine-textured sand. In an environment like this, where everything was constantly washed and rearranged, Shawn could not imagine anything ever going wrong. He had not felt so peaceful since he was a child. He had never felt so free.

He turned to look back at his brothers. They were halting at the edge of the water, afraid to get wet.

"Come on," he shouted, and walked out farther to show them he was not afraid. The deeper he went, the more hypnotized and tranquilized he felt. He couldn't understand why he had been so tense and worried the past few months. How could you be afraid of anything in a world where there was a sky and sea like this one?

"Come *on*," he repeated.

Obediently, Chris took a few steps into the water. "It's squishy!" he protested.

"Come on out here, you sissy!" Shawn demanded.

Chris waded just up to his knees. "It's cold, too," he said.

Rick and Mark stayed where they were, trying to decide who was right.

"It's not cold when you're used to it," Shawn said. "You come right out here where I am. Now!"

Chris was a naturally cooperative person. He continued to wade out, cringing each time a wave broke over his legs. "My clothes are getting all wet!" he said.

Mark edged into the water, looking down all the time. "Are there any sharks in this part of Florida?" he asked.

"No, they're in the other part." Shawn giggled. He was high on ocean. He had rapture of the deep from the waist down.

Rick stayed on the shore. He wanted to see if anything happened to any of them before he ventured out.

Chris was close to Shawn now. "You're crazy," he said. "It's too fucking cold to be getting this wet!"

Shawn was tired of his whining. "How do you like

this?" he asked and, using both hands, splashed a tidal wave over Chris, soaking his hair and face and shirt.

Chris was rendered speechless. "Look what you did!" he finally screamed. He dripped like an umbrella.

Shawn's answer was to giggle uncontrollably.

That cracked Chris up and he splashed Shawn back. That was enough to bring Mark into deep water and they began a spectacular three-way water fight that lasted nearly a half hour.

Rick sighed. *Kindergarten,* he thought. He confined his wading to the shoreline and smiled at his brothers from time to time, to show them he forgave their immaturity.

While they were playing, the sun came out and everything changed abruptly from gray to sapphire. It was like being inside a jewel. Their happiness bordered on hysteria.

When they had exhausted themselves, they came back to shore and found a place to sit, near a car whose radio was playing music they liked. Since it was too cold for most people to go in the water, the beach was full of parked cars. There were innumerable games of Frisbee going on and a lot of people on bikes. Nearby, in a life-guard tower, a young man was reading *A Farewell to Arms.* Everyone, everywhere in sight, looked unspeakably happy.

"Why didn't we do this sooner?" Shawn said.

"I'm going to live in Florida the rest of my life," Mark said.

"That probably won't be much longer," Rick said. "How much money do we have left now?" He smiled sweetly at Shawn.

"We have enough," Shawn said, which wasn't true. They had spent three thousand dollars in only five months

on the road. They were now down to less than nine
hundred. If they kept living in motels and no one was
working, they would be broke within the month. "Let's
walk," Shawn said, getting up. "Which way do you want
to go?"

Chris pointed north, and it was that decision that first
led them to the Ormond pier. At first it was just a ghostly-
looking scaffold in the distance, but gradually, because it
was the only landmark, it became the goal of their walk.
They agreed to walk to the pier, turn around, and go
back.

Since the pier was actually about six miles from the
heart of Daytona, they had to walk for hours to get to it.
By that time it was late afternoon, low tide, and the boys
were exhausted. But the pier was worth it. It was immense, as tall as a double Ferris wheel, by Mark's calcu-
lation, and extended hundreds of feet into the ocean. The
end of the pier was T-shaped and there were several fishermen casting off the end. At the entrance to the pier
there was a small clapboard building where one could
rent equipment and buy food. The supports of the pier
were steel and concrete, but the top structure was of
wood: wood rails, wood planking, and wood benches.
It was the only part of the beach where there was not a
crowd of tourists.

They climbed the hill to the pier entrance without saying a word to each other.

Inside the clapboard building there was a middle-aged
man behind a counter. He was blond and sunburned and
looked like an ex-golfer. He wore a dark blue Izod shirt
and plaid pants and a white belt. Behind his head was a
blackboard, on which was written *On Duty: Jack
O'Brien* and underneath that, a tally of how many of each

kind of fish had been caught off the pier that week. "You guys want to go out on the pier?" he asked. His voice was amiable, but he kept an eye on Rick, who was handling things on the counter.

"Yes," Shawn said.

"Four people is four dollars. You don't plan to fish?"

"No."

"Want anything to eat, then?"

Shawn turned to Mark. "Are you hungry?" It was a rhetorical question.

Mark looked coy. "They have cookies," he said.

Shawn bought a half-dozen cookies and they went out onto the pier.

It was like being on the deck of a large ship. One could look through the slats in the planking and see the beach a hundred feet below. Then, as they walked out farther, the ocean was underneath, swirling and lapping against the supports. It made them all nervous, but they walked out very bravely, staying a polite distance from the serious fishermen. The railing was lined with tame seagulls and pelicans, waiting to see if any of the fishermen got lucky. A few of them eyed Mark's cookies, but he stared them down.

They sat for a long time on one of the wood benches, watching the sun set behind the hotels on the strip. The water was quiet and bright with streaks of light. When a wave came in, it would rock the pier, ever so gently. None of them spoke. They all understood that there was something special about this place. They knew they had finally found a home.

Thirteen

The sun was blindingly bright, making squiggly reflections on the water below. Chris sat alone at the end of the pier, his legs dangling over the ocean, drinking Budweiser out of the can. He had serious things on his mind.

His brothers were distributed over the length of the pier. Rick was the farthest away, at the shore end, smoking a cigarette. Mark was midway down the pier, trying to get a pelican to eat from his hand. The pelican and Mark had been at a standoff for fifteen minutes. Mark kept saying friendly, reassuring things while the pelican looked at him from various angles. It would lower its head and look at Mark through the top of its eyes, then it would stretch its neck out long and look down on him. Both Mark and the pelican seemed content to let this ritual go on forever. Shawn was on a bench a few feet from Chris. He had lured a young female tourist onto the pier and was working on her. She wasn't bad-looking, but she was incredibly stupid. Shawn was trying to give her directions to the hotel. She couldn't get north and south straight in her mind. Shawn had told her about a thousand times that if the ocean is on your left, you're going south.

Chris was annoyed because he wanted to talk to Shawn. He looked far out to sea at the big waves. If you followed them with your eyes, it made you dizzy. *I shouldn't sit like this when I'm drinking,* Chris thought and pulled his legs up. Something important was on his mind. It was such a big idea, he was afraid to discuss it with anyone yet. He was thinking they should stop living in hotels and get their own apartment.

Their financial situation had improved drastically in the last few months. He and Shawn had sold their class rings, which brought in five hundred dollars. There had been some discussion, mostly by Rick, that Chris sell his medal, too, since it was sterling and had an obsolete saint on it anyway, but fortunately that idea had been voted down.

Chris and Shawn each worked twenty-five hours a week lifeguarding. It was a wonderful job because no one ever really needed their life saved. Most of the time you just sat in the tower and read books. Once in a while, little kids would try to drown each other or do something that looked dangerous, so you just blew your whistle and pointed at them. It gave Chris a nice feeling of power. The main hazard of the job was sunburn.

Mark kept earning money, almost without meaning to. He would offer to watch people's things on the beach while they went in the water, and afterward they would force five-dollar bills on him. He started getting food for the night manager of Corsair, who was always hungry and couldn't leave his desk. Now Mark kept his eye out for anyone who looked like they might want an errand run. He averaged between ten and twenty dollars a week on that sort of thing.

Then there was the pier. The boys spent most of their time there, so it was inevitable that they would become friends with the O'Briens, who leased and managed the pier. The O'Briens had no children and the Cunnigans had no parents, so there was an automatic attraction. Also, the O'Briens had managed the pier for five years and were very tired of being on duty seven days a week, twelve hours a day. One afternoon Shawn had offered to watch the cash register, and after he had proved competent and trustworthy, the O'Briens became dependent on the Cunnigans, letting them take over whenever they wanted to get away. All these sources of income had put the boys on a new footing. They now had an income they could actually live on. In fact, they took what was left of Shawn's old college fund, plus the class-ring money, and opened a savings account at Sun Bank. Things were going so well, they felt nervous about it, making jokes about getting a stock portfolio soon.

Their success had a strange effect on Chris. It had kindled in him a powerful desire for a permanent home. At first he just looked at it from an economic point of view. They could save money by paying rent instead of hotel bills, and buying groceries was cheaper than eating out. But as soon as the idea formed in his mind, it became an obsession, a longing, a passion. He began reading the classified ads in newspapers, studying each apartment listing. He found some one-bedroom places without air conditioning for as little as $145 a month. Little fantasies began to come to him at night in bed, or up in his life-guard tower. He pictured himself in the kitchen of an apartment, forcing nutritious food on Mark, the way he had when they were living at home. He could see himself on Sunday mornings, getting up before the others to put on coffee. Such thoughts made him unspeakably happy.

He would have mentioned the idea to Shawn right away, but his own emotionalism frightened him. He didn't want to appear feverish or fanatical on the subject. He just wanted to suggest it to Shawn casually, like any good business proposal. But whenever he thought of the apartment, he would begin to daydream about what kind of dishes they would have or how they might save up for a stereo, and his own intensity would frighten him. He had almost felt ready to talk to Shawn today, but now Shawn was wasting his time with this idiot girl.

"All right, you're going south on the strip, right? So you go beyond Seabreeze Avenue . . ."

"What's that?" The girl giggled. She seemed to think her stupidity was amusing.

Shawn sighed. "It's the only street with a sign that says Seabreeze Avenue. You can read, can't you?"

"Come on, fella," Mark said to the pelican. "I won't hurt you."

Christ, Chris thought, *they'd probably do better if Mark tried to feed the girl and Shawn tried to make it with the pelican.*

"Do you live near the Plantation?" asked the dumb girl. The Plantation was a bar for tourists.

"South of that," Shawn said. "Listen, where do *you* live?"

"I live with my mom," she said. She found herself very funny. She laughed and laughed.

Chris got up. "Draw her a map," he snarled as he walked past them.

Mrs. O'Brien was on duty this morning. She was reading a horoscope magazine. She was a short, plump woman who always wore a sun visor, even indoors. "What's your sign?" she asked Chris as he approached.

"Sagittarius," he said, throwing his empty into the trash. "Is that good?"

"You're very intelligent, but you have no tact." She watched his face.

"I think I've got tact," he said. "What's Capricorn?"

"Very ambitious," she said. "Sexually inhibited."

Chris grinned. "That's Rick. Shawn's a Libra and Mark's Aquarius."

"That's why Shawn likes to argue and Mark has such a good imagination," she said.

"Maybe so," Chris said. "But I *do* have tact." He sat down in a deck chair. He liked Mrs. O'Brien.

"I was wanting to ask you a question, Chris," she said, "Jack brought it up the other night. How is it that you boys are here on weekdays? Shouldn't you be in school?"

Chris was horrified. It had never even occurred to him that they should pretend to be in school during the week. "We were given the semester off," he said.

"Really?" she asked. "Why?" She wasn't suspicious, only curious.

"Because of the tragedy in our family," Chris said. His mind was going a hundred miles an hour.

Mrs. O'Brien was fascinated. "What tragedy, dear?" she asked.

Chris gauged her and decided the more lurid the story was, the better she would like it. "Our father shot our mother," he said. He made his voice very quiet. "He was drunk," he added with a very realistic note of hatred.

Mrs. O'Brien put her magazine aside. "Good heavens, dear, I had no idea."

Chris pretended to struggle for control. "It's all right," he said. "I'm supposed to talk about it. That's what the therapist told us. The more we talk about it, the better we can accept it." He was ashamed not only of his lying but of the talent with which he did it.

"You . . . you didn't see it happen, did you?"

Chris thought it over. "I didn't, but Mark did. He's the one the doctors are really worried about."

Mrs. O'Brien leaned over the counter and looked down the pier at Mark, who was swearing at the pelican. "I can't believe it," she said. "He seems so well adjusted."

"That's the problem," Chris said. "He won't—this is what the doctor said—he won't acknowledge what happened. He's holding it all in. He has a lot of nightmares and things."

Mrs. O'Brien came all the way around the counter and put her arms around Chris. "You poor boys. I can't believe it. Who takes care of you?"

"We live with our grandparents," he said. "My mother's parents. Of course, the whole thing is very hard on them, too." Chris felt guilty, but he was sure he had taken her mind off why they weren't in school.

"It's so hard to believe," Mrs. O'Brien said. "The way you boys act, I'd never know you'd been through something like this."

"We try to keep up a front," he said. "Mostly for Mark's sake."

"I can see you don't want to talk about it anymore," she said gently. "I understand." She hugged him again. She tried to think of something nice she could do for him. "Would you boys like to make some money this afternoon?" she asked. "I was thinking of doing some shopping."

"Sure," Chris said, "we'd be happy to."

She picked up her purse and looked at him lovingly. He was looking at the floor. "You know," she said, "things like this test our faith, but we should never lose our trust in God."

Chris was exasperated. It never failed. Every time he lied or cheated or did anything like that, someone always mentioned God to him. "No, ma'am," he said, keeping his eyes on the floor.

She left quickly. She could see he wanted to be alone.

"I'll never get to Heaven," he said quietly after she had gone. He sighed, got up, and went behind the counter. He carefully counted all the money in the cash register. Then he erased Mrs. O'Brien's name from the blackboard and wrote *On Duty: Rick Cunnigan.*

Then he went out onto the pier. Rick was just starting another cigarette. He was up to two packs a day. Chris was thinking about mentioning something about that to him sometime, but not today. Rick was looking out to sea, lost in thought. Since they'd come to Florida, he'd worn his sunglasses nearly all the time. When he heard someone behind him, he whipped around like a startled animal.

"Mrs. O'Brien went shopping," Chris said. "It's your turn."

Rick threw his cigarette into the ocean. "Great," he said. He stood up and stretched.

As Rick started to walk away, Chris said suddenly, "I counted the register, so don't—" and then he stopped, embarrassed.

Rick stopped in midstep. He turned around, lifted his sunglasses, and looked at Chris with cold eyes. "Don't what?" he said. There was a chilling undertone in his voice.

Chris was actually frightened of him. "Don't do *anything,*" he said and walked away quickly, afraid to look back.

Shawn was just getting rid of his girl friend. Chris

passed her and she looked at him angrily, as if he had sabotaged her chances with Shawn. Chris began to feel a little paranoid.

He sat down on the bench next to Shawn. Shawn was watching seagulls, so Chris watched seagulls too. "Did she ever get the address right?" Chris asked.

"I gave up," Shawn said. "Think how long it would take a girl like that to take her clothes off."

A fishing boat, the *Sea Love,* drifted by on its way to the marina. The captain knew the boys by sight and waved at them. They both waved back.

"Something's on your mind, Christopher John," Shawn said.

Chris felt his heart rate pick up. "Yes," he said.

"Well, are you going to tell me about it?"

Chris reviewed his arguments again. But immediately his mind was dominated by fantasies: closets and drawers and watching television in the evening. "I'm not ready to talk about it yet."

Shawn looked alarmed. "It's not some woman, is it?"

Chris laughed. "No."

"Oh, Christ," Shawn said. "I was afraid it was Steven all over again. You're not in trouble, are you?"

"No, I'll tell you later. I really will."

"Whatever. Tell Mark to get off that fucking railing."

"Get off that fucking railing, Mark!" Chris shouted.

March 27

Dear Guys—

This is an important letter, so if anyone's in the bathroom, wait till they come out before you read this. I got married today.

It was very complicated. You have to swear your life away to get married in the state of Indiana. I had to swear I was 18. I had to swear I wasn't a blood relation of Amy's. I had to swear I hadn't been married before (did they have to ask?). Then I got into all kinds of trouble because they wanted my birth certificate. Being a teenage runaway, of course, I didn't have one. So I told them it was destroyed in a fire. They got real suspicious of that and started calling all these places in Ohio, while I was just dying, thinking, *this is the end*. Anyway, they got in touch with some kind of bureaucratic institution that confirmed I was born at St. Elizabeth Hospital and that I really was 18. Amy laughed about all this, which didn't help.

The week before that, we had to go to some sleazy clinic and have blood taken to make sure Amy and I were free from venereal disease and RH factors. All this stuff is good, because you have to really be in love to put up with this sort of shit.

Anyway, after all the paperwork was done, we went downstairs and they brought out this judge, who looked REAL DRUNK and he made us swear to a few more things and we all signed something and then we were married. As you may have noticed, Chris, this was not a Catholic wedding.

I certainly hope I don't get any letters from CERTAIN MEMBERS OF THE FAMILY, asking me if I'm sure of what I'm doing. If I wasn't, I wouldn't, right? In fifteen or twenty years, you'll see I was right. At the moment, you'll just have to trust me. I don't want any grief from ANY of you.

I took a high school equivalency test. Sample question: The Bill of Rights is in, A. The Constitution, B. The

Declaration of Independence, C. The Gettysburg Address, or D. The Phone Book. Any idiot could pass this thing, even you, Mark. This is something all of you should do because they give you something that's just as good as a diploma and now I get to go to college in the fall, if I get all the grants I think I'm going to get. You have to swear to almost as many things to get financial aid as you do to get married.

I'm glad to hear you guys are doing so good. I really miss you. Amy was saying maybe we could afford to drive down there for a week or so this summer. Wouldn't that be great? But if we do come down, I want Mark to stay away from my wife. She keeps saying over and over how *cute* he is.

Take care of yourselves.

                                                          STEVE

It was after 3:00 A.M. Shawn sat on the curb, watching traffic on the strip. The city was getting busy again. It was the beginning of Student Weeks, when all the kids come down for spring vacation. All the signs which had said WELCOME RACE FANS now said WELCOME STUDENTS. The restaurants and bars extended their hours and the lights on the strip got brighter and the senior citizens all went into hiding.

Kids were driving up and down the strip in candy-colored Fords and Chevys and Rabbits, drinking and laughing and fondling each other. Under the bright streetlights, they looked unreal.

Shawn couldn't sleep. Steven's letter had made him sad, but he wasn't sure why. Maybe he was lonely for his brother, or anxious for him, or maybe he was merely jealous of someone who could go to college when he couldn't. He didn't know. He just felt as if someone had torn a hole in him and the wind was blowing through. He felt all alone.

He heard Chris coming up behind him. He knew it was Chris without looking. The pain inside Shawn flared suddenly and he realized what it was. He wanted his mother. After all these years, it was still the same. After all they'd been through, that was all it boiled down to. He was still a little kid missing his mother.

Chris sat down on the curb and stuck his feet out into the street exactly the way Shawn did, and watched traffic with him. Then, after a few minutes, he began to talk. "I've been looking at apartments in the newspapers for the last few days. They're so much cheaper than the hotel, and now that we've got regular money coming in, I think it would be a good thing to do. We could rent one furnished, you know, so it wouldn't cost that much to get set up; just a set of Corelle dishes, some stuff to cook in, sheets, towels, that kind of stuff. We could take some money out of the bank for that. And for the deposit and stuff. It wouldn't be that much." Chris paused for a minute, but Shawn was looking away and had nothing to say, so he went on. "There's one right now, on Peninsula Drive, furnished, and it rents for a hundred and forty-five a month. I mean, it wouldn't be a palace for that kind of money, but it would have to be better than a hotel room. Just one bedroom, but you and I could sleep in the living room. Once we got set up, Shawn, think of the money we'd save because we'd be eating at home, and it would be good for Mark, because, you know, he doesn't eat right when we eat out, and also it would be good to have something permanent, because a hotel is sort of uncertain and the rates change all the time. I know this is a lot to throw at you at this hour of the night, but I can just . . . I've been thinking about this a lot and it seems like an awfully good idea to me, unless I'm overlooking something. Do you think it would be remotely possible for us to do something like that?"

Shawn finally looked around. He looked at Chris a long time. "Of *course* we could," he said. "Of *course* we will."

Fourteen

By summer, Shawn had come to believe that luck came in cycles. Last winter, in Grand Rapids, they had hit a low cycle. Anything that had happened to them at that time was a change for the worse, things steadily declined and there was nothing anyone could have done to make it better.

Conversely, since they'd come to Florida, nothing could go wrong. They were in a high cycle and everything that happened was a change for the better. They had jobs, they had money, they had a place to live, even Rick was fairly easy to get along with. And the surroundings, of course, were beautiful. Nothing but beaches and bars on the whole peninsula, and the pier at the north end, and the marina and lighthouse at the south end. It was as if they'd designed the whole place according to their fantasies. But the happiness itself caused Shawn a certain amount of worry. He would watch his younger brothers playing in the ocean or sunning on the pier and see how healthy and tan they were and it would prove to him that he had been right in taking them away from home; he would just be taking pride in how well he was taking care of them, then a current of fear would hit him. How long could such incredible luck last? Life wasn't really like this. Shawn felt certain that if things kept getting better, they would reach the apex of their cycle of luck and things would take some kind of horrible plunge.

One Saturday morning he was helping Mr. O'Brien take inventory of the pier office. Mr. O'Brien had been teaching him what kind of lures caught which kind of fish. Shawn liked to know as much as he could so he could do a better job when he was on duty.

"You kids sure do love this pier, don't you?" Mr. O'Brien asked. He had emptied his junk drawer onto the counter and was sorting fishing line and paper clips and little knives into piles. "Peggy says you spend as much time up here as we do."

Shawn had climbed onto the Pepsi machine to reach a high shelf. "Some places just get to you," he said. "I'd feel funny if we didn't come up here every day."

Jack O'Brien smiled. "That's how Peggy and I always felt. We used to come down here every summer and fish and then we heard the lease was up and we grabbed it. We thought this was the best place in the world to live."

Shawn finished the shelf and rested awhile, sitting up on the Pepsi machine. He liked being up high. "I agree with you," he said.

"Are you going to keep living with your grandparents for a while?" Mr. O'Brien asked. He seemed to have something on his mind.

Shawn wished Chris hadn't made up that dumb story in the first place. Mrs. O'Brien was always crying over them now and Mr. O'Brien kept asking how their grandparents were. "Yes, it looks that way," he said.

"You're nineteen, isn't that right?" Mr. O'Brien asked.

Shawn could see now that he was driving at something. "Yes."

"Well, I was hoping, I was thinking, this fall, when your brothers are in school, if you're looking for something to do, maybe you'd like to look after the pier full time. Peg and I could just sit in now and then. Kind of oversee things."

"Really?" Shawn said. "You mean it?"

"Well, it's not as much fun for Peg and me to be up here all the time as it used to be. I sure don't want to give up my lease on this pier, but, you know, we're not getting any younger and these twelve-hour days . . . Well, you're young. You could handle it better. I'd pay you all right, too. I wouldn't take advantage of your age. Do you think you'd like that?"

"Oh, yes! Absolutely."

"You wouldn't be too tied down. I mean, Peg and I would help out a lot on the weekends, if you boys wanted to go somewhere. Are you sure you'd enjoy it?"

Shawn jumped down. "I know I would. I'd do a very good job. Really I would." He was thinking of all the things they could have if he was working full time.

"Well, that's great," Mr. O'Brien said. "You want to shake on it?"

They shook hands. And as they did it occurred to Shawn that that was just one more stroke of good luck. Happy as he was, he felt sure now that it had been one thing too many. It was time now for some kind of catastrophe.

The boys came down to the pier every evening after dinner. It became a rather special ritual with them. They would drink coffee and sit on the edge of the pier and watch the ocean until it got dark. This became the time of day when they talked seriously to each other. Things could be said during this twilight break that could never have been mentioned during the day. After it got dark, they would lock up the pier office and walk home along the strip, stopping off somewhere to get drunk if they had the money and the inclination.

Tonight there was a wind blowing and the weather had been rainy and chilly all day, so they drank extra coffee (except Mark, who preferred hot chocolate) and sat close together at the far end of the pier. They sat on the planking rather than on benches. It was almost like being out on a ship.

Mark had his guitar and was playing. He didn't play songs, just explored chord patterns with his fingers, looking for sounds he liked. Rick smoked. Shawn and Chris were both daydreaming. It was twilight and the sky was translucent, pearlized; the water below, deep, oily, and blue with silver-black streaks. Between guitar licks they could hear the water lap against the pier supports. No one had talked for a long time.

Chris pointed out to sea where a few bright lights were shifting across the water, like planets. "Shrimp boats," he said softly.

Rick held his lighter over his head and flashed it a few times. One of the boats turned its lights off, then on again. "He saw us," Rick said, pleased.

Mark stopped playing and laid his fingers across the strings to quiet them. "What's high school like?" he asked.

Shawn had leaned his head back against the railing, almost asleep. He sat up rather suddenly at the question. It seemed horrible that Mark would have to ask such a question, but, of course, it made sense. Mark had never been to high school and might never go. Shawn looked at Chris and saw the question had troubled him, too.

"You didn't miss much," Chris said finally. "The girls are nice, but the learning part seems a little stupid when I look back on it. It seems like they taught us an awful lot of crazy things."

"Teach him some high school stuff," Shawn said to Chris. "You're brilliant. You can remember all that stuff. Teach him some algebra or something so he won't feel left out."

"Algebra?" Chris said. "Are you kidding? I don't understand algebra."

"You got an A in it. I remember you did. I wanted to kill you."

"I understood it up until the test and then I forgot it. I wouldn't know how to do algebra now if my life depended on it."

"I don't want algebra anyway," Mark said. "I hate math. Teach me some French." He had always been resentful when his brothers talked French in front of him.

"*Mon frère Guy est dans la marine,*" Chris said.

"My gay brother is in the Marines?" Mark guessed.

"Not quite," Chris said. He appealed to his brothers. "What else did we learn in French?"

"*Je me demande s'il est dangereux de patiner,*" Shawn said.

Chris translated for Mark. "I wonder if it would be dangerous to ice skate."

"I can't use that in Florida," Mark complained. "Teach me something I can use."

"*J'aime foutre les jeunes filles,*" Shawn said.

"What's that?" Mark asked.

"Never mind," Chris said.

Mark felt there wasn't much use for French as long as they lived in Florida anyway. "How about geometry?" he asked. "What's that like?"

"Oh, Christ," Chris said. "Let's see. Space is made up of an infinite number of points and between any two points is a line and three points, not on a line, make an angle and the number of degrees—"

"I'm fucking glad I never went to high school," Mark interrupted.

"Wait, there's more," Shawn said. "There are two houses in Congress and Moby Dick is really Jesus Christ and if you get in a car with an older woman, you'll get VD. Now you've got a complete high school education."

"That's horrible," Mark said. "You guys did all that studying and all you can do is recite a bunch of stuff you don't understand. I'm disillusioned."

"You learn the important things in elementary school," Chris agreed. "High school is just to keep you off the streets for a few more years."

"Congratulations," Rick said suddenly. "You two have done it again."

"What?" Chris asked.

"You and Shawn. It's fascinating to watch your technique. In five minutes you gave Mark the impression that high school is totally meaningless and unimportant and he's better off without it, when all the time you know damn well you've ruined his life, because all he's got is a fucking eighth-grade education." He threw his cigarette into the ocean. "I suppose if one of us came up with a terminal disease, you two would find some way to make it sound like something fun."

"We weren't doing that," Chris said. "We were just telling him what we could remember. It sounded silly because most of what you learn in school is silly."

Rick turned to Mark. "What kind of a job do you think you're going to get someday?" he asked. "When you tell people you only finished the eighth grade, you're going to have to stand in line to get a job as gravedigger at the dog cemetery."

"I am not!" Mark shouted. "Besides, I'm going to school someday."

"What, when you're thirty?" Rick asked. "Let's face it, Mark. You and I got the worst deal out of this. Shawn's got his education. Chris is close enough and smart enough to take an equivalency test. But you and I are the ones who'll never make it. That's why they can make jokes about it. They know *they'll* be all right."

"That's about enough, Richard," Shawn said. "We don't like to see anyone dominate the conversation."

"You see?" Rick still directed his whole argument to Mark. "I'm making him nervous. He hates to hear that he hasn't given us everything we need. He hates to think he's not perfect. He knows fucking well he's wrecked your life and mine, but he doesn't want you to figure that out."

"Quit putting it all on Shawn," Chris said. "You left home of your own free will. Nobody forced you."

"That's it," Rick said to Chris. "Do your job. Back him up. Keep him from looking bad. You two make the best team since Nixon and Haldeman, since Captain Bligh and Mr. Christian."

"Now hear this," Shawn said. "I don't want any more discussion on the merits of my leadership, or someone will take a swim who doesn't want to."

"Totalitarianism!" Rick said to Mark. "You see? If there's any dissent, he wants to suppress it."

"What's totalism?" Mark asked Chris.

"Never mind," Chris said. He was watching Shawn to see how angry this was making him.

Shawn put his coffee aside roughly, spilling some of it out. "What is your problem?" he shouted at Rick. "What the fuck do you want from me? Why do you always take these sneaky little shots at me? If there's something you don't like, why don't you come right out and accuse me?"

"You're a tyrant," Rick said. "You're a dictator. You think you're God. You're afraid to make a mistake, or if you make one, you're afraid to admit it. You rescued us from our terrible home and brought us here to this beach you created and you think we ought to bow down and worship you. But you know damn well that none of us, yourself included, has any chance at any kind of future except Steve and he has to whore his way through college!" Rick was very worked up.

"Okay, that's quite enough," Shawn said. "I don't want to hear any more of this."

"You see?" Rick appealed to Mark again. "He doesn't answer me. He just threatens. Doesn't that tell you something? That's the way he operates. He's got you so submissive, you don't even think anymore."

"Yes, I do!" Mark said. "Don't I?" he asked Chris.

Chris kept his attention on Shawn, who had gotten to his feet. He wasn't making any move toward Rick, but he was on his feet.

"Was it any better at home?" Shawn asked Rick. His voice was unusually agitated. "Tell me that. Did you prefer things at home? Did you like getting smashed up all the time? Tell me what we did that's so terrible when you compare it to how things used to be."

"Maybe you thought you were protecting us," Rick said. "But if we could have stayed at least through high school, we'd have gotten out of there anyway and then, at least, we'd have had an education. We wouldn't be criminals like we are now."

Shawn went over to Rick and knelt down and took him by the shoulders. Chris could see the argument had become too important to Shawn. Rick was completely detached, but all Shawn's emotions were on the surface, as if the outcome of this argument would be the final judgment on his life. "I was afraid he'd kill you," Shawn said. "Don't you understand? I was afraid for you, especially you younger ones. I was eighteen. I could have just moved out if I hadn't cared about you. But I couldn't leave you there with him."

"It wasn't that serious," Rick insisted. "He never seriously injured any of us. You've just told yourself that as an excuse. The real reason you took us away is because you want to feel like a hero. This gives you the chance to play the role you're playing now. The whole thing is mostly a power trip for you."

Shawn's grip on Rick tightened, causing Rick to flinch a little. "How can you say that? How can you say I'm selfish? I was concerned for you."

"But you've ruined our lives!" Rick said. "That's what you won't face! No matter how nice things are now, later on it'll be horrible. So whatever your motivations were, *you did the wrong thing!*"

"That's not true!" Mark shouted.

"There!" Rick shouted at Shawn. "Aren't you ashamed when you hear him defend you like that? Knowing what you've done to him, doesn't it bother you that he'd do anything for you? If I were you, I'd be *ashamed.*"

That last word seemed to signal Shawn as if it were the gunshot at the beginning of a race. He threw his body against Rick's, knocking him flat, and pinning his arms with one hand, used the other one like a hammer to smash Rick's body. It was nothing like a normal fight. Shawn drove his fist systematically into Rick's stomach and chest and rib cage, as if he were a wrecker trying to bring down a stubborn wall. It was a murderous and relentless kind of beating, the kind one gives to a wasp that won't stop moving. It was exactly the way their father had always beaten them and the familiarity of it was chilling to watch.

Rick was totally impotent against such an onslaught. He was outclassed by size, weight, age, and experience, but beyond that, he was dealing with irrational anger. Shawn's eyes were animal, unreachable, and his face registered a certain pleasure, or at least an abandonment of conscience. Rick felt clearly that there was no human being in control of Shawn, no one he could appeal to. Instead, there was something psychotic in control, something Rick hadn't known was inside his brother. He made no attempt to fight back or even to struggle free. The best he could do was move in such a way that few blows landed near his lungs or heart and to pray that he would live until this was over.

After the first wave of horror passed, Chris was able to react. He managed to get a grip on Shawn's hitting arm and, with Mark's help, dragged Shawn, still struggling, off Rick.

Rick managed to pull himself up into a sitting position. His shirt was ripped all down the front and his mouth was filling with blood. His hair hung over his eyes. He stood up, panting and unsteady, holding his chest and hanging on to the railing for support. He tried to walk, and was able to do it as long as he held on to something. He looked at Shawn again and saw the muscles relaxing, saw the human look come back into his eyes. Rick pushed his hair back from his face. "Tell me again," he said, as bitterly as he could, "what were you trying to protect us from?" He turned away from the three of them and began working his way haltingly down the pier, gradually gaining more and more control over his body and eventually disappearing in the darkness.

Shawn had to gulp air because of the energy he'd expended. His body had relaxed, so Chris and Mark let go of him. As they did, he grabbed the railing. "I haven't done anything like that in years," he whispered. "*Years.*"

"Anybody would have done it," Chris said. "He was trying to provoke you."

Shawn shook his head, still not able to breathe normally. "No," he said. "He's right. He's right about me. I'm just like Dad. Someday, I won't be able to control it." He looked out at the water, desperate.

"That's not true," Chris said passionately. "He did it to you. He knows you've got a temper. We all know that. He just knew what would set you off. It was like a trap."

Shawn sat down on a bench, still looking far off into the water. "You won't remember it," he said. "I had to have therapy right after Mom died. I was beating up kids at school. I couldn't control myself. It took two years. I had to see that doctor for two years, but then I didn't need to do it anymore. I could control it. I thought I had it controlled forever. Even then, even when I was a psychotic little kid, I never hit any of *you.*" He was unable to go on.

"Let's go home," Chris urged him gently.

The next day was Sunday. Mark was watching television and eating a bowl of Trix. Shawn was reading the paper. Chris was in the kitchen.

"I don't personally care if he ever comes home," Mark said. "It's nice and quiet here without him."

Chris brought a cup of coffee to Shawn. "Don't drive yourself crazy," he said. "This is Florida. It's summer. Even if he was outdoors all night, it wouldn't hurt him."

"I just wish I knew how badly he was hurt," Shawn said in a low voice. "If I knew he wasn't somewhere bleeding to death..."

There was a knock at the door. They looked at each other.

"He's supposed to have a key, unless he lost it," Chris said. He opened the door and instinctively took a step backward. There were two policemen in the hall.

Fifteen

One of the policemen was black, the other, white. They were both young and terrifyingly tall. The black one had a holstered gun. "Is your name Cunnigan?" he asked Chris. He seemed to be the senior officer. The white guy hung back and watched everything he did.

"Yes," Chris said. "I'm Chris Cunnigan."

He gestured Chris aside and came into the room. "This would be Shawn and Mark?"

The white cop edged into the room behind him, looking as if he expected an ambush.

"That's right," Shawn said, getting up.

"Okay, the three of you are under arrest. You have the right to remain silent. Anything you say from this point on can and will—"

"Jesus Christ!" Mark said. "They really say it!"

The black officer gave him a look and went on. "You have the right to be advised by an attorney. If you cannot afford an attorney—"

"We know all this," Shawn said.

"I have to say it anyway . . . one will be appointed to you by the court."

"What's the charge?" Shawn asked. He felt the best strategy in this situation was to be as polite and respectful as possible.

The white policeman, meanwhile, had begun to drift around the room, looking things over. Chris watched every move he made.

"Runaway, truancy, possible grand theft, and, if you're Shawn, contributing to the delinquency of minors and aggravated assault. At least, that's what you've been accused of. We'd like you to come into Daytona for questioning and then we'll see if any formal charges should be made."

"Accused by whom?" Shawn asked, even though he already knew.

"Your brother Richard. We found him by the river this morning. We thought he was drunk, but apparently he'd been in some kind of fight. He was beat up pretty bad."

Shawn didn't react to that at all. "And he made up all this stuff about us?"

"That's what we want to find out. That's why you need to come into town with us."

"He told you where to find us?" Chris asked. He didn't seem able to grasp the situation. He looked lost.

"We've got a bunch of speed back here!" called the white policeman, who had drifted into the bedroom. "Dietac and Dexatrim and about five packages of—"

"Hey! Has he got a search warrant?" Shawn demanded.

"Oh, crap!" said the black officer. "Sergeant Warner! Get your ass out of that back room. This kid knows the law better than you do!" He said to Shawn, confidentially, "This is his first time out."

Sergeant Warner was furious. He stalked back into the

room. "If they've got that stuff, it's a good bet they've got something illegal around somewhere."

"You make all the bets you want," said the black officer, "but you stay out of that back room. You didn't see anything that wasn't legal. On the other hand, what you just did was illegal, do you follow?"

"Okay, Josh," said the white officer. "But while I was making that illegal search, I did find one other thing." He held up Shawn's switchblade and flicked it open for emphasis.

The black officer gave Shawn a disappointed look. "What's *that* about?" he asked.

"Self-defense," Shawn said. "And he still doesn't have a warrant."

The black officer looked tired. "If you want to defend yourself, you ought to learn karate. I'll tell you what. I'll pretend I didn't see the knife, if you pretend you didn't see Sergeant Warner go in the back room. And I think I'd like to give you a little frisk, too, in case you carry something to defend yourself against policemen."

"That seems fair," Shawn said agreeably.

They had to put their hands on the wall and stand with their legs apart. Sergeant Joshua, the black officer, searched Shawn and Sergeant Warner did Chris and Mark. Chris didn't like being handled. "I'm only wearing cutoffs," he said. "You act like I've got a machine gun somewhere."

"You'd be surprised where some people keep their weapons," Sergeant Warner said. He stood up and noticed Chris's neck chain. "This one's Catholic," he said to Sergeant Joshua.

"Put it in your report," said Sergeant Joshua. "Maybe they'll make you a detective."

"Do you want us to pretend we didn't hear him say that?" Shawn asked.

"Please," said Sergeant Joshua.

"I was just making conversation," said Sergeant Warner. He finished with Chris and started on Mark.

"I saw a movie once where a policeman was frisking Clint Eastwood," Mark said, "and Clint Eastwood kicked him right in the teeth and stole the police car."

Sergeant Warner kept a close watch on Mark the rest of the time they were together.

They rode in the back of a police car to Orange Avenue, where the Daytona Beach police station was. Despite their vast knowledge of television police procedure, they were slightly surprised by the cage wire in the car, by the fact they had to be photographed and fingerprinted and had to give up their watches to a total stranger. It was disturbing to be in a place where everyone but them had a gun strapped on. While they were being processed, two policemen dragged in a black man who was screaming like a lunatic. They had to drag him because he refused to walk. But the worst part was when they were separated and put in those little rooms to be questioned. If they could have stayed together, none of it would have been so frightening.

Douglas Frazier, an assistant D.A., was twenty-eight years old. He was blond and baby-faced and could easily have passed for a minor. This was one reason, he felt, they always assigned him to the Juvenile Division. Kids preferred talking to someone like him. Frazier preferred juvenile work anyway. At least with kids, there was some small amount of hope. Once they were twenty, he had found, there was no turning them around.

Some cases interested Frazier more than others. The Cunnigan case had been on his mind since the moment he saw Rick and talked with him. The poor kid looked as if he'd been through a hurricane. At first he wouldn't talk about anything, wouldn't even give his name. Then, suddenly, he seemed to change his mind and started pouring out an extraordinary story, accusing his brothers of everything short of manslaughter. Frazier could see the hatred in Rick's eyes when he talked about his brothers. The only conclusion he could draw was that either Rick was a congenital liar or his brothers were monsters. He couldn't wait to hear the other sides of the story. He hung around the police station all morning, drinking machine coffee and reading *The Wall Street Journal*. Finally someone came and told him the rest of the Cunnigans were ready for questioning. Because of certain things Rick had said, he decided to talk to Shawn first.

Shawn was a taller, stronger, more self-confident version of Rick. He had the same light-brown eyes and slightly wavy hair and the same steeliness about his eyes. If Rick had learned to mask his emotions, it was from this brother he had learned it.

Frazier sat in the chair that faced Shawn's. "You're Shawn Michael Cunnigan and you're nineteen."

"That's right." Shawn's eyes were neither friendly nor unfriendly, but very direct. *Intelligent*, Frazier thought.

"I'm Doug Frazier. I'm with the district attorney's office. I guess you already know your brother Richard has made some accusations about you. I'd like to get your side of things before I file any charges."

"All right, go ahead," Shawn said.

"Did you get your phone call?"

"Yes." They had called the O'Briens and told them

Mark was sick and they wouldn't be at work for several days. They had wanted to call Steven, but didn't want to risk making the long-distance call on a police telephone.

Frazier wrote on his legal pad, *Shawn—19.* "And you didn't want an attorney, is that right?"

"That's right," Shawn said impatiently, "and I know my rights and I don't smoke and I don't want a glass of water."

Frazier laughed. "Coffee?"

Shawn laughed. "I don't want anything. Just ask me the damn questions."

That was interesting. Most kids wanted to stall. "Your brother has accused you of assaulting him last night on the Ormond fishing pier. Would you like to talk about that first?"

The eyes went steely again. "We had a fight."

"From the looks of Rick, it was a very one-sided fight."

Shawn shrugged. "I'm older. I'm bigger."

"Do you and Rick have a lot of fights?"

"We have a lot of disagreements. I never had a physical fight with him before last night."

"Not even when you were children?"

"No."

"Come on, Shawn, all little boys fight with their brothers."

"I never hit any of them until last night. Ever." The eyes were impassive.

"All right." Frazier wrote it down but didn't believe it. "What was this unprecedented fight about?"

"It was about me. He was saying some things about me I didn't like."

"Rick insulted you?"

"He challenged me. He . . . Have you got all the stuff about our leaving home?"

"I have Rick's version of it."

"All right. We left home. I thought we should. I thought we had to. I'm the oldest, Mr. Frazier, so I have to make the decisions. Rick has always . . . he's always questioned my judgment. He's always implied that I'm an incompetent leader. It never bothered me because I thought he didn't really mean it. But last night he said things about my sincerity. He said I was selfish, that I've done things for selfish reasons. He said I didn't care about him or any of them and that isn't true. I couldn't stand to hear him say it."

Frazier was trying to write all this down. "So you lost control of yourself and beat the shit out of him."

"Yes, sir, I did."

"Well, that's clear enough. What would you say was your motivation for encouraging your brothers to leave home?"

Shawn's steady eyes wavered, dropped suddenly. "I wanted to keep them from being hurt," he said quietly. "That's why . . . I'm very upset about what happened with Rick yesterday. I *hate* seeing people hurt. I hate violence. I hate it even more when I see it in myself."

"Rick says your father was abusive."

The eyes stayed down. "Yes."

"He beat all of you. Often?"

"Yes."

"How did he hit you? Was it with an open hand? Or with some kind of object?" Frazier thought his own voice sounded a little unsteady.

"Fist," Shawn said—his voice was getting lower and lower—"he'd get us on the floor and hit us with his fist. Over and over. I was always . . ." He looked up, "I was always coming home from school and finding someone all bloody. I never knew what I was going to find. I never knew which day it was going to happen, or which brother it was going to be. You see? I couldn't take it. I had to get them out of that house."

"So you left home on the night of August twenty-ninth last year?"

"That's right."

"All your brothers went with you voluntarily. You didn't threaten or force any of them."

"No."

"And you encouraged your brother Christopher to steal your father's car."

The eyes changed to a new expression. An expression Frazier couldn't put a name to. "We didn't steal any car," he said.

Frazier flipped some pages in his pad. "Your brother Rick says it was a 1978 Chevrolet Caprice, light blue, blue interior, license number PG 7021. He says your brother Christopher drove it from Dayton to Kentucky to Indiana, to Michigan, back through Indiana, back to Kentucky, through Tennessee, Georgia, and finally here to Florida, where you abandoned it in Jacksonville. He says you changed license plates three times and the last one on the car was FLH 909."

"That was our father's car you described, and that first license number. And those were the places we went, but we didn't steal Dad's car." The eyes never wavered. Not even a flicker. If he was a liar, Frazier thought, he was a very good one.

"How did you get from place to place?"

"We hitchhiked."

Frazier enjoyed a challenge. He was rarely up against such intelligent opponents. Kids' lies were usually pitifully easy to expose. "You understand this doesn't agree with your brother's story?"

Shawn shrugged. "I guess he was angrier at me than I thought."

Frazier nodded. "I have everything I need from you, Shawn. I'll talk with Chris and Mark and file charges against you this afternoon. Then we'll try and get you a hearing as soon as possible, maybe this week. Until then, we'll have to hold you here in detention. Do you have any questions?"

"Can we all be in the same room tonight?"

"If that's what all of you want."

"Can I ask you something that isn't related to this?"

"Sure."

"How tough was law school?"

Frazier smiled. "It can be done," he said.

Frazier opened the door. "Christopher John?" he asked softly.

"Yes, sir."

"I'm Doug Frazier. I work in the district attorney's office. How old are you, Chris?"

"I'm seventeen, sir."

Frazier wrote on his pad, *Chris—17.* "Did you get your phone call, Chris?"

"We didn't each need one. We just used one for all of us, sir."

"Why don't you call me Doug, instead of sir? Otherwise, it feels like we're in the army. Do you want an attorney?"

"No, I don't want one."

"I'm going to ask you basically the same questions I asked Shawn. So, I'll start off by asking you about the incident on the pier last night."

Chris drew back a little. "Yes, sir?" he asked faintly.

"Quit calling me sir. Rick has charged Shawn with assault. Shawn admits to it, but says it was an isolated incident. I'd like to know, have you ever seen Shawn display violent behavior like this before?"

"No, sir," Chris said emphatically. "He never hit Rick before. He's not like that."

"He's never hit you or slapped you? You've never had fights with him? You've never seen him hit anyone before this?"

"No!"

"Would you say Shawn has a bad temper?"

"Well, yes, he yells and screams a lot, but he can't help that. He doesn't *hurt* people."

"Tell me about your father, Chris."

The eyes dropped. Just like Shawn's. "Tell you what?"

"About the beatings."

"He used to beat us. Once a week, at least. He drank a lot. I guess he couldn't help it." Chris raised his eyes reluctantly, to see if that was enough.

"Shawn seems to feel that you boys were in immediate danger from your father. That he had no choice but to take you away from home."

"Yes, I think that's right," Chris said.

"Were you afraid for your life at home?"

"Sometimes."

"How did you feel about stealing the car?" Frazier kept writing on his pad, giving the question no special emphasis.

"Stealing the car?" Chris repeated.

Frazier looked up. "Your father's car. The night you left home. A 1978 Chevrolet Caprice. I understand you were the driver."

Chris's eyes became wider. "Who told you I stole a car?"

"Richard said you did."

That was what Chris wanted to hear. Shawn hadn't confessed to it. "I didn't steal any car. I can't believe Rick would say that, unless he's trying to get us in worse trouble than we're in."

Frazier frowned. He'd thought Rick was the one telling the truth. But this one didn't look like the type who would lie. "What kind of life have you had since you left home?"

Chris gave it some thought. "It's been very good, if you consider everything. I mean, we've managed. I probably shouldn't talk this way, because I know we've broken the law and everything, but it makes you feel kind of . . . *proud* when you find out you can take care of yourself."

"How did you manage?" Frazier asked. "How did you have enough money to survive?"

"Shawn took his money out of the bank, so we had that to start with. And we sold our class rings and worked different places. We work on the pier now. We've got everything we need."

"Do you look up to Shawn? Do you admire him a lot?"

"Yes," Chris said shyly.

Frazier stood up. "Just one other thing, Chris. How did you get from state to state if you had no car?"

Chris's eyes were pure and clear. "We hitchhiked," he said.

Mark Cunnigan was skinny and badly in need of a haircut. Frazier had never seen a guiltier expression in his five years with the D.A. *I'll get the truth out of this one,* he thought. "Mark Joseph Cunnigan? And you're fourteen, right?"

"*Fif*teen."

"Fifteen." Frazier erased and rewrote. "I'm Doug Frazier from the district attorney's office."

"You're the district attorney?" Mark was clearly impressed.

"No, I work for him."

"Are you a lawyer?"

"Yes."

"Do you just prosecute kids like us, or do you do hardened criminals, too?"

"Just kids like you. Could *I* ask *you* a few questions, Mark? I've talked to everyone but you. I'd like to go over all the things I discussed with your brothers."

"Okay."

"So, we'll start with what happened on the pier last night."

Mark's face became anxious. "Shawn isn't like that!" he said. "He never did anything like that before in his life!"

"That's what I was going to ask you. You wouldn't call him a violent person?"

"No, no, he's great. He's great to get along with. You've got to understand what a pain Rick is. Did anybody tell you that?"

"Not really."

"Rick's a bastard. Really he is. I don't know what he's told you about the rest of us, but he's out to screw us. If you're writing this down, you better not use that word."

"I'm not quoting you directly. Do you mean you think Rick provoked Shawn to hit him?"

"Yes, sir. I've wanted to hit Rick for years. I wish Shawn would have done it sooner. I know how that sounds, but I'm trying to have you see the real situation. He had it coming."

"That doesn't alter the fact that it's a crime to assault someone. I kind of get the impression, Mark, that you want to protect Shawn a little bit. Are you pretty fond of him?"

"He's the closest thing I've got to a parent," Mark said.

Frazier pretended to take notes for a minute. "Does he take pretty good care of you boys?"

"Yes," Mark said enthusiastically. "He took care of me when I was sick last winter and he worries about money all the time and he's always asking us if we need things. He'd do anything in the world for one of us, I *know*." Mark's eyes were bright.

"It's too bad he's not running for office," Frazier said.

"Well, you asked me and I'm telling you," Mark said firmly.

"When you were still at home, were things pretty tough, living with your father?"

Mark's eyes did not drop, like Shawn's and Chris's. "Yes. He was drunk all the time and the only thing he liked to do was beat up on us. He broke my arm one time. We were all scared to death of him. It's bad when you have to be scared all the time. You can't ever relax."

"I understand. Did any of you ever hit him back?"

"No," Mark said. "You don't hit your father."

"Since Shawn's been taking care of you, has he encouraged you to commit any illegal or immoral acts?"

Mark frowned. "He and Chris fixed me up with a *girl*," he said. "But I didn't do anything."

Frazier laughed. "No, I mean, does he encourage you to shoplift, smoke pot, drink, anything like that?"

"None of the other things you said. They let me drink a little."

"How much?"

"A few beers. I've never had more than two at a time. If I try to drink three, I throw up."

"So do I," Frazier said. "Were you pretty nervous about stealing the car?"

Mark frowned again. "We didn't steal a car. I just told you we didn't steal anything."

"You didn't run away in your father's car?"

"No, sir. We talked about it, but we decided not to because that would make it easier for the police to find us."

"How did you get around?"

"Hitchhiked."

Frazier rose. "That's all I need, Mark. You'll have to stay here in the Detention Center until your hearing. Do you want to be in the same room with your brothers?"

"Yes, please. I'll see you in court!" Mark smiled at Frazier.

Frazier smiled back.

Rick sat with his legs over the arm of his chair, reading *Newsweek*. Since Shawn had left no marks on his face, it was impossible to tell he'd been in a fight, until he tried to walk. He looked up when Frazier came in.

"How can you read with those sunglasses on?" Frazier asked.

"I'm used to it," Rick said. "Have they apprehended the rest of the gang by now?"

"Yes," Frazier said. "I've just been talking to them. Listen, do me a favor and take those things off. I can't talk to someone I can't see."

Rick took off the glasses and looked blankly at Frazier.

"All three of them said they didn't steal a car. That puts a little doubt on that aspect of your story."

Rick shrugged.

"Since it's three to one, I'm inclined to disbelieve you now."

No change of expression. "I suppose you are."

Frazier felt frustrated by Rick. He was a slippery surface. Talking to him was like trying to climb a marble wall. "Do you want to change your story?"

"No," Rick said calmly. "*I'm* telling the truth. You're the prosecutor. You figure out what's what. It's not my problem if you're confused."

"Their stories matched perfectly."

"So they had it rehearsed. They're sharp kids. Of course, that's just my opinion. Just an opinion from one of the accused."

"You seem so angry with them," Frazier said. "Why is that?"

"I don't know," Rick said. "Now you want me to be a psychiatrist."

"Do you hate your brothers, Rick?"

Rick's expression became chillingly hostile. "Whether I do or not," he said, "has nothing to do with my guilt or innocence."

Frazier was shaken. "If you don't cooperate with me, it makes it harder for me to be fair with you."

Rick put on his sunglasses again. "Why should I care if your job is hard or not?"

Frazier stood up, angry now. "Here's what I'm going to do," he said. "I'm going to check records in Jacksonville and Dayton. I'll find out if the car you describe was abandoned or reported stolen. I'm going to contact your father and see what he says about all this. If I can't get any indication your story is true, I'm not going to waste a judge's time with it."

"Fine," Rick said.

"You still want to file an assault charge against Shawn?"

"Yes."

"I need to know a little more about it, then. Do you feel he was trying to frighten you, or seriously hurt you, or—"

"He was trying to kill me," Rick said.

"I don't think—"

"I believe his intention was to kill me," Rick repeated. "I think that's a felony, isn't it? Of course, since it's my word against his, you can switch that around however you want it, too."

"I take it you don't want to room with your brothers."

"You take it right. Put me in with some killers or something."

Frazier closed the door on Rick.

It was after midnight. Mark, Shawn, and Chris were together in a room that was very much like a college dormitory, only the door locked from the outside. It had no windows and no furniture except four cots and an overhead light fixture. The only decoration in the room were the things that had been written on the wall. The most prominent message, written with something like charcoal, said *Prepare to be screwed.*

They had been in detention four days. They had been issued clothes that didn't fit them and they had to call for someone to take them down the hall when they wanted to use the bathroom. They were brought food on trays three times a day. Their only occupation was talking about the hearing and comparing notes on how their questioning had gone. They felt slightly reassured by the fact they'd all said the same thing about the car and that everyone, even Rick, had apparently left Steven out of things. But their worst fear was that their father would be contacted, which would bring the whole story out. Shawn was pretty sure they called the parents in cases like this.

Frazier came to see them every day. He always said he was sorry about the delay, and he always looked guilty, as if something were happening and he couldn't tell them about it. They were sure he was piling up evidence that would put them away for years.

Chris hadn't slept at all. His body refused to relax until he knew what his final fate would be. By the fourth night he felt exhausted, but still couldn't fall asleep. Mark, he noticed bitterly, was sleeping like a baby, lying on his stomach and hugging the pillow with both arms. Neither his sleep patterns nor his appetite had suffered in the least from their situation. Chris envied Mark's ability to adjust. When Chris thought about their apartment, locked up and abandoned, or of the pier, which he might never see again, it made him sick.

He stood up and walked around. He couldn't tell in the dark if Shawn was awake or not. He was lying on his back with his hands under his head. Chris came closer and saw that Shawn was wide-awake and looking at him. "Insomnia?" Shawn asked.

Chris sat down on the edge of his brother's cot. "What do you really think is going to happen to us?" he asked.

"I was hoping you wanted to make small talk," Shawn said.

"Tell me what you're really thinking. Not the stuff you say in front of Mark."

Shawn's eyes looked uncertain, as if he didn't know whether to be honest or not. "It depends on what charges are filed. If they nail us for grand theft, it's going to be hard. Depending on what Rick says about the fight, I might be charged with another felony, for the way I hit him. Then you have to take my age into consideration. I'm old enough to be tried as an adult. If they pin all that stuff on me, I could get put away for a while. I'm just hoping now, it's someplace like this and not an adult facility, because . . . Chris, do you want me to tell you this or not?"

Chris had been choking up. He brought himself under control. "Yes."

"I'd say the rest of you are in pretty good shape. Again, the car is a big problem for you, but you can step around that if you say I influenced you to do it. The court will feel sorry for you younger guys. Homeless, battered children with nobody to look after them except their Fagin-like brother. You see? Just look sincere and frightened. You'll probably get a lecture about truancy and then they'll try to find someplace for you guys to go. I don't think there's any danger they'll send you back to Dad, once they know about him. But you might have to stay with Aunt Ann, or get put in a foster home. If you have anything to say about it, just make sure you stay together if that's possible at all."

"I don't want to get separated from you," Chris said. "I want to go the same place you go."

Shawn looked pained. "I don't think so, Chris. Because of our ages. They're going to hold me a lot more responsible than you. I'm not trying to scare you, but there are some serious things I could be charged with. I'm in a hell of a lot of trouble."

Chris's eyes were filling up with tears. "I won't be able to stand it if they do anything to you," he said.

Shawn pulled himself into a sitting position. "Don't be such a baby, Christopher John. I mean it. We've still got the hardest part of this ahead of us and I don't want you falling apart on me. I need you. Look at it this way. I know I'm not going to get the death penalty, so whatever they do to us is temporary, right? When I get out, you and I can go to Harvard together, all right? We'll be roommates."

Chris laughed even though he was still crying. "All right."

"I want you to go over there and get to sleep. Otherwise the judge will think you're a drug addict."

"Okay," Chris said. Still he didn't move.

"Do you want something else?"

"Yes."

"Well, what is it?"

Chris threw his arms around his brother. "I love you."

Rick's roommate was black. He said he was eighteen, but Rick thought he was younger. His name was TJ and he was serving a sentence of ninety days for destruction of public property. He had uprooted a swing-set in a playground in Holly Hill. He gave no real explanation for why he had done such a thing. "Damn swings" was his only comment on the subject. Rick was put with TJ because TJ liked having roommates. Also, neither of them was considered dangerous or violent.

Rick was feeling sicker every day from having no access to pills. He didn't know which of his feelings were real feelings and which were pill reactions. Also, they had taken away his sunglasses. He felt very tired and depressed. He didn't care what happened to him anymore.

TJ had heard all about the Cunnigans. Rick liked talking to TJ because TJ didn't listen. It was like talking into a tape recorder and then erasing the tape.

"I didn't tell them about my other brother," Rick said. "There were five of us who ran away. One of them got married and moved to Indiana."

"That's two mistakes right there," TJ said.

"I could have told them about him," Rick said. "I could have had him torn away from his love nest and extradited here, but I never even mentioned his name, and, of course, they didn't either. So *he's* safe and sound. I don't suppose they give me credit for that, though. They probably think I'm a regular Judas Iscariot. I can just hear what they're saying about me."

"You got good ears," TJ said. "Look here." He had found a crayon under his mattress. He began to write on the wall: *fuck, fuck, fuck, fuck, fuck, fuck.* "This is how I feel about the justice system in the state of Florida," he explained as he wrote.

"No matter what I did," Rick said. "I was never really one of them. They never really let me in."

"That's how I feel about the human race," TJ said. He stopped writing *fuck* and began writing *shit*. "I'm not one of them. I came from another planet, you know. Hundreds of years ago." He looked at Rick to see if he would accept this.

"It would be just my luck," Rick said, "to get put in with an alien."

"I'm radioactive, too," TJ said. "You probably sterile just from talking to me."

Rick didn't want to talk about TJ's radioactivity. "Even as a little kid, I wasn't one of them."

TJ stopped writing. "You must be one of *them*," he said, "or you'd shut up about *them*. All you can talk about is *them*. Why don't you ask me what my home planet was like?"

"What was it like?"

"It was shitty," TJ said. "It looked just like Philadelphia." He thought this was funny. He laughed and laughed.

"Do you have any brothers or sisters?" Rick asked.

TJ cut the laughter and looked at Rick levelly. "Don't ask me silly questions," he said. "I'm just like you, man. I don't have anybody. I don't love anybody and they don't love me. Only I'm smart enough not to talk about it." He lay down and closed his eyes. "You got to shut up now, Richard. I have to recharge my batteries. I have to scan for messages from my home planet. They come in through the fillings in my teeth." TJ closed his eyes.

The next time Frazier came to visit Rick, Rick told him he wanted to drop the assault charges against Shawn. He gave no reason.

Sixteen

Monday morning was cold for late June. The air was clear and shimmery and the breeze fluttered the holly in front of the police station. It was the first daylight the Cunnigans had seen in seven days.

It was also the first they'd seen Rick. He walked with a slight limp and kept his eyes down. He and his brothers did not talk.

They were waiting for the police car to come and take them to their hearing. When it pulled up in front of the station, Mark ran over to it. "Josh!" he said. "Sergeant Warner! Do you remember us?"

"How could we forget? But my name is Sergeant Joshua. Don't be calling me Josh like we went to school together."

Chris and Shawn stood together, looking down Orange Avenue toward the Halifax River. A causeway had just opened to let a fishing boat through. This backed up traffic all the way to the police station.

"Take a good look," Shawn advised. "In case they put us away for years and years, this is the last view of the real world you'll get."

"I wish we could go over to the ocean for a minute," Chris said.

"I don't think so, Jack," muttered the guard who was watching them.

Then they were herded into the police car. Shawn was jammed against Rick. "You all right?" he asked gruffly.

"I'm just fine," Rick said. "And you?"

That was the extent of their conversation.

They took Nova Road to U.S. Route 92. "This is the way you'd go to Disney World, isn't it?" Mark asked.

"Yeah," said Sergeant Joshua. "You can get to Orlando this way."

Mark leaned on the cage wire so he could talk more intimately to Sergeant Joshua. "They were always promising to take me to Disney World, but they never did. Now if I get sent up the river, I'll never get to go. Hey! Look at that! There's a Krispy Kreme! Remember that from Georgia?" he asked his brothers enthusiastically. "I didn't know they had them down here!"

Sergeant Joshua looked at Sergeant Warner. "Are you hungry?"

"Why?"

"We could buy them some doughnuts. They been eating shit all week. Besides, I want one myself."

Sergeant Warner shrugged. "You just better get them to the hearing on time."

"We got time," said Sergeant Joshua. He bought three dozen doughnuts, which was good because Mark ate a dozen by himself. They took so much time, they had to run the siren all the way to DeLand, and even then they were five minutes late.

Frazier was pacing the lobby of the county courts building. "You're late!" he shouted.

"We had to eat breakfast," Mark said.

"Well, let's get you upstairs. There's nothing worse than holding up a judge."

Frazier took them to Room 5 on the second floor of the building. It was very small, with green carpet and plastic walnut paneling. There was a judge's bench, a conference table with five chairs, an American flag, and a bailiff, who seemed to be standing at attention. "You're late," the bailiff said to Frazier.

"I know," said Frazier. "Sit!" he ordered the boys. "Stand up when he tells you to."

"All rise!" shouted the bailiff immediately.

"What did we sit down for?" Rick demanded.

"Shhh!" said Frazier.

A side door opened and Judge Abrams came in. He was middle-aged and short, with curly gray hair and longish sideburns. He walked as if his robe were annoying him.

"The Honorable Judge Daniel G. Abrams!" shouted the bailiff, as if addressing a very large group.

Judge Abrams made a gesture for them to sit down and glanced at the bailiff, as if slightly disgusted by the voice tone.

"Your Honor!" the bailiff continued, still screaming. "Before the Court today are Shawn Cunnigan, nineteen, Christopher Cunnigan, seventeen, Richard Cunnigan, sixteen, and Mark Cunnigan, fifteen. Shawn is charged with possible grand theft and contributing to the delinquency of minors. Christopher is charged with possible grand theft and runaway. Richard is charged with runaway and truancy. Mark is charged with runaway and truancy. The incident for which they are charged occurred on the night of August twenty-ninth of last year, when Shawn encouraged his brothers to leave their home at 3336 Cornell Drive in Dayton, Ohio. Richard has stated to the Court that, on that night, the family car was stolen, but his statement is not corroborated by his brothers, nor by any evidence found by the Prosecutor. The Cunnigans have, since the date of runaway, lived in Indiana, Michigan, and, most recently, in Daytona Beach. They have been residents of Volusia County for six months. Shawn is currently employed on the Ormond Baited Steel Fishing Pier. None of the Cunnigans have attended school since the date of runaway. Shawn is a high school graduate. Christopher would have been in the eleventh grade, Richard in the tenth, and Mark in the ninth. Other than truancy, the prosecutor has found no evidence of any criminal or delinquent behavior since the date of runaway."

Judge Abrams watched the bailiff a few seconds to make sure he was finished speaking. "I'm tired just from hearing all that information," he said. "It'll take all morning just to get your names straight. Which of you is Shawn?"

Shawn signaled with his hand.

"So you're the ringleader," Judge Abrams said.

"I guess so, Your Honor."

"Don't guess," the judge advised. "You *know* you are. The oldest child is always that way. I have kids of my own. If my oldest daughter told the others to jump off the roof, they would. Isn't that pretty much your situation?"

"Yes, sir, pretty much so."

"You're nineteen years old." The judge was reading the Complaint as he talked.

"Yes."

"Before you got this idea about leaving home, were you planning to go to college?"

"Yes, sir. I was going to Ohio State."

"That's a good school," said the judge. He took out a pair of half-glasses, still studying the Complaint. "What was your grade point average in high school, Shawn?"

"Three point four."

The judge removed his glasses and looked intently at Shawn. "You're no dummy, then, are you?" he asked.

"I guess not, Your Honor."

"Stop guessing about everything. I won't accept any more answers from you where you guess."

"I'm no dummy, Your Honor," Shawn said, smiling a little.

Judge Abrams abruptly turned his attention to Rick, who was sitting sideways in his chair, with his back to his brothers. "Which one are you?" the judge demanded.

"Richard," said Rick, as if he were ashamed of the fact. "Rick."

"Rick, would you mind facing the bench? I don't like looking at half of you that way."

Rick turned around and hunched over the table.

"I'm not trying to badger you, son, but I'd appreciate your sitting up a little straighter, too. It looks as if you're bored with the proceedings."

Rick tried to sit up. "Sir, it hurts my back to sit up all the way."

"What's the matter with your back? Have you got back problems?"

"No, Your Honor, I hurt myself. I had an accident on the pier." He grazed Shawn with a glance.

"Nothing serious?" the judge asked.

"No, sir, it just hurts if I sit up like that."

"Well, by all means, then, slouch," said Judge Abrams. "I don't want you in pain."

"Sir, there isn't any way I could have a cigarette, is there?" Rick asked.

"No, there isn't. Let's get this car business out of the way first. Did they steal a car or didn't they?" He looked at Frazier.

"Your Honor," Frazier said. "Rick has told me they stole their father's car. The others all claim they hitch-hiked from state to state. We have no evidence a car was stolen. There was no police report filed in Dayton and there is no record of such a car turning up in Jacksonville, where Rick says it was abandoned."

"So, Rick, it's just your word against theirs," said the Judge.

Rick focused his eyes on a point in front of him on the table. "I was lying to Mr. Frazier about the car," he said.

Everyone in the room, except the bailiff seemed surprised by this.

"Really?" asked the judge. "You just made up a story about a car being stolen?"

Rick looked up with blank eyes. "Yes, Your Honor."

"Why would you do something like that?"

Rick glanced at Shawn again. "I was angry. I had been in an argument with Shawn and I was angry. When Mr. Frazier was questioning me, I thought that would be a good way to get Shawn in trouble. So I exaggerated."

"You didn't exaggerate if you made the whole thing up. You *fabricated*," the judge told him. "Do you realize you caused Mr. Frazier's office a lot of work and aggravation because you didn't tell the truth?"

"Yes, sir, I'm sorry about that," Rick said.

The judge looked at him, narrow-eyed. "Why don't you tell me about this argument you had with Shawn?"

Rick hesitated, just for a second. "It was about my hurting myself. We were working and I did something careless and hurt myself. Shawn yelled at me and that set it off."

Judge Abrams sat back in his seat. "You must have quite a short fuse, Rick," he said after a while. "Just because someone yells at you, you decide to falsely accuse them of committing a felony?"

Rick didn't answer. He and the judge looked at each other for several seconds.

"I think we've discussed that subject enough," Judge Abrams said finally. "Which one of you is Christopher?"

"I am, Your Honor. You can call me Chris, if you want to."

"All right, Chris. I'd like you to tell me a little about your home. What were things like before you left?"

"Sir?" said Chris nervously.

"What was wrong, that made you want to leave home?"

"Well, the main thing . . ." Chris faltered, "I mean the reason we left home . . . our father was . . . he would hit us."

The judge laid the Complaint aside so he could speak very directly to Chris. "You had an abusive father?"

Chris was terribly uncomfortable. He wished someone else could answer *these* questions. "I guess so, Your Honor."

"Don't *you* start guessing," the judge said gently. "Just tell me how it was. Did you father abuse you or not?"

"Yes, sir, he did."

"I know this is hard, Chris. But I have to understand your situation or I can't make a fair decision. I need for you to tell me specifically what your father did to you. Could you tell me about that?"

"He just beat us up," Chris said softly, keeping his eyes on the table.

"He hit you with his fists?"

"Yes, sir."

"Often?"

"Yes, sir. Every week."

"Did he ever hit you hard enough to cause an injury?"

"Sometimes."

"Can you remember any specific injuries he caused to any of you?"

Chris cleared his throat. "He broke a rib of mine. He broke Mark's arm once." Chris nearly mentioned Steve, but caught himself. "He knocked Shawn out once. But usually it was just cuts and bruises."

"And this happened, roughly, once a week?"

"Usually. He would drink a lot on the weekends and then it was pretty likely to happen."

"Had this just been happening recently, or had he done it for years?"

"Years."

"Did he do this when you were small children?"

Chris's voice shook. "When we were children he would spank us and whip us with things . . ."

"What things?"

"Belts and shoes and things. Whatever was around. Then, as we got older, he started slapping us and cuffing us around. He'd yell at us for not fighting back."

"He wanted you to hit back?"

"Yes, sir. He thought there was something wrong with us for not hitting him back."

"Did it ever occur to you to do that?"

"Yes, sir, it occurred to me, but I couldn't do it."

"I can understand that. Where was your mother during all this?"

"Our mother died ten years ago, in a car accident."

The judge noticed that all during this questioning, Shawn had leaned toward Chris, as if to give him invisible support. "I'm sorry I have to ask you questions that are painful to answer, Chris. You were only seven when she died?"

"Six. I guess it was eleven years ago."

"I see. So you spent most of your childhood with just your father."

"That's right."

"And you all pretty much lived with the fact your father was going to beat you up occasionally. Until last August when Shawn suggested you leave home."

"That's right."

"Did anything special happen to trigger that desire, or was it just a cumulative thing?"

"Sir?"

"Do you think Shawn was just fed up, or did something particular happen?"

Chris thought. "Well, Dad had just . . . hurt me that morning. I guess maybe that triggered it. But I also think . . . are you sure you don't want to ask Shawn about this?"

"No, I'm interested in your opinion."

Chris glanced at Shawn. "Well, I don't really know, but I think he was worried about going away to school in the fall. I don't think he wanted to leave us with Dad. I think he felt guilty about going off somewhere without us."

"Are we allowed to object or interrupt or anything?" Shawn asked.

"No," said the judge. "You'll get your chance in a little while. I've been neglecting Mark, though. I can see he's anxious to talk. Mark, you must have been very young when your mother died."

Mark had to figure it out. "I was four."

"That's pretty small. Who in the world took care of you?"

"They did. Chris and Shawn did. They dressed me and stuff, until I was old enough to do it for myself, and I can remember them taking me to kindergarten, the first day."

"Your father didn't do any of these things?"

"No. I don't think he knew how. He kind of avoided us when he could. But I did okay. They took good care of me."

"But who took care of the house? Who did the cooking?"

"Chris does all that stuff," Mark said. "I don't know where he learned it."

"I didn't learn it anywhere," Chris said, sounding embarrassed. "I just did it. Somebody had to."

"When you were only six years old?" the judge asked.

"Somebody *had* to," Chris insisted.

"Well, don't be ashamed of it, it's admirable. Mark, I'm sorry to interrupt you. Go on."

"They've done a lot of admirable stuff," Mark said, warming to the subject. "But *they* won't tell you about it. Chris and Shawn hardly ever did anything with kids their own age. They were always with Rick and me. They took us to the movies or they'd play ball with us. I think every single Saturday of my life, we went somewhere together."

Shawn interrupted now. "That was for a reason. Saturday was a bad day at home. It was better to get them all out of the house."

"Your father was more inclined to be violent on Saturday?"

"Well, yes. He had all day to . . . get in the mood."

"And another thing," Mark said, feeling it was still his

floor, "lots of times when I did something wrong, Shawn would say he did it, so Dad wouldn't hit me."

"Not very often," Shawn argued.

"Constantly," Mark argued back. "You did that constantly."

"Judging from your tone," said Judge Abrams, "you think quite highly of your older brothers, don't you?"

"Yes, sir, I do," said Mark, looking defiantly at Shawn.

"Tell me something, Mark. Back on August twenty-ninth, when Shawn suggested that you leave home, did you have any reservations about the idea?"

"No, sir."

"Why not?"

"I thought, if Shawn thought it was what we should do, then that was good enough for me."

"I see." The judge sat back in his chair. "We need to take a little recess, I think, so Rick can have his cigarette. We'll start up again in about five minutes."

"Five-minute recess!" screamed the bailiff.

"Good God!" said Judge Abrams to the bailiff. He held part of his robe in his hand, so he could climb down easily from the bench.

Rick got up and also left the room, not looking at anyone.

"How are we doing?" Shawn asked Frazier.

"Just fine. Just be honest. That's the main thing."

"What happened to the assault charges?"

"Rick wanted to drop them."

Shawn looked out in the hallway, where Rick was smoking. "Why?"

Frazier shrugged. "I think he's having second thoughts about lots of things. At first he really seemed to want to do you in, but that's softening. I'll tell you something,

Shawn. I feel bad about this now. Until just now I thought you and Chris and Mark were lying about the car. I realize now why Rick made it up. Listen, I'm going to go get a Coke. Does anybody want to come with me?"

"I'm a little hungry," Mark said hopefully.

Frazier grinned at him. "Let's go see what we can find."

That left Shawn and Chris alone with the bailiff. Because the bailiff was there, they had to communicate with their eyes. It was no problem for them to do so. They'd had years of practice.

"All right," said Judge Abrams when they reconvened. "I think we talked enough about the past. Let's talk about the present. Shawn, tell me about your job."

"It's the pier up in Ormond Beach. Jack O'Brien manages it and I, we all, help him out. We look after things when he isn't there."

"Mr. O'Brien must trust you implicitly, if he leaves you alone with his business."

"We do a pretty good job for him. We all love that pier."

"And Mr. O'Brien pays you enough that you can support yourself and your three brothers, is that right?"

"Yes. We're doing all right, right now."

"Where are you living?" The judge flipped back through the Complaint. "Peninsula Drive. An apartment?"

"Yes. It's a little small for four people, but we're okay."

"So you're working full time, living in reasonably good circumstances. Who takes care of the domestic side of it? Chris?"

"Yeah," Chris said. "They help me, though. If I ask them to help me, they do."

"And we have a savings account!" Mark said, unable to control himself any longer. "We have four hundred and five dollars at the Sun Bank."

"Really?" Judge Abrams looked at Frazier. "I think that's a first. I don't think we've ever had runaways with a savings plan, do you?"

"These guys are unique," Frazier agreed.

"No stocks and bonds, though, right?" the judge asked Mark.

"Not *yet*," Mark said.

The judge smiled at him, then made his face very serious. "Of course, there are other kinds of poverty. Chris, did you tell me what your grade point was?"

"No, sir. It was three point eight."

"Three point eight! Rick, do you know yours?"

"Three point five."

"And Shawn's was three point four, as I remember. Mark, how were your grades?"

"Pretty good, except in math."

"Mostly A's and B's?"

"Yes."

"Shawn, when you were still planning to go to college, had you picked out a major?"

Shawn reddened a little. "Prelaw," he said.

"Really? Were you thinking of becoming a judge one day?" Judge Abrams grinned at Frazier.

"No, sir. I wanted to be a prosecutor," Shawn said.

Frazier grinned at the judge.

"But of course that's all over now, isn't it?" Judge Abrams said to Shawn. "You'll never get to law school now, will you?"

Shawn looked hurt. "I guess I won't," he said.

"Chris, did you have any career plans?"

"I was thinking maybe medicine," Chris said quietly.

The judge actually scoffed. "No chance of that now," he said. "Rick?"

"Accounting."

"Mark?"

"Theater."

The judge paused a minute for emphasis. "You all had plans, then. You all had ambitions for yourselves. And now they're ruined. Completely." He looked at Shawn. "You see the real crime you committed? It would be hard for me to argue you didn't do your brothers a favor by taking them out of a violent home and providing for them as competently as you do. But in the process, you've cheated them and yourself out of a decent future. Boys with minds like yours should never drop out of high school. That's a crime. Don't you agree with me?"

Shawn said, "Yes, I do, but—"

"It's a serious crime, in fact. Do you know what you've done to Mark? Can you imagine how you've crippled him, leaving him with just an eighth-grade education?"

"I know, Your Honor," Shawn said, upset. "But I didn't know what else to do. I didn't think I had any alternative."

"Why did you take it all on yourself? There are agencies that could have helped you. If you had told the police the situation in your home, action would have been taken, believe me."

"I thought of that," Shawn said. "But if I did that, they might have come and taken them away. They might have put them in some god-awful foster homes or something. We might have all been split up. I wanted to take care of them myself. Like I always have."

"You talk as if they were your children."

"I can't help it! They're my brothers. You heard how it is. We've always been together."

"Calm down a minute, Shawn. I can hear you. Do you agree with Chris? Were you unable to handle the prospect of going away to school and leaving your brothers behind?"

"I don't know. How could I go anywhere? I didn't know what Dad would do from one day to the next."

"So you thought, in the long run it was better to break the law and throw away your collective educations, than to face the prospect of being separated."

"Yes, Your Honor. I'm sorry, but that's how I felt. That's how I still feel. I'd do it over, if I had to."

"I appreciate your honesty. I suppose more irrational acts are committed because of familial feelings than for any other reason. What you did was undoubtedly irrational. It was poorly thought out and suggests desperation. As I've pointed out, you did your brothers irreparable damage. There can't be any question about that."

"Yes, sir," Shawn said.

"Have you made any contact with the boys' father, Mr. Frazier?" asked the judge, sitting up.

"We can't locate him, Your Honor," Frazier said. "We've tried to skip trace him all week. He apparently left the Cornell Drive address sometime in September last year. His employment records at Delco Moraine show him leaving September seventeenth. Since then Mr. Cunnigan hasn't apparently been in touch with his family, or anyone else we could locate."

"Sounds like he ran away, too," said the judge. "Apparently he wanted to take advantage of your absence, as if any sane judge would ever send you back to him. So, there's no chance I can send you back home, but I've got to send you somewhere."

Realizing this was it, the boys grew very quiet.

"I have an awful lot of things to consider when I make these kinds of decisions. My options include having you placed in foster homes, contacting your relatives to see if they could take some of you, placing you in a county or state facility. When I make this decision, I try to take everything into consideration. I have to consider your ages and educational needs. I have to, unfortunately, consider how overloaded the state of Florida is with runaways and how all our agencies, charities, and support groups are overloaded. I have to try and consider your feelings. I want you to try and understand what a difficult decision I have to make. I don't think in a case such as this, I should overlook the bond between you. You've gone through a lot, made sacrifices, just because it was important to you to stay together. I don't like to see families any more fragmented than they have to be." He sat back in his chair. "You've not done such a bad job, Shawn. For someone your age, thrust into your position, you haven't done a bad job at all. You make enough money to provide for their needs. They seem healthy. They're clean. They're polite. If Mr. Frazier did his homework, they aren't drug addicts or criminals. On the whole, Shawn, you do as well as most of the parents I can think of. A lot better than some. I don't really think an alternative arrangement would improve on what you've been doing."

Shawn sat up straighter. He thought he was hearing it right, but he wasn't sure.

"Until these boys are adults in the state of Florida, they are remanded to your custody, Shawn. With certain stipulations." Judge Abrams paused while Shawn and Chris both made the same sound, between an exhale and an outcry. "I'm sure you're anxious to hear the stipulations. I want these boys placed in the proper grades and enrolled in high school by the next term. I demand, I *sentence*, each one of you to stay in school until you graduate. You've lost a year, but you seem bright enough to catch up. Shawn, I want you to give some serious thought to saving that money for college. With all these financial geniuses in the family, you ought to be able to arrive at some solution. You will be on probation for a period of time until this court is convinced it isn't necessary. Until that time, you will report each month to a court-appointed probation officer and I want to hear glowing descriptions of your good grades and responsible behavior. If I see one questionable report, Shawn, we'll make other arrangements. Is that understood?"

"Yes, sir," Shawn said.

"There's more. Shawn, I think I have to take some kind of punitive action with you because you took such a terrible risk with these boys' lives and security and because you showed a shameless disregard for their educational needs, which, believe me, outrages me more than anything else you did. What time do you get off work in the evening?"

"About six."

"I'd like to have you report to the Juvenile Detention Center in Daytona at seven o'clock every evening for the next two weeks. I'd like you to spend a couple of nights thinking about the seriousness of what you did. I'm not trying to hurt you by doing this, but you need to understand that what you did was wrong and the Court doesn't condone it. Just ten days ought to be enough. You can have your weekends free. Do you understand why I'm giving you this sentence?"

"Yes, sir, I do," Shawn said.

The judge smiled at him. "I'd like to see someone like you make it to law school. You have convictions. You have courage. All you need to learn is not to say *I guess* to a judge and you might have a fine career ahead of you."

"Thank you, sir," Shawn said.

"Make sure I'm kept advised of their progress," the judge said to Frazier. "They're a nice group of boys."

"I was wondering, Your Honor, if I might serve as their probation officer," Frazier said. "Since the circumstances are unusual."

"Yes, and since you're getting attached to them," the judge said, smiling. "I think that would be all right." He glanced at Mark. "Make sure that one gets a haircut," he concluded. "You're all dismissed, as I'm sure the bailiff will tell you."

"Court is adjourned!" screamed the bailiff.

Back at the police station, they were given back their personal property and Frazier gave them instructions on when and how they were to report to him. There was a minor crisis when Chris's St. Christopher couldn't be found, but it was just in the wrong envelope.

Then they walked up Orange Avenue together, toward home. Rick walked a little behind the others. It was a little past noon and the air was warming. The river was full of sailboats.

"We haven't eaten for hours!" Mark commented. No one paid any attention to him.

Chris put his arm around Shawn's shoulder. "We'll miss you tonight when you're up the river, serving your time. We'll put a candle in the window, won't we, Mark?"

"We don't have a candle," Mark said. "We could use a flashlight, but it would wear out the batteries."

"That's right," Shawn said. "Your big brother is going

to prison for you and all you can do is mock and insult me. Callous, ungrateful children. But just you wait till September. When you guys go off to school and I'm sunbathing up on the pier, we'll see who's laughing then."

They stopped on the bridge for a minute, watching the sailboats and the pelicans over at City Island. Shawn and Rick stood side by side at the railing. "Thank you for everything you did," Shawn said.

"What did I do?" With his head down and sunglasses back on, there was no way to make real contact with Rick.

"You lied for us. You lied about the car and you dropped the assault charge against me."

Rick looked up. The sun caught his glasses and obscured his eyes even more. "I didn't do it out of any great feeling for *you*," he said. "I just went along with your story because I realized nobody was going to believe me anyway. Nobody ever believes me. I just figured, why fight it?"

Shawn, hurt, pretended to watch a boat. "Well, thank you anyway," he said.

"Fuck off," Rick said angrily. "Don't thank me. I didn't do anything for you. I wouldn't go around the block for you."

Shawn turned around, leaning his back against the railing. He looked suddenly tired. "Richard, how much more money do you need?"

"What?"

"I don't want to play anymore, Rick. I don't care anymore. You've been stealing my money since we left because you want to go to Chicago, or some place like that. Isn't that true?"

"Who told you that?" Rick demanded.

"I just know," Shawn said. His voice was tired and resigned. "I know everything. I'm omnipotent."

"How long have you known?" Rick insisted.

"A long time. I didn't say anything because I thought you'd change your mind. I thought deep down . . . but I was wrong. No matter what I do, you hate me, isn't that right?"

Rick frowned. "I think," he said slowly, "maybe we'd all be happier if I went somewhere on my own."

"Right. Fine. Phrase it any way you want. Just tell me how much money you need and we'll give you a head start and then we'll tell Frazier you're gone. Just make sure they don't find you, because I don't want to go through another hearing."

Rick was silent for several minutes. "I don't need any money. I have enough now. I could go anytime."

"Well, do it, then," Shawn said. "If it's what you want, do it. I'm tired of fighting something I can't fight."

"What about your probation?" Rick asked.

"We'll give you a good head start. Then we'll tell Frazier you took off in the middle of the night. He knows you don't like us. It won't affect anything else."

"I have to get my stuff out of the apartment," Rick said.

"Fine. Go. We'll give you some time. Just please don't steal anything else from us, because we can't afford it."

Rick still hesitated. "You won't call the cops on me the minute I'm gone, will you?"

"No! Of course not!"

Rick crossed the bridge, passing Chris and Mark, who looked at him but said nothing.

"Richard," Shawn said.

Rick stopped.

"If you mess up or get in trouble and you want to come back here, you can. All right?" Shawn was looking at the river, not at Rick.

"I won't be back," Rick said.

Shawn seemed to be summoning his last ounce of strength. "But you need to know that if you want to come back, you can. I want you to know that."

"All right," Rick said. "I know it." He hesitated one more minute, then started in the direction of their apartment, picking up speed as he went.

Shawn looked after him until he was completely out of sight. "We'll give him an hour before we go home," he said quietly.

Rick tried to pack as quickly as he could, so he wouldn't have to see them again. He took his money from the place he had been keeping it, and a good supply of pills and one of the switchblades. He knew Shawn would authorize that. Those things, a change of clothes, and a carton of cigarettes were all he took. He left a lot of his things behind. Mark could always use them.

Chris had left a cereal box out on the kitchen counter the day they were arrested. Rick put it away in the cupboard. He held his key for several minutes, deciding whether to take it with him or not. Finally he let it drop on the kitchen table. He knew he'd never come back, no matter what happened to him.

He knew where the Greyhound station was and how to read the timetable and how to purchase a ticket. He had rehearsed these steps hundreds of times before. After he bought his ticket to Chicago and fed himself, he still had forty-five minutes to kill. He picked up his overnight bag and went to the men's room.

There was no one else in there, which was fortunate. Rick picked out the cleanest stall and bolted himself inside. Then he let his body sag against the wall and waited for the first sob to come up into his throat. Once he started crying, he was glad he had forty-five minutes. It was going to take that long to get it all out.

The beach was crowded, noisy with radios, cluttered with parked cars. Shawn sat in the sand, abstracted, staring at a point of space that was being continually intersected by a Frisbee. Mark, on his left, was eating ice cream. Chris, on his right, was watching him to see if he was all right.

"Steve will be down in two more weeks," Chris said, testing the waters.

"Steve. That's another one I lost," Shawn said.

Chris was determined to cheer him up. "When they come down, we ought to do something special."

"Like take me to Disney World," Mark said immediately. "The way we've been *meaning* to."

"All right," Shawn said. "If you want to blow a hundred dollars of my money looking at a big mouse, who am I to stop you?"

"Really?" Mark said. "You mean it?"

"Whatever you want," Shawn said.

"This is probably a bad time to mention it," Chris said. "But we need laundry detergent."

Shawn gave him a look. "All right, we'll go to the store this afternoon."

"We don't have to do anything about it today," Chris went on, "but if we're going to be in school, Mark and I both need some clothes. Everything we've got is wearing out."

"All right! All right!" Shawn said, pretending to be exasperated. "Bleed me white! Take all my money! I suppose *you're* still hungry, aren't you?" He looked at Mark, who had just stuffed the last of his ice cream into his mouth.

"A little," Mark said.

"Jesus Christ," Shawn said.

Chris touched his sleeve very gently. "I imagine he's gone by now," he said.

Shawn looked at Chris. "Do you want to go home?" he asked.

Chris nodded.

"Come on, then," he said, getting up. He started off down the beach, with his hands in his pockets.

His brothers flanked him, doing their best to imitate the way he walked, finding excuses to touch him, wondering if they would ever be able to tell him how they felt about him.

About the Author

JOYCE SWEENEY was born in Dayton, Ohio. She has wanted to be a writer since the age of eight. A graduate of Wright State University in Dayton, she has done graduate work in English and creative writing at Ohio University. *Center Line* is her first novel and the winner of the First Delacorte Press Prize for an Outstanding First Young Adult Novel. Ms. Sweeney lives with her husband in Ormond Beach, Florida.